Praise for STEPHANIE BOND

Of *Body Movers*

"There should be a notice on her books:
For a really GOOD time, read Stephanie Bond!"
—*America Online Romance Fiction Forum*

"Need a lift, feeling down? Pick up Stephanie Bond's
latest and your mood cannot help but improve."
—*CataRomance.com*

Of *Body Movers: 2 Bodies for the Price of 1*

"Readers will stay up late to finish the book,
eagerly anticipating each page."
—*RomanceDesigns.com*

"Body Movers is one of the most delightful series I
have read in quite some time.
Stephanie Bond shows her audience what a
wickedly funny mystery should be all about."
—*Suspense Romance Writers*

Of *Body Movers: 3 Men and a Body*

"Stephanie Bond's Body Movers series
is an absolute hoot!"
—*TheRomanceReadersConnection.com*

4 1/2 stars! "Bond continues her popular
Body Movers series with a fast-paced and wickedly
humorous story that skewers fame and celebrity
obsession with deadly accuracy."
—*Romantic Times BOOKreviews*

STEPHANIE BOND

6 KILLER BODIES

MIRA

Recycling programs for this product may not exist in your area.

ISBN-13: 978-0-7783-2707-3

6 KILLER BODIES

Copyright © 2009 by Stephanie Bond, Inc.

www.MIRABooks.com

Printed in U.S.A.

Acknowledgments

Having a trilogy out back-to-back is so, so exciting—but it makes for a manic writing schedule! Without the padding of downtime between books, things tend to get a little crazy...including the author. So most of my thanks for this book go out to...well, everyone who put up with my preoccupation with writing BODY MOVERS books 4, 5 and 6 this year while juggling other writing projects in between!

Thanks to my editor Brenda Chin for keeping everything going without missing a beat and helping me to plan ahead. Thanks, too, to Margaret O'Neill Marbury and Valerie Gray for championing the BODY MOVERS series within MIRA Books. Thanks to my agent Kimberly Whalen of Trident Media Group for keeping everyone on track. As always, thanks to my critique partner, Rita Herron, for your weekly support and keeping me sane.

And finally, thanks to my husband, Chris, my family, friends and neighbors for making allowances when I was in my cave writing about bodies—dead ones and naked ones. By the time this book is released, I hope to have rejoined civilization!

1

"Carlotta, this isn't your fault."

Carlotta Wren turned her head to look at Detective Jack Terry, who was dividing his attention between her and Atlanta's evening rush-hour traffic. They were heading north to Buckhead so Jack could drop her off at Peter Ashford's home. She was still reeling from watching her good friend Cooper Craft be arrested as The Charmed Killer, a monster who had murdered nine women, leaving a charm in the mouths of his victims as his signature. There was only one problem: Coop wasn't a serial killer.

"I know it isn't my fault." Carlotta dabbed at her wet eyes with the handkerchief Jack had given her. "Because it's *your* fault, Jack."

He frowned. "Mine? How do you figure that?"

"You tipped off the GBI that Coop was coming to see me at Neiman's." Carlotta worked at the store as a sales associate, although lately not up to her potential, considering all the...*diversions* of her life. Missing fugitive parents. A delinquent brother dodging loan sharks. Serving as an on-again, off-again body mover for the county morgue. "Insinuating" herself into police investigations (according to Jack's partner, Detective Maria Marquez).

Jack's mouth tightened. "It was better for Coop to be taken into custody sooner rather than later, and in a public place. At least no one was hurt."

"Jack, you can't possibly believe that Coop committed those horrific crimes."

He slammed on the brake to keep from rear-ending the car in front of him. "Damn traffic. Where the hell are all these people going?"

The way Jack deflected her question made her wonder if he thought the GBI had arrested the wrong man. "Jack, answer me."

His jaw hardened. "It doesn't matter what I believe. I'm not on the case, remember? But trust me, the GBI wouldn't have made an arrest without evidence."

"What kind of evidence?"

"I don't have specifics."

"DNA?" she prodded. "The Chief Medical Examiner told me that the state crime lab was supposed to return DNA evidence any day."

Jack frowned. "Why would Bruce Abrams be talking to you about the case?"

"Because he knows Michael and I are…connected." Michael Lane, her former coworker, was on the run after committing some pretty heinous acts himself, including trying to kill Carlotta and, after escaping from a hospital mental ward, stalking her. Until Coop's arrest, Michael had been the primary suspect for The Charmed Killer.

And Michael was still out there somewhere.

"Plus," she continued, "I played the sympathy card by telling Bruce my father's name had popped up on a list of potential suspects, thanks to your crackerjack profiler, Detective Marquez." She gave Jack a wry smile. "I'm sure she's behind Coop being fingered as The Charmed Killer."

"Regardless of the outcome, Maria is just doing her job."

"Do you know, she actually warned me about the men I let into my life? I thought she was talking about you."

He gave a rueful laugh. "Not bad advice, considering who you're living with."

"You were happy when I took Peter up on his offer to stay with him until things settle down."

"I wouldn't use the word 'happy.' I thought you'd be safe with him. But that was before Ashford bought you that stupid tricycle."

"It was a scooter, Jack. And it was a thoughtful gesture considering I didn't have transportation. Now I'm back in the same spot. I don't suppose you've found the person who planted the explosive under my Monte Carlo?"

He frowned. "No."

"Do you still think it was Michael?"

"Maybe."

"Who else could it have been?"

Jack shifted in his seat. "Coop."

Carlotta's eyes went wide. "Coop? Jack, that's crazy. Coop would never do something like that. Why would he want to hurt *me?*"

"When your car blew up in the mall parking lot, you told me the only places it had been parked earlier that day was in your garage at the townhouse and at Coop's place when you allegedly paid him a—" Jack took his hands off the wheel to draw quotation marks in the air "—*visit.* I can't ignore the fact that Coop had a window of opportunity to plant the device."

"When I allegedly paid Coop a *visit?*" Carlotta shook her head. "Jack, if you want to know if I slept with Coop, or with Peter for that matter, why don't you just ask me?"

"Because, as you so often remind me, it's none of my business." Then he nodded to her lap. "What's that you're holding?"

She glanced down at the mangled piece of paper, feeling sick all over again. Just before his arrest, Coop had brought her the results of the drug test she'd asked him to conduct on a sample of Wesley's hair. The report stated that her brother tested positive for opiate/Oxycodone, confirming her worst fears. When she'd confronted Wesley about stolen refills of a painkiller and a single tablet of generic OxyContin she'd found on his bathroom floor, he'd told her he'd only taken the drugs temporarily to alleviate the pain he'd experienced from when one of his loan sharks, The Carver, had cut part of his name into Wes's arm.

But the drug test indicated a more pervasive problem... didn't it? Coop had said over the phone that he wanted to explain the test results to her in person. But before he'd gotten the chance, the GBI had descended and arrested him.

"It's nothing," she murmured, pushing the paper into her purse. If Wesley was caught taking drugs, his probation would be revoked. All this time, she'd been worried about keeping her brother out of jail, and now, inconceivably, Coop was in lockup. "What's going to happen to Coop?"

Jack sighed. "He'll be arraigned within a few days."

"Do you think he'll get bail?"

"That depends on how good his attorney is, the mood of the judge, and the D.A."

"Kelvin Lucas?"

"Right. Since this is the biggest case Fulton County has seen in a while and since one of Lucas's A.D.A.'s was murdered, I'm sure he'll handle this case himself."

She touched her throbbing forehead. "I can't believe this is happening. The idea of Coop being The Charmed Killer is ludicrous."

Jack clenched his jaw. "Right now, jail is the best place for him to get sobered up and dried out."

The vision of Coop in a cold, empty cell made her lungs squeeze. He must be feeling dazed and utterly confused. And so alone.

Jack leaned on the car horn, which was ridiculous considering traffic was at a standstill. "This is bullshit." He reached under the seat and pulled out a siren to set on the dashboard, then switched on the blue light. Begrudgingly, the cars ahead of him eased over to the shoulder to allow him to pass.

"Are you taking advantage of your position as a law enforcement officer to get around traffic?"

"You bet your sweet ass I am."

He pulled ahead, slowed at a red light, then proceeded through when the coast was clear.

"You're only making it worse for everyone else."

"Yeah, well, I'm not feeling too generous today."

Carlotta observed Jack under her lashes. His rugged features and big body were rarely at ease, but a muscle worked in his jaw, and his grip on the steering wheel was more fierce than necessary. Despite the fact that he'd given Coop up to the GBI, Jack, too, was disturbed about the arrest. But was he disturbed because he'd been duped by someone he considered a friend of sorts, or because he believed Coop was innocent?

But if Jack thought Coop was innocent, why would he give him up? Because he couldn't resist being part of an investigation he'd been dismissed from?

She knew the detective well enough to know that he wouldn't tell her what was going on in that thick head of his, not if he thought she might go off on her own tangent. She'd have to finesse information out of him.

"Coop's fall from grace a few years ago is going to hurt him, isn't it?"

Jack nodded. "He was drunk when he stopped at the scene of an accident and declared a woman dead when she wasn't. Frankly, Coop was lucky he was only stripped of his title as Coroner and had his license to practice medicine suspended. The woman barely survived. If she'd died because of Coop's negligence, he would've been looking at serious time. It doesn't take a psychiatrist to see how something like that could mess with a person's head."

"But he seemed to be dealing with everything okay," Carlotta said. "I didn't know him when it happened, but Coop seemed at peace with working for his uncle at the funeral home, and moving bodies for the morgue."

Jack shrugged. "Things change."

"Not without a reason," she insisted.

"Everyone has a breaking point," Jack said. "It doesn't have to be a major incident."

She was tempted to let Jack in on what her brother, Wesley, had told her about following Coop to a neurologist's office, and their concern that Coop was sick. But their suspicions were mere conjecture, and Jack had already betrayed her confidence by informing the GBI when she'd called to let him know that Coop, who had been missing for a day, was on his way to see her at Neiman's. She wouldn't be so forthcoming with information the next time.

Jack took a call on his phone and from the one-sided conversation, she gathered he was talking to his partner, Maria, who needed a ride somewhere.

"I'll be there as soon as I can," he said, and Carlotta thought she detected a note of intimacy in his voice.

The GBI had kept Maria on The Charmed Killer case, but had removed Jack, partly because of his association with Carlotta, who had been indirectly connected to some of the victims—either as a body mover on the crime scene, or a passing acquaintance. And the last body had been a speed bump for her scooter. She hated that Jack had to maintain his distance from the investigation just because she'd been implicated in the crimes. Now that an arrest in the case had been made, she assumed Jack and his gorgeous partner would be reunited.

Not that she cared if Jack and Marvelous Maria were sleeping together. Okay, maybe she cared a *little*. Carlotta and Jack had rolled around a few times, but Jack was his own man. And she was supposed to be giving her relationship with Peter a fair chance. She and Jack had agreed to stop falling into bed with each other, yet their lives still intersected enough to keep the temptation alive.

Jack Terry managed to push every emotional button she had—Carlotta alternately hated and desired him, loathed and admired him. Right now, she desperately wanted him to tell her that everything was going to be okay, but she was terrified to ask.

Instead she nursed the ache in her chest and watched out the car window as the houses became increasingly posh until Jack slowed at the entrance of Martinique Estates. He could've pulled up and allowed her to punch in Peter's access code, but Jack preferred to flash his badge at the guard. The long black gates opened and he drove the familiar route through the manicured neighborhood to Peter's palatial home.

When Jack pulled the sedan into the circular driveway in front of the brick house, Carlotta's stomach clenched at the thought of going inside. Peter wasn't a big fan of Coop's primarily because the man had shown a romantic interest in Carlotta. No doubt Peter would feel vindicated that the good doctor had been so publicly exposed.

Peter opened the door and waved.

Jack grunted.

Carlotta didn't want to get out of the sedan, but she didn't have a choice. Wesley hadn't finished installing a security system in the townhouse, and it wasn't as if Jack had offered her a place to stay. She supposed she could get a hotel room, but that seemed silly considering Peter had offered her the run of his mansion. Especially since her budget didn't allow for extended hotel stays.

She couldn't explain it, but she felt as if she lived in two worlds—in one world was Peter and his home in the suburbs that offered her shelter from the other world of Wesley's problems, Jack's issues and Coop's crises. Peter's world should be more attractive, but it left her feeling isolated.

"Looks like Ashford's waiting for you," Jack said.

"The GBI will be in touch. I'm sure they'll want to question you again."

"I'm not giving them any ammunition against Coop," she said.

His expression hardened. "Do yourself a favor, Carlotta, and tell the truth. Coop can fend for himself."

She frowned. "I guess he'll have to fend for himself since his friends have turned on him."

Jack didn't say anything, just stared ahead.

She wondered again if Jack was simply toeing the company line when it came to fingering Coop as a mass murderer. Carlotta opened the car door, then looked back. "Jack, aren't you forgetting something?"

"What?"

"My red panties? The ones you stole and said you'd keep until The Charmed Killer was behind bars."

He was quiet for the longest time, studying her. Then the smallest of smiles curved one corner of his mouth. "If it's all the same to you, darlin', I think I'll hold on to those panties for a while."

She exhaled. "No problem."

Carlotta climbed out of the sedan and walked toward Peter's house, her heart lighter. In a roundabout way, Jack had just told her that he, too, didn't believe Coop was The Charmed Killer.

Today, that was enough for her.

Tomorrow, she had her work cut out for her. If The Charmed Killer—whether it was Michael Lane or someone else—had involved her in order to frame Coop for the murders, the criminal had messed with the wrong shopgirl.

2

"Thanks, guys," Wesley said, waving from the stoop of the townhouse at the motley crew of loan shark staffers who had helped him install a security system. Mouse, his collections partner now that he was working undercover in The Carver's organization, had surprised him by offering up the group of "security experts" to expedite the job.

He went back inside and surveyed the damage. The walls were badly pocked and scarred where wires and sensors had been installed. A wireless system would've been less invasive, but he knew how easily those systems could be hacked into. Mouse had agreed the old security systems were more reliable, and the man should know. He'd compromised more than one alarm system in the process of collecting on overdue accounts.

Wes sighed. He'd have to patch the walls and paint everything before he and Carlotta moved back in, but she'd been wanting to spruce up the place for a while now anyway. Wesley walked into the kitchen to stare up at the small black device lodged in the wall above the window over the sink that had been exposed during the installation.

A listening device, Mouse had said—a good one. Professional grade. Configured into the wiring of the house for ongoing power. And, according to the manufacturer's date stamped on the frame, it had been installed about ten years ago.

About the time his father had left town.

Wesley's heart thudded at the implication. Had his father installed the device so he could listen to conversations between his children over the kitchen table? When Randolph Wren had approached Carlotta at a Florida rest stop a few weeks ago, he'd indicated that he'd been keeping tabs on them...was this how?

Wes wasn't schooled in listening devices, but he knew enough about basic electronics to understand that most bugs used a radio transmitter. Meaning the person listening in had to be within a certain proximity to pick up sound.

Usually within a few blocks.

Which meant their father could've parked nearby, listening to whatever conversation had been going on in the Wren kitchen. If that was the case, then Wesley conceded that Randolph would've likely overheard many arguments. Wes had been a pain in the ass to his older sister. Looking back, he was surprised she hadn't given up on him and shipped him off to foster care. Hell, she'd been a kid herself when their parents had left town.

A sudden headache exploded under his scalp. He needed a hit of Oxy. He groaned at the blinding pain, then felt around the couch until he located his backpack. From a pocket, he pulled out an Oxy tablet and considered swallowing it to allow for a long, slow bleed of sweetness. Instead he decided to chew it, breaking the time-release coating for a blast of euphoria and instant pain relief.

He sat on the couch and leaned his head back, yielding to the floating sensation. His brain worked more slowly under the influence of Oxy, but without the headache, at least he could think.

From Wes's backpack his cell phone rang, drilling into his buzz. It was the ring of his regular phone, not Mouse calling him about a collections job. He considered letting it go, but after several rings, he pulled out the phone to check the caller ID screen.

Atlanta Police Department.

Crap. Suddenly, he thought of the piece of paper he'd mailed four days ago to the APD with three possible name variations for the identity of the headless body in the morgue. He'd sent the note anonymously, not wanting to be fingered as the guy who'd pulled the teeth out of the severed head (at Mouse's direction). Was it possible they'd tracked the envelope or its contents back to him?

Then he forced himself to relax. It was probably just Jack Terry calling to hassle him about the undercover work he was doing in The Carver's organization as part of his plea agreement with the rat bastard D.A., Kelvin Lucas.

He connected the call. "Yeah?"

"Wes?"

Wes frowned at the familiar voice. "Coop?"

"Yeah, it's me. Did I catch you at a bad time?"

"No." Other than the fact that he was high as a kite. "What's up, man?"

"Uh, nothing good, I'm afraid. I need a favor."

Wes sat up. He didn't think he and Coop would ever be friends again after Wes had stupidly agreed to aid in the theft of a celebutante's body they'd been transporting. "Whatever you need, Coop."

"I'm in a bit of a jam. I've been arrested."

"For drinking?" He'd smelled alcohol on Coop once recently in the morgue lab, and the man's voice sounded a little slurred now.

"Uh, no. Actually, for murder."

Wes's head went back. "What?"

"They think I'm The Charmed Killer."

Wes gave a little laugh. "You're punking me."

"Wish I were. They cuffed me in front of your sister a few minutes ago and hauled me away."

Wes's breathing became shallow as he realized Coop was serious. He swallowed nervously. "So what am I, your one phone call?"

"Something like that." Coop sighed. "Looks like I'm going to need a good lawyer. I thought I might give your attorney a call."

Wes frowned. "Liz Fischer?"

"She's a criminal attorney, isn't she?"

"Yeah."

"And she knows the D.A.?"

"Yeah. He digs her, I think." Liz was a looker with long legs and big knockers.

"Can you give me her office number?"

Wes grimaced, remembering Liz had left town. "Coop, man, she's out of town for a few days."

"On vacation?"

"I guess." Actually, when she'd called Wesley, she'd been kind of vague, saying she needed to get away to think. And she hadn't sounded well. "Let me give her a call on her cell and see what the deal is."

"Okay. If she's interested in taking me on, have her call the jail."

Wes wet his lips. "Uh, Coop?"

"Yeah?"

"You didn't…you're not…I mean…did you…do it?"

"What do you think?" Coop asked with a laugh, his words running together. "Tell your sister I'm sorry I embarrassed her at work."

Wes frowned. Coop was wild for Carlotta, just like Peter Ashford, and Jack Terry were—poor saps. "I will." When a dial tone sounded in his ear, Wesley slowly disconnected the call. He shook his head to clear it, trying to process what Coop had just told him. The police suspected Coop of killing all those women? Wesley tried the idea on for size, his mind wandering back over all the crime scenes on which he'd been a body mover. No, he couldn't believe it. Coop would never do something so gruesome. He'd never hurt anybody, much less a woman.

So why would the police arrest Coop if they didn't have evidence of his guilt?

He turned on the broken television and tuned into *CNN Headline News.* Sure enough, a "Breaking News" banner scrolled across the screen that a suspect in The Charmed Killer case had been taken into custody. He watched, incredulous, at the footage of a handcuffed Coop being led to a police car. His head was down and the one time he looked at the camera, Coop looked unfocused and disheveled.

Wes punched in Liz's number and paced in an attempt to walk off some of his buzz, just to cut through the Oxy fog. After a few rings, Liz answered.

"Hello?"

Like Pavlov's dog, his dick jumped. Liz was a great lay. "Liz, it's Wes."

"Hi," she said, sounding surprised. "I didn't expect to hear from you."

"Are you back in town?"

"I'm driving back now. I'd like to see you."

Inexplicably, the face of Meg Vincent popped into his mind, probably because he'd inadvertently shouted his cock-tease coworker's name the last time he'd balled Liz…not that Liz had minded. "Uh, sure. Actually, though, I'm calling for a friend of mine."

"Oh?"

"Do you remember Cooper Craft?"

"The body mover who used to be Coroner?"

"Yeah. He was just arrested and he needs an attorney. He called me and asked about you."

"I don't handle DUI's, Wes."

"Do you handle murder?"

"Murder?"

"This is nuts, but apparently, they think Coop's The Charmed Killer."

Liz was silent for two heartbeats. "When did this happen?"

"Within the hour, I think."

"Bye, Wes. I'll be in touch."

He ended the call and continued watching the news, losing count of the number of times Coop's name was mentioned. Poor Coop. And Carlotta must be going out of her mind. He picked up the phone and pulled up her number, wondering if he should hold off telling her about the bug he'd found.

As he listened to her phone ring, Wes wiped sweat from his forehead with his sleeve. It would be nice if the Wrens could winnow things down to just one crisis at a time.

3

"I always had a bad feeling about Craft," Peter said.

Carlotta looked up at her first love and former fiancé in dismay. When fugitive Michael Lane had broken into their townhouse and had been living in their parents' room unbeknownst to her and Wesley, Carlotta had gratefully accepted Peter's invitation to stay in one of his spare bedrooms while the police processed the town home as a crime scene and Wesley installed a security system. But after only a week and a half, she was starting to rethink her living arrangements. Peter would be happy, she realized, if she gave up her friends, and forgot all about the life and the relationships she'd built after he'd dumped her.

"Peter, Coop isn't The Charmed Killer. He wouldn't hurt anyone."

"Not if he was in his right mind," Peter said gently. "But people change under the influence of drugs and alcohol. Even nice people can do terrible things. The police must have evidence or they wouldn't have arrested him."

"They arrested you for Angela's murder, and you were innocent," she reminded him.

"The police had a reason to arrest me—I confessed, remember?"

She bit her lip and softened toward him. "Yes." He'd confessed to a murder he didn't commit to prevent his wife's dirty secrets from being discovered and her reputation tarnished. It was noble of him.

Peter reached for her hand and pulled her against him. "I'm sorry this happened, Carly. I know you were close to Cooper. But I'm glad it's over."

"But it's not over," she protested.

"You realize, don't you, that Coop's arrest gets your dad off the hook?"

Carlotta balked. She'd held off telling Jack or the GBI that Peter had remembered a romantic liaison between her father and one of the victims. Maybe she should've come forward.

And sacrificed her father for Coop?

She shook her head. "Coop is innocent, I tell you."

"Let the police do their job," he chided against her hair. "Meanwhile, have you given any thought as to when we can take that Vegas vacation I won at the club auction?"

She closed her eyes briefly. "I haven't. But Jack said the GBI would be wanting to talk to me again. And I'd have to ask my boss about taking time off."

"With all you've been through lately, I don't think your boss would mind."

She nodded. "I'm off tomorrow, but I'll talk to Lindy when I go in Saturday."

"Good," he said with a smile. "I think we could both use a break."

She manufactured a smile in return. "You're probably right." Actually, she suspected that Peter was hoping that a change of venue would allow them to consummate their relationship. They had tried on two occasions and both times, Peter had come up a little too quick on the draw. They both agreed they were putting too much pressure on themselves, but Carlotta was admittedly worried that the one aspect of their previous relationship that had been rock solid—the sex—was now such an awkward challenge. Something so natural shouldn't be so difficult…should it?

From her purse her cell phone rang. Thankful for the distraction, Carlotta pulled away and reached for her bag, half relieved, half panicked to see Wesley's name appear on the caller ID screen. "It's Wes. I'll take this upstairs, then change into something more comfortable."

Peter nodded. "I'll get dinner started."

God help her, she was beginning to hate those words. Carlotta turned toward the stairs and connected the call as she climbed toward the second floor. "Wes?"

"Hi, Sis."

"I guess you heard about Coop?"

"Yeah, he called me."

Carlotta gripped the phone. "Is he okay?"

"As good as can be expected, I guess. He wanted to get in touch with Liz Fischer."

Carlotta frowned. "Liz?"

"He needs an attorney, duh."

"Yes, well, Liz is certainly all that." And more, considering Liz had been their father's mistress, was a booty-call for Jack Terry, and had also bedded Wesley, who was at least twenty years her junior.

"Coop said he was with you when he was arrested?"

Carlotta walked into the spacious suite where she

was staying and sat down on the bed. "Uh…yeah. He came to the store to say hello. Jack had told me that Coop had been M.I.A. for a day, so I made the mistake of calling him to let him know Coop was okay. The next thing I knew, the police were everywhere. They handcuffed Coop right in front of me."

"So Jack gave him up? Asshole."

Her phone beeped and she glanced at the screen. "Hold on—that's Hannah on the other line."

"Okay."

She clicked over. "Hannah?"

"Jesus Christ, I'm watching the news. Tell me it isn't true."

Carlotta sighed. "I'm sorry, but it's true. I'm heartsick."

"But Coop isn't a serial killer! That's crazy."

"I agree." Carlotta hardened her jaw. "So what are we going to do about it?"

"Break him out?"

Carlotta gave a little laugh. "Hang on a minute, will you? Wes is on the other line."

"Okay."

Carlotta clicked over. "Wes? Hannah is as upset as we are."

"I forgot to tell you that Coop said he's sorry he embarrassed you at work."

Coop was in jail, but he was worried that he'd embarrassed her. Carlotta blinked back sudden tears, then took a deep breath. "I think we need to do something."

"Like what?"

"Prove Coop innocent."

"I'm in," Wes said.

"Can we get together tomorrow?"

"I could do one o'clock."

"Where?"

"How about the townhouse? I'll show you the new security system."

"Great. Hang on. Let me talk to Hannah."

"Okay."

Carlotta clicked over. "Hannah? Wes and I are going to prove Coop's innocence. Do you want in?"

"Abso-fucking-lutely."

"Pow-wow at the townhouse tomorrow at one o'clock."

"I'll be there. Can I bring Chance?"

Carlotta rolled her eyes. Chance Hollander was Wes's partying, trust-fund, pornographic, drug-dealing, slob of a friend. And apparently Hannah had grown a soft spot for him and his gigantic shlong. "Only if you keep him on a leash."

"See you then."

Carlotta ended the call, then clicked back to Wesley. "We're all meeting there tomorrow."

"Okay, see ya. Night, Sis."

"Good night." She disconnected the call, and exhaled. She'd confront Wesley with the results of the drug test another time.

Carlotta sighed. It would be nice if the Wrens could taper things down to one crisis at a time.

4

The next morning, Wesley approached the metal detector in the government building where he worked for Atlanta Systems Services—ASS for short—his body screaming for a hit of Oxy. A war raged in his head, his hands shook as if he had palsy, and his nerve-endings fired at will. It had taken him twice as long to ride to work because he'd had to concentrate to keep from swerving his bicycle into traffic. He was hoping the worst of the pain would be over before he clocked in, but it seemed to be escalating. He used his sleeve to wipe the perspiration from his forehead.

Yesterday his coworker Meg Vincent had nailed him for using his community service job as a cover for tapping the city's legal databases to gather information on his dad's case. When he'd left at noon, she hadn't decided whether or not to turn him in. Considering that he'd left her high and dry at a hoity-toity reception with her parents earlier in the week, he wouldn't blame her if she did. Meg's father, a renowned geneticist, had hired a P.I. to tail Wesley, presumably to uncover enough dirt on him to keep Wes away from his precious daughter. According to Dr. Vincent, the only reason Meg had invited Wesley to the reception was to make her father crazy. Too late, Wesley realized Dr. Vincent had probably just been taunting him, hoping he'd react exactly the way he had. When he'd tried to apologize to Meg for leaving the reception, she'd cut him off with her revelation that she knew what he was doing at ASS. So, after pissing her off, his balls were now in her hands.

Wesley thought it would be better not to be high in case the police were waiting for him at the ASS office to toss him in the clink for abusing his community service job and violating probation. But with a vise tightening around his temples, he was rethinking that thought.

"You okay?" a security guard asked as he walked up to the detector.

"Hungover," Wes said, trying to look sheepish instead of like a domestic terrorist.

The guard grinned. "Been there. Eat a banana, man—always helps me."

Wesley nodded his thanks, then stepped through the detector and retrieved his backpack from the scanner belt.

To delay his arrival as long as possible, he took the elevator to the top of the building, then rode back down to the seventh floor. When the doors opened, he looked out expectantly. When he didn't see any police uniforms or his boss Richard McCormick standing there ready to call him on the carpet, he stepped off and strolled toward his assigned work area.

Meg Vincent was already sitting at the four-plex workstation they shared with Ravi Chopra and Jeff Spooner, but she didn't even glance Wes's way when he dropped into his chair. He sat there for a few minutes, listening to himself breathe, waiting like a peasant for Her Highness to acknowledge him.

His head was a metal bucket full of rocks. It hurt to blink. Through the haze of pain, though, he perceived that she was wearing snug black pants and a pale green blouse that was done up one button too high for him to appreciate it. A flowered headband held her dark blond hair away from her face. The purple smudges under her eyes made them look even greener, but he was relatively sure whatever sleep she'd lost hadn't been over him.

She sighed in his direction. "You're high."

He licked his dry lips. "I wish." His voice reverberated like a jackhammer in his head.

Meg twirled a mechanical pencil between her fingers. "What's stopping you? I'm sure you have a stash of pills in your backpack."

He did, inside a hollow ink pen to thwart a search in case he was shaken down. "Have you told McCormick about the test data?"

"Not yet. If I told him, he'd fire you, you know."

He nodded, even though it hurt like hell. "And my probation would be revoked."

"You'd go back to jail?"

"Yeah."

Ravi and Jeff walked up, arguing good-naturedly about an episode of *Star Wars: The Clone Wars*. Ravi was of Far Eastern descent. Jeff, on the other hand, was from a galaxy far, far away. The guys stopped and looked back and forth between Wes and Meg.

"Somebody die?" Jeff asked.

"You," Meg warned, "unless you give us a few minutes of privacy."

"Uh, sure," Jeff said nervously. The sloppy geek was head over heels in love with Meg. "We'll get some breakfast out of the vending machine. Come on, Ravi."

Ravi was a germ-a-phobe who wouldn't touch the buttons on the vending machines without wearing his latex gloves. Ravi looked panicked, but he, too, did pretty much everything Meg told him to do. The two of them headed down the hall in the opposite direction. Meg waited until they were out of earshot before turning back to Wes.

"So what's the deal with your parents?"

He swallowed. Talking about his parents always made him nervous and defensive. "What do you mean?"

"I mean, did they just up and abandon you and your sister?"

"They left me in my sister's care," he corrected, "because my dad had to leave town."

"Because it was either leave town or stand trial?"

"Yeah," he mumbled, trying to tamp down his irritation that she was judging Randolph without knowing what had happened. "But he's innocent of the accusations."

"So why not stay and defend himself?"

The sixty-four thousand dollar question. The question that his sister had asked so often over the years. The question that niggled the back of his own mind. "I guess he had his reasons."

Her mouth flattened. "And your mom? She had her reasons for leaving her kids?"

Wes had met Meg's mother at the reception that he'd ducked out of. Mrs. Vincent had been a warm, caring person who obviously adored her daughter and husband. Wesley had blushed under the woman's welcome, and had fought the urge to stay and soak up her attention. It was apparent Dr. Vincent hadn't shared Wesley's shady background with Mrs. Vincent. Just as it was apparent Meg couldn't comprehend her mother leaving her.

"She knew my sister would take good care of me," Wes said.

"How old were you?"

He squinted. "Nine, I think."

Sympathy clouded her eyes. Normally her reaction would've irked him, but at the moment, he needed her on his side.

"That must've been tough on you and your sister," she offered.

He shrugged. "I'm sure it's been tough on my parents, too."

"So you haven't seen them since they left?"

He shook his head, unleashing an earthquake. He sucked air through his teeth against the sharp pain.

"And the charges against your father still stand?"

He nodded with as little movement as possible.

"So they're fugitives?"

"You could say that," he conceded. "But I think they'll come home soon."

She frowned. "Why would you think that?"

His mind slogged away. He debated telling her that his father had been in touch with Carlotta recently. But he'd already told his attorney Liz, and regretted it.

"I don't want to get you involved," he said, trying to sound as mysterious as possible.

Her eyebrows shot up. "You're protecting me?"

"Yeah. The less you know, the better."

She sat back and crossed her arms. "Give me one

good reason why I shouldn't tell McCormick that you're here simply to dig into your dad's case."

He shrugged. "It's more interesting if I'm around?"

She made a face. "More dangerous maybe."

Even though the muscles in his face ached, he grinned. "Same thing."

As he waited for her reaction, sweat dripped down his back. He couldn't read Meg at all. She was smarter than anyone his age he'd ever met, let alone a girl. Top that with the fact that she had a killer body and was as cool as hell, and he was pretty damn fascinated by her. She'd once announced that he could be her boyfriend if only he'd "straighten up," which left him feeling alternately irritated and turned on.

Meg held up the *AJC*, which heralded THE CHARMED KILLER CAPTURED? "Isn't this Cooper Craft the guy you worked for?"

He set his jaw. "Yeah."

One eyebrow arched. "You were apprenticing with The Charmed Killer?"

"He's innocent. No way Coop did those things."

"Really. And you think your dad is innocent, too?"

"That's right."

She dropped the newspaper and studied him. "You're either the most brilliant guy in the room or the worst judge of character ever."

He shrugged. "Maybe."

"What about your sister?"

"She doesn't believe Coop is guilty, either."

"No, I mean, what does she think about your father?"

"She's willing to give him the benefit of the doubt."

Meg drummed her fingers on the desk, and the rhythmic movement sent thunder rolling through his head. Just when he was on the verge of screaming, she stopped.

"And you think the records in the courthouse database might shed some light on your father's case?"

He shrugged. "I don't know. I thought it was worth a try to find out."

"Isn't the police record public?"

"Just the arrest report. I'm hoping to find the transcript of the grand jury."

She began drumming her fingers again.

He reached across and covered her hand with his. "Please don't do that."

Beneath his hand, her fingers were cool and baby soft. The Oxy magnified the sensation of her skin against his—it was electric and left him with images of her touching him elsewhere.

Meg yanked her hand out from under his as if he'd burned her. She looked flustered, then her gaze hardened. "Let me get this straight. You hacked into the city computer system and risked going to jail to help the man who abandoned you?"

It occurred to him that she might be wired—not out of the question since her father had hired a P.I. to follow him—so he decided not to say anything. Instead he nodded.

She chewed the side of her mouth and was quiet for so long, he was sure she was going to turn him over to McCormick. "I'll make you a deal," she said finally.

Warning flags rose in his mind. "What kind of deal?"

"I won't turn you in…if you'll let me help you sift through your father's records."

Wes squinted. "Why would you do that?"

Her expression was haughty. "You're not really in a position to ask, are you?"

"No," he mumbled in agreement, relieved, but still wary. Because of all positions he'd imagined himself in with Meg, this wasn't even in the top five.

5

"I'd like to see Cooper Craft, please." Carlotta's grip on her shoulder bag was slippery—she was a nervous wreck at the prospect of facing Coop, but she'd barely slept last night from worrying over him. She desperately needed to make sure he was okay.

The lady officer behind the counter at the Atlanta City Detention Center leaned forward and eyed her suspiciously, as if she might be hiding a metal file in her slingbacks. "Are you his attorney?"

While the idea of impersonating Liz Fischer gave her a little thrill, she decided it would be too easy to check. "No."

"Reporter?"

"Definitely not."

"If you're some kind of serial-killer groupie, you're wasting your time." The officer's eyes narrowed. "I've heard about kooks like you."

"I'm not a groupie. My name is Carlotta Wren. Brooklyn at the midtown precinct can vouch for me."

"Yeah, I know Brook," the woman conceded with a wary nod. "But that ain't gonna get you a free pass into my jail."

Carlotta realized she would have to change tactics to get past the cranky gatekeeper. She glanced at the officer's name badge and offered her a sad smile. "Officer McHenry, is it?"

"Uh-hm."

"Officer McHenry, surely there must be some way for me to see Coop."

"No can do. In case you haven't read the papers, sweetie, this is a high-profile case. Technically, he's not supposed to see anyone except his lawyer and immediate family. So unless you're his sister, you ain't getting in."

Carlotta angled her head. "What if I'm his girlfriend?"

"Uh-uh."

"Fiancée?" she asked hopefully.

The woman's eyes widened. "You're engaged to this guy?"

Beneath the ledge of the counter Carlotta discreetly moved a costume jewelry butterfly band to her left ring finger, then lifted her hand in reply. "I just need fifteen minutes."

"I don't think—"

"Ten minutes?" She worked up some tears to seal the deal. It wasn't hard because she was starting to feel panicky about not seeing Coop. She couldn't bear him thinking that she'd set him up to be arrested. "Just long enough to break it off. Surely you can understand."

The woman crossed her arms and nodded. "Girl, you gotta get out of that mess, for sure."

Carlotta sagged in relief. "I knew you'd understand."

"Course, he'll have to agree to see you," Officer McHenry said, picking up the phone. "Give me your name again."

She told the woman, then chewed on a ragged thumbnail. Would Coop blow her cover and refuse to see her?

The woman talked to someone in low tones and was on hold for several long minutes. Finally, she replaced the receiver and tapped on a keyboard before pushing it toward Carlotta.

"Sign the computer log," she said. "I'll need your purse, and I have to search you."

The officer had typed Coop's name in the Inmate column. In the Visitor column, Carlotta typed in her own. Under "Relationship to Inmate" she hesitated, but with Officer McHenry watching, she slowly typed in F-I-A-N-C-É-E. If Peter knew she was pretending to be engaged to Coop, he'd have a stroke.

The officer waved Carlotta around to a door that she held open. When Carlotta walked through, the woman said, "I have to warn you—your man's in a bad way."

Her heart skipped a beat. "What do you mean?"

McHenry took her purse and set it aside, then began to methodically pat her down. "He's a drinker, right?"

"He's had some issues with alcohol," Carlotta hedged.

"Well, there's no alcohol here," the cop said pointedly. "Take off your shoes."

She stepped out of the slingbacks. So Coop was going through withdrawal. Jack had commented that at least in jail Coop could dry out.

"Nice shoes," the officer said, setting them back down for Carlotta to step into.

"Thanks. I work at Neiman's at Lenox. Come by sometime and I'll give you my friends-and-family discount."

McHenry brightened. "Oh, you're the one who hooked Brooklyn up with a coupon."

Carlotta smiled. "That's me."

The officer, now in a better humor, handed Carlotta off to another uniform, and as she was led through a series of doors and hallways, she was passed to a pair of guards. Her pulse ratcheted higher as her heels clacked, echoing on the tile floor. They delivered her to a small room with four partitioned booths that faced a glass wall. Carlotta had to suppress her dismay. She'd expected to be in the same room with Coop when she talked to him.

Another visitor—an older woman—was talking to an inmate on the other side of the glass.

"You can take the booth on the far end," a guard said, nodding.

Carlotta swallowed hard and moved woodenly to a metal folding chair in front of a grubby wooden ledge scarred with letters and names. She lowered herself to the cold, hard surface of the chair. The guard stepped out of the room and the steel door closed with a clang. The scene was surreal, like something in a movie. At the sight of Coop dressed in a gray jumpsuit and being led in shackles and handcuffs to a chair on the other side of the glass, she grew light-headed. Starbursts flashed behind her eyes as she blinked back tears.

He looked pale and gaunt, his eyes behind his glasses dark and sunken. He seemed lethargic as he held up his hands for a guard to unlock the cuffs, but he managed a small smile when he turned toward her and sat down. He gave her a small wave, then reached for the phone with a shaky hand.

Moving in slow motion, she did the same, wracked with anguish over what he must be going through.

"Hi," he said into the phone.

It was strange to watch someone talk and hear it through the earpiece. "Hi," she returned with a croak. "How are you?"

A light came into his eyes. "Engaged, apparently."

She smiled sheepishly, her cheeks warming. "I had to fib or they wouldn't let me see you."

"I don't mind," he murmured, then nodded to the butterfly ring on her left hand. "But that's a pretty sad engagement ring I bought you."

"I had to improvise."

"I'm just glad Peter hasn't convinced you to wear *his* ring."

Carlotta bit her lip. "You have bigger things to worry about, Coop."

He sighed and averted his glance. "So it seems."

"I'm so sorry."

He frowned. "About what?"

"Jack told me you were M.I.A. So when you called and said you were coming by the store with Wesley's drug test results, I called Jack to let him know you weren't missing after all. I didn't mean to set you up."

He looked at her with quiet, hooded eyes. She could tell he didn't know whether to believe her. "What's done is done."

"Coop," she said earnestly, "where is your fight?"

"I'm tired," he said quietly.

"You're sick. You're going through withdrawal from the alcohol. You'll feel better soon."

He nodded, but without conviction.

Fear squeezed her heart. "Coop, you'd tell me if something else was wrong, something more…serious?"

"There's no need to worry, Carlotta."

She wet her lips. "Coop, Wesley saw you at the hospital and he followed you—"

"Stop," he cut in, his jaw hardening. "Don't say another word. Whatever Wesley saw or thought he saw, it has nothing to do with this, understand?"

She nodded, aware that she had hit a nerve. Afraid that Coop would abruptly end their conversation, she changed tack. "Your arraignment is Monday?"

"That's what my lawyer tells me."

"I hear Liz Fischer is representing you."

"At least in the arraignment. Then we'll see."

She didn't even want to think about the case going to trial. "Liz will take care of you," she said, trying not to let her disapproval of the woman show. "Besides, anything could happen over the weekend. Michael Lane might be taken into custody. Or—" She sighed. "I hate to say this, but The Charmed Killer could strike again and at least everyone will know you're innocent."

He blinked slowly. "I'm prepared for things to run their course."

Carlotta bit her cheek in frustration. Even though she knew in her heart that Coop wasn't The Charmed Killer, she ached for his reassurance. Then there was the matter of what he'd said to her just before he was arrested. He said he'd done something terrible, that he'd killed someone. But he'd been drinking, and at the time when she'd pressed him, he'd brushed it off as a bad joke.

She held her tongue now only because she worried their conversation might not be private, and that Coop was still too foggy to express himself clearly. She didn't want to be responsible for him saying something to further incriminate himself.

"How are *you?*" he asked.

"Worried sick about you."

His mouth twitched. "Still living with Peter?"

"Staying with him, yes."

"I'm glad you're safe. Did you talk to Wesley about the drug test results?"

"Not yet. I'm waiting for the right time."

"Don't put it off too long."

"I won't." Carlotta wet her lips, then put her hand on the window. "Coop, I'm afraid for you."

He lifted his large hand to mirror hers against the glass. "Don't be. Everything will work out, you'll see."

She felt the heat from his skin through the cool glass. Memories of their weekend in Florida came flooding back to her. They had been the victims of bad timing and if she could go back...

Tears clogged her throat. "We want to help, me and Hannah and Wes. Tell me what we can do."

He gave her a wry smile. "Water my plants?"

"I'm serious, Coop."

"You can't help me, Carlotta. This was bound to happen, one way or another."

Her mouth parted in confusion, but before she could ask him to explain, the door opened and a guard stepped into the room. "Time's up."

Carlotta's throat convulsed. "I probably won't be able to talk my way in again. I told the woman at the front desk I had to see you so I could break our engagement."

He gave a little laugh. "Well, it was fun while it lasted."

A tear slid down her cheek. "Coop, I…" She didn't know what to say. She wasn't in a position to make promises, and she was acutely aware of how the situation might distort emotions.

"Hey, how about a smile before you leave to get me through?" Coop asked.

She inhaled deeply, then gave him the best grin she could manage.

"That's better," he said.

"Call me if you need anything at all."

"Thanks for coming," he said, then returned the receiver to the cradle.

Realizing that he hadn't responded to her offer of help, she hung up the phone on her side and watched with growing panic as he was handcuffed and led away. The shuffling of his shackled feet sickened her. She choked back a sob.

"Ma'am, are you okay?" the guard asked kindly.

She covered her mouth and nodded, then followed the man blindly back to the lobby area where she retrieved her purse. When she emerged, she looked up and nearly swallowed her tongue.

Jack Terry was standing in the lobby, leaning on the counter talking to Officer McHenry.

He, on the other hand, did not seem surprised to see her. He straightened and crossed his arms. "Officer McHenry, is this the fiancée?"

The woman looked at Carlotta. "Sorry, girl. Detective Terry from the midtown precinct is set up to receive a text when Craft receives visitors."

"Ms. Wren and I are acquainted," Jack said dryly. "Carlotta, can I have a word with you?"

"Actually, I'm in a hurry," she said, moving toward the door.

"Actually, that wasn't a question," Jack said, walking up next to her. He grasped her elbow and ushered her outside.

"Jack, you're manhandling me!"

"You're lucky I don't shoot you," he said in a lethal tone, shepherding her to his sedan sitting at the end of the walk. "I told you to stay out of this."

Detective Maria Marquez stood next to the car, every inch of her tall, curvy frame oozing authority and sexuality. With luxurious hair the color of caramels, luminous skin the color of toffee, and enormous almond-shaped eyes, the woman looked utterly edible. Carlotta slid Jack a sideways glance, wondering if he'd taken a nibble yet. He was a red-blooded male, and Maria had intimated to Carlotta that she was attracted to Jack, although she wasn't looking for a liaison with a coworker. Carlotta wondered, though, if Maria was skittish for other reasons. Once she had overheard Maria on the phone talking to someone in an angry tone, asking them not to call her again. Maria had moved to Atlanta from Chicago "for a change" she'd said. She was a profiler for the Atlanta Police Department and had been assisting the GBI in the investigation of The Charmed Killer while Jack had been banished because of his relationship to Carlotta and her family.

Carlotta was sure that Maria's profiling had led to Coop's arrest. She frowned at the woman, but Maria seemed amused to see her. "In trouble again, Carlotta?"

It didn't help that the woman's melodic voice was like a snake charmer's flute.

Carlotta yanked her arm out of Jack's grasp. "I have a right to see Coop!"

A couple of passersby looked their way.

Jack glowered at Carlotta. "How about we not do this in public? What are you driving these days? Did Ashford buy you a pink Lamborghini?"

She rolled her eyes. "No. I'm getting a rental this evening. Peter dropped me off at MARTA and I rode to Underground, then walked here."

"Which means you didn't tell him where you were headed."

She pressed her lips together.

Jack sighed. "Well, at least I'm not the only person you lie to."

"I didn't lie. If Peter had asked me if I was headed to the city detention, I would've said yes." Probably.

"Get in the car," Jack said. "We'll take you to work."

"I'm going by the townhouse first."

"Why?"

"If you must know, Wesley wants to show me the new security system."

"Okay, we'll take you there."

She climbed into the back of the sedan, feeling morose. When Jack and Maria assumed their positions in the front, Carlotta crossed her arms. "Why are you so angry that I came to see Coop?"

Jack turned around in his seat. "Did you and Coop get engaged and not tell anyone?"

"No," she mumbled.

"Then you lied your way in to see him. How do you think that's going to look to the GBI?"

"I don't care."

Maria turned around. "Carlotta, if you care about Cooper, you'll listen to Jack. Stay out of this investigation."

Carlotta's acidic retort was cut short by a pointed look from Jack. Instead she sat back in a huff, stewing.

After they'd ridden in silence for a few minutes, Jack made eye contact through the rearview mirror. "So... how did Coop look to you?" he asked quietly.

Carlotta hardened her jaw. "Not good."

She averted her gaze and was quiet for the remainder of the ride. Jack and Maria talked in low tones, their heads and bodies leaning in. At one point Maria reached over to pick lint off Jack's jacket—the man had certainly started dressing better since Maria had been assigned as his partner. And he didn't seem to mind the extra attention. In fact, Carlotta had to tap his shoulder after he missed the turn to the townhouse she shared with Wesley.

"Sorry," Jack offered. "I just assumed my car knew the way since it's been to your house so many times on distress calls."

"Very funny." But it was true. Since she'd first met Jack when he'd arrested Wesley for hacking into the city computer, their lives had crossed and folded back onto each other's several times.

He pulled into the driveway behind Hannah's van. Wesley's bicycle sat nearby, and Chance's BMW.

"You having a party?" Jack asked.

"Yes. And you're not invited." She unbuckled the seat belt and reached for the door handle. "Thanks for the ride."

"Carlotta."

She stopped and looked back to see Jack's meaty

finger wagging at her. "Stay away from this investigation. Let the professionals handle it."

"I don't know what you're talking about," she said, feigning ignorance.

"I mean it, Carlotta. Behave."

"Why, Jack, I'm a Southern lady. Of course I'll behave. Toodles."

The sound of his snort resounded in her ears as she swung out of the car and slammed the door.

6

Carlotta bounded up to the townhouse, amazed at how much she missed the place. There really was no place like home.

"Carlotta?"

At the sound of Mrs. Winningham's voice, she stopped and swallowed a groan. She looked up to the see her neighbor standing at the fence, wearing a big sun hat and a bigger frown. "Hi, Mrs. Winningham."

"We need to talk. You have a serious problem."

Carlotta laughed. "You're going to have to be more specific, Mrs. Winningham."

"Fire ants."

"Beg your pardon?"

Her neighbor gestured to the Wren's yard. It was the bane of the woman's existence because crabgrass and dandelions had all but choked out the more desirable blue-green fescue. "See those two piles of sand over there and there? You have fire ants."

"I guess that's a bad thing?" Carlotta asked.

"Have you ever been bitten by a fire ant?"

"I can't say that I have."

"Well, it's not pretty." The woman shook her finger.

"If you don't get rid of them, they'll spread to my yard, and I can't risk Toofers getting into their nest. They'd eat him alive."

While Carlotta wasn't crazy about the tuft-headed, snarling little beast, she agreed that death by fire ants would be a painful way for the mutt to go. "I'll talk to Wesley about it," Carlotta promised.

"Did you hear the police arrested The Charmed Killer?"

Carlotta's throat convulsed. "I heard that an arrest had been made."

"Finally I can sleep at night."

"That's good, Mrs. Winningham." Would everyone who'd read of Coop's arrest assume he was guilty? Of course they would. If she didn't know Coop, she would, too. After all, he was a former medical examiner who worked around death, and had been demoted to a body mover because of a drinking problem. It had all the makings of a movie of the week. She moved toward the house. "Take care, Mrs. Winningham."

"Don't forget about the ants!"

She jogged up the stairs to the door and twisted the knob. When she pushed the door open, a faint *beep, beep* sounded. The sound of voices in the living room stopped. Wesley, Hannah and Chance all looked her way.

"The sensor on the door works," Wes said. "Where've you been? I was getting ready to call."

"Sorry. I went to see Coop."

From the couch, Hannah pushed to her feet. "How is he?"

Chance looked stricken at Hannah's interest. Carlotta winced—she still had to process the idea of Hannah and Fat Chance as a couple. "Coop was calm." She turned to Wes. "Except when I mentioned that you'd followed him at the hospital. Then he was furious."

Wes explained to Hannah how he'd followed Coop to the office of a neurologist.

Hannah paled. "Something's wrong with him?"

"He brushed it off," Carlotta said, pushing her hair back from her face. "He insisted it had nothing to do with any of this."

"And you believe him?" Hannah asked.

"I don't know. But since he was so agitated and our conversation was probably being recorded, I didn't want to force the issue."

"Has he talked to Liz?" Wesley asked.

"She's going to handle the arraignment on Monday."

Chance scratched his head. "I don't understand what we're all doing here."

Hannah frowned at him. "We're going to help prove that Coop didn't commit these murders."

"Isn't that what the police are for?" Chance asked.

"The police have already made up their minds," Wes offered.

"And what if the guy is guilty?"

"He isn't," the rest of them chorused.

Chance's eyebrows went up. "And you know this how?"

Hannah scoffed. "Because some things you just know about some people." She gave Carlotta a meaningful look, and Carlotta realized Hannah was referring to Carlotta's support earlier in the week. Hannah had been accused of stealing purses at Bedford Manor Country Club events where she'd sometimes worked as a server. Carlotta had defended her friend to the victims who had been quick to judge Hannah because of her goth makeup and clothing. And piercings. And tattoos.

Carlotta smiled, then noticed all the holes in the drywall in the living room and beyond, in the hallway and the kitchen. She gasped. "Did the police do this when they processed the house for evidence?"

"No," Wes said. "The holes are from the installation of the security system. You're welcome," he added dryly.

"No, I appreciate it," she assured him, but her knees felt weak. "I just didn't expect this much…destruction." Between the damaged walls and the black splotches of fingerprint dust around light plates, door facings, and doorknobs, the place looked like a war zone.

"You wanted to repaint anyway," Wes said. "I figured this would give us a reason to redo everything."

She nodded, pursing her mouth. "You're right. Now we don't have a choice."

"But we *do* have sensors on all the doors and windows."

"I'm really impressed you did this all by yourself," she said.

"Uh, Chance helped a little."

Chance grinned up at Hannah. "Yeah, I helped."

Hannah tweaked his chubby cheek. Carlotta threw up in her mouth a little. Quickly changing the subject, she pulled the notebook she'd been using to record details of the crimes out of her bag. "Let's go in the kitchen to talk."

"But it's more comfortable here in the living room," Wes said.

She frowned at him. "We can talk better at the table."

He looked like he wanted to argue, but he followed

her. In the kitchen, though, he kept looking toward the window over the sink. He was acting strange. As soon as this little pow-wow ended, she was going to talk to him about the drug test results.

"Okay," Carlotta said, opening her book. "I've been keeping notes on everything that's happened with The Charmed Killer case. I made copies for you, Wes, and for you, Hannah."

"We'll share," Chance said happily.

Carlotta narrowed her eyes at him. "Anything we talk about is confidential."

"I can keep my mouth shut," he groused.

"I'll make sure of it," Hannah said to Carlotta, giving Chance a glare.

Carlotta passed around the copies. "I figure since we were on the scenes of most of the crimes, we're in a good position to help figure out who's behind these killings. Until we have something else to go on, I'm operating under the belief that it's Michael Lane." She held up a picture of Michael. "The body of the first victim, Shawna Whitt, was found about the same time he escaped from Northside Hospital."

"Remind me how she was killed," Hannah said, skimming through the notes.

"It looked like she'd died of natural causes, but before we moved the body, Coop found a charm in her mouth—a bird, like this one." She pulled out a silver charm and set it in the middle of the table.

"Is that the charm?" Wes asked in alarm.

"No. I bought it from a kiosk in the mall."

"Could be a chicken," Hannah added.

"The Whitt woman's cause of death was ruled natural causes," Carlotta said, "and her body was cremated."

"Natural?" Chance asked. "How did they explain the chicken charm in her mouth?"

Everyone was quiet for a few seconds. Finally, Wes said, "No one did." He shot a glance toward the kitchen window.

"So Coop could've put it there himself?" Chance asked.

"No," Hannah said firmly.

"I was there," Carlotta said. "I saw him pull the charm out of the woman's mouth. Now, what very few people know is that later, I found an entry Shawna Whitt made on a Web site set up for people who were charm fans. So, she was into charms, even though a bracelet wasn't found in her home. She'd also asked for recommendations for online dating services."

"So she could've met the creep there," Hannah said.

Carlotta nodded. "Then we have the second victim, Alicia Sills."

"Carlotta, Wes and I went to pick up her body," Hannah said to Chance.

"How'd she die?"

"It looked as if she'd fallen from a stepladder and hit her head," Carlotta offered. "But when we moved the body, a charm shaped like a cigar fell out of her mouth, like this one." She dug the charm out of a baggie, then set it next to the chicken.

"The autopsy stated she died of blunt force trauma," Wes supplied, "but the M.E. couldn't determine if it was from the fall or if someone had hit her." He glanced toward the window again, as if he was afraid someone would appear.

"Was Coop there?" Chance asked.

"No," Wes said. "He called and asked me to do the pickup."

"Did he give a reason?" Chance pressed.

Wes scratched his head. "I just remember him saying it would be better if I did it."

Silence boomed around the table. Carlotta decided not to mention that Peter believed Randolph had had an affair with the woman years ago—not yet anyway.

She cleared her throat. "The third victim was Pam Witcomb, street name Pepper. She was stabbed in a room at the High Crest Motel."

"Pepper?" Chance asked. "I know a prostitute named Pepper."

Hannah glowered.

"Might be the same woman," Carlotta said, although she found it hard to believe that Chance knew only one Pepper. "She hung out on Third Street and West Peachtree."

"Dang," Chance said. "I think I might have lost my virginity to her."

Carlotta gave him a tight smile. "Not relevant, but thanks for the image. Anyway, the charm in her mouth was a car. I don't know the exact one, but let's use this one for now." She set the generic car charm with the others.

"How did you know Pepper hung out on Third and West Peachtree?" Chance asked Carlotta.

"I met her one night while I was waiting for Coop—" She stopped and swallowed. "To pick me up."

"So Coop saw her, too?"

"I...suppose so. But they didn't talk or anything."

Still, a disquieting sensation began to niggle at the back of her mind.

"What about the fourth victim?" Hannah asked quickly. "She was an assistant to the District Attorney, wasn't she?"

"Right. Cheryl Meriwether. She was found shot to death in her home. The charm in her mouth was a gun." She set a charm of a handgun on the table.

"Did Coop know this woman?" Chance asked.

Wesley shrugged and looked to Carlotta.

"Not that I know of," she said. Although he had attended her memorial service....

"Since she worked in the D.A.'s office, he might have known her from...before," Wesley said, his eyes darting back to the window.

"Before what?" Hannah asked.

"Coop made a mistake a few years back when he was the Chief Medical Examiner," Carlotta said. "The story is that he was drinking and driving and came upon a car accident. He stopped to help and declared a woman at the scene dead."

"Except she wasn't dead," Wes supplied. "And because she didn't receive medical care right away, she almost *did* die. Coop lost his job."

"Jack said he had to spend some time in jail," Carlotta murmured.

"So maybe he knew this Meriwether chick from then," Chance said.

"Maybe," Carlotta agreed quietly, making more notes.

"What about the next victim?" Hannah pressed, sounding desperate.

Carlotta took a deep breath to clear her head. "Number five was Marna Collins. She died in her home of cyanide poisoning. The cop who was first on the scene told me there was no sign of forced entry, and that the M.E. pulled a handcuffs charm from her mouth. I don't know if it looked like this one, but it's the only one I could find." She set the silver charm on the table.

"Next was Wanda Alderman. Suffocated, again in her home. They didn't realize she was a victim at first because she'd swallowed the charm, a barrel or a keg. It was found during the autopsy. Again, I didn't see it, but this was the only barrel charm I could find."

Carlotta stopped and massaged her temples. "The seventh victim was the burned body that was dumped in front of my scooter on the street."

"They still haven't made an identification?" Hannah asked.

"No. And Jack said it could take a while."

"What kind of charm was in the mouth?" Wesley asked.

"I don't know, but I'll keep trying to find out. Wes, can you keep your ears open at the morgue?"

He nodded.

"So the killer meant for you to run over the body," Chance said to Carlotta.

She nodded. "I'm assuming."

"What kind of car was the body tossed out of?" Chance pressed.

"I can't say for sure." She'd played the last seconds before the accident over and over in her mind so many times. Her memory was starting to return flashes of vehicles, but she couldn't be sure if they were simply vehicles at the scene in the aftermath, cars she'd seen in commercials, or even figments of her imagination. "It might—" Carlotta swallowed, having never uttered the words before. "It might have been a white van."

In the silence that followed, Chance looked around the table. "What does Coop drive?"

"A white van," Wes mumbled.

"And a Corvette," Hannah added quickly.

Carlotta fought a growing tide of alarm. "Wesley, since you picked up the last two victims that were found together, what can you tell us?"

"The eighth and ninth bodies were Georgia State students, two girls." He squinted, as if he were trying to recall details. "Amy Hampell…and DeeAnn or Diane Easton, I think. They were parked, smoking a joint from the looks of it. Died of carbon monoxide poisoning. Our UNSUB stuffed a rag in their tailpipe, then stuffed charms down their throats."

"UNSUB?" Chance asked.

"Unknown subject," Wes supplied. "Police speak."

"And the charms in their mouths were books," Carlotta said.

"Both of them?" Hannah asked.

Wes nodded. "Maybe because they were students?"

"Is Coop into co-eds?" Chance asked.

"I think he's just into Carlotta," Wes said with a laugh.

Hannah flinched.

Carlotta bit her lip, recalling the slinky blonde who'd been all over Coop the night she'd seen him drinking at Moody's cigar bar.

"Was the car found near his house or where he works?" Chance asked.

Carlotta exchanged a glance with Wes, then said,

"No, but it was found close to a cigar bar where Coop sometimes hangs out."

Chance threw up his hands. "I don't even know the guy and I'd convict right now."

"Don't say that," Hannah said. "Coop isn't a killer."

"Okay. But assuming that's true, how the heck are we supposed to help him? Unless someone else walks into the police station and confesses, the guy is sunk."

They all looked at Carlotta. Her face felt hot. "Well…the way I see it, we have two choices. We can either try to prove that Coop didn't do these things, or we can find the person who did."

"Michael Lane?" Wes asked.

She nodded.

"How are we supposed to do that?" Hannah asked.

"I don't have all the answers yet. Meanwhile, let's divvy up some of these leads and unanswered questions. I'm going to keep trying to track down where the charms might have been purchased, and I'm going back to the beginning to look into the background of the first victim. Hannah, can you and Chance find out where someone would get cyanide?"

They nodded. Carlotta figured with Chance's drug connections, he'd have the answer in a couple of phone calls. "Also, Chance, can you ask around and find out if Pepper's friends know anything about a man who might have been stalking her?"

He struck a serious pose. "Will do."

"Wes, I need for you to stay on top of the identification of the burned body, and find out what you can about Coop's case through Liz." She gave him a pointed look.

"No problem."

Carlotta tried not to think about his methods for gleaning info out of Liz. "I'm also going to try to figure out where Michael might be hiding." She closed her notebook. "Call me if you find out anything."

Hannah and Chance got up to go. "Do you need a ride?" Hannah asked.

"That would be great, thanks." She looked over to find Wesley chewing on a fingernail, still seemingly fixated on the kitchen window. His eyes looked dilated. Carlotta sighed. She couldn't put off the drug talk any longer. "I need a minute to talk to Wes."

7

Carlotta studied Wesley with growing concern. The fact that he was so distracted by the kitchen window to the point of not noticing when his buddy Chance said goodbye told her how much the drugs were messing with his concentration. Was he hallucinating?

"Wesley," she said sharply.

His head came around. "Huh?"

"How did the reception go the other night?"

"Uh, not so well."

"What happened?"

"Meg's dad doesn't like me."

She smiled. "No father likes a guy his daughter likes. What matters is whether Meg likes you."

"I don't think Meg likes me anymore, either."

"Why not?"

He sighed. "Because I was stupid. I let her dad make me mad and I left the reception without telling her."

Carlotta's eyes widened. "You just left her there? I can't believe she's still speaking to you."

"Only to say mean things," he said morosely.

"Have you apologized?"

"Not exactly."

She arched an eyebrow. "What are you waiting for?"

"It's complicated."

"Not as complicated as you men want to make it," she countered. "If you like this girl, buy her flowers and tell her you were an idiot."

"I'll think about it," he hedged.

Carlotta crossed her arms. "We need to talk about something else."

His Adam's apple bobbed. "What?"

"Um…we have fire ants."

"Huh?"

"In the front yard, apparently. Mrs. Winningham is about to have a fit. Can you take care of it?"

He pushed his hand into his hair. "I'll figure something out." His glance slid back to the window. "I really need to get going, Sis."

She caught his arm. "Wait, there's something else."

He sighed. "*What* already?"

"The fact that you're taking Oxy."

He looked surprised, then recovered with nonchalance. "I'm not, I told you."

She reached for her purse and pulled out the piece of paper that Coop had given her, then extended it to him. "This says different."

"What is it?"

"The results of a drug test. On you."

He glanced over the sheet. "A drug test? But how? What did you test?"

"Your hair."

"But how—" He stopped, his face going stony. "The haircut you gave me the other day."

"Right."

His face went red, then he flailed his arms. "I can't believe you'd do something like that behind my back!"

"I had a feeling you were lying to me."

The veins in his neck bulged. "You had no right! It's none of your business."

She blinked at his belligerent response, but held her ground. "You're my brother. I'm not going to stand by and let you do something that could kill you, or at the very least, send you back to jail."

He pursed his mouth. "I only took a few pills for the pain."

"I understand why you started taking them, Wes, but you need to stop."

"Where did you have this test done? This could be bogus for all I know."

"Coop did the analysis himself."

"Coop?" Emotions played over his face—anger, frustration, shame. He turned his back to her and jammed his hands on his hips.

She waited, wanting to reach out to touch him, but sensing he wouldn't welcome it.

"Wes, I need for you to get straight," she said quietly. "With Coop in jail, I'm barely hanging on here. I need your help to deal with this."

Finally his shoulders fell. "Okay, I'll quit." He turned around, his expression bleak.

"Can you do it on your own?"

He scoffed. "Hell, yeah, I can do it on my own. I can quit any time I want to. This stuff isn't cocaine. I'm not some hard-core addict shooting up in an alley."

"Good," she said, relieved. "So you'll just…quit."

"I said I would," he snapped.

"Okay," she soothed, grateful he at least acknowledged he had a problem. That was enough for now. "I'm here if you need me."

She noticed that his gaze had slid back to the window over the sink.

"Wes, is something wrong? You keep looking—"

He cut her off by clamping a hand over her mouth.

Her eyes widened. He lifted a finger to his mouth, then pointed to the top of the window.

Carlotta squinted at what looked like a dark hole the size of a golf ball, then realized it wasn't a hole, it was…something. "What—"

Wesley covered her mouth again and shepherded her into the living room. "Keep your voice down."

When he released her, she whispered, "What's going on?"

"That thing over the window is a bug."

"A what?"

"A listening device. We—I mean, *I* found it when I installed the security system."

"What's it doing there?"

"I don't know. But from a date stamped on the base, it looks like it was installed about ten years ago."

Her eyebrows shot up. "Do you think Dad did it?"

"That's what I thought, so he could listen in to make sure we were okay."

Wonder flowered through her chest at the prospect. "When he spoke to me at the rest area, he did say he was keeping tabs on us. Maybe this is how."

"I figure he has a handheld receiver and parks near the house to listen in. The transmission range couldn't be more than a mile or so."

So Randolph had planned to be nearby, at least on occasion. Her mind scrolled back over all the conversations between her and Wesley that had taken place over the past ten years. The times her little brother had cried into his dinner plate. Knowing that Randolph and Valerie might have overheard how much their children were suffering, yet still hadn't come back, was almost worse than being ignored. Then another thought occurred to her.

"What if someone put it there to listen in on Dad?"

Wesley pulled his hand down his face and nodded. "That's a possibility."

"Wes, there's something else I should tell you. The Charmed Killer's second victim, Alicia Sills, worked in Dad's office building."

"Yeah. So?"

"So…Peter remembers that Dad and the woman were…friendly. Very friendly. And since Randolph's name has already come up as a possible suspect, it doesn't look good."

"Did Peter tell the police?"

"No. He left it up to me to decide, and I haven't said anything."

"Do you still have Dad's client file? The one I took from Liz?"

"It's at Peter's, but I haven't gone through it yet. I guess part of me doesn't want to dredge it up again, and another part of me wants to get past this situation with Coop before dealing with it."

Wes nodded, looking as concerned and confused as she felt. "I'm getting closer to pulling Dad's records from the city databases."

"Are you sure you won't get caught?"

"Why don't you let me worry about something?"

She smiled. "Deal." From her purse her cell phone rang. She pulled it out and checked the caller ID. It was June Moody, the owner of Moody's Cigar Bar who had befriended Carlotta, and who had developed a soft spot for Coop. "I need to take this."

"I'm gonna take off," Wes said, moving toward the door.

"I'll lock up. Tell Hannah I'll be right out. Oh, and Wes?"

He turned back.

"Apologize to Meg."

He looked pained, but nodded.

Watching him go, her heart gave a squeeze. She connected the ringing phone. "Hi, June. How are you?"

"At the moment, I'm worried half to death about Coop and the things they're saying on the news. Can you tell me what's going on?"

"I went to see Coop this morning. He's in good spirits," Carlotta lied, massaging her temple. "This is all a mistake. I think the GBI was pressured to make an arrest, and because Coop was so close to the crime scenes, he was a good candidate."

"And because he's drinking again?"

"That doesn't help," Carlotta agreed. "But Coop wouldn't want you to worry about him, June. I'll keep you posted."

"Okay." The woman sounded somewhat relieved.

"Is Mitchell still in town?" June's son, a sergeant in the army, was in Atlanta on leave from his post in Hawaii.

"For another week or so." But from the sound of June's

voice, their relationship was still strained—or maybe she was just concerned about her surrogate son, Coop.

"Try to enjoy the time you have left with him," Carlotta said, trying to sound upbeat. "I'll drop by the bar soon."

"Okay, dear. Bye."

Carlotta ended the call, but lying to June had taken its toll on her. The idea that she had to manufacture optimism sickened her. She leaned over to grasp her knees. A terrible storm of frustration and anger at the state of her life swirled in her stomach, spreading to her chest. Coop…Wesley… her father. A wall of tears pressed behind her eyes and cheeks. A sob rose in her throat, choking her. She wanted to scream, to cry, to do *something*.

Possessed with a fierce need to vent, she ran into the kitchen and raised her voice in the direction of the listening device imbedded in the wall. "Randolph, you're a coward!" she yelled. "Do you hear me? You're a coward, and I will never forgive you for what you've done to me and Wesley!"

She stopped and stared at the device, as if she half expected her father to answer. He didn't, of course. Even if he were listening, why would he respond after all this time?

She gripped the edge of the breakfast bar for support. A dark cloud threatened to engulf her. Was this what a nervous breakdown felt like?

She shook her head to clear it. She couldn't do that to Wesley, she had to get a grip. She had her job, and other people needed her.

The front door opened and Hannah's voice rang out. "Carlotta? You okay?"

She swallowed hard to rally herself before she turned

and walked into the living room. At the concern on her friend's face, she smiled. "I'm fine, just checking on a couple of things. Let's go."

But she felt Hannah's gaze on her as they backed out of the driveway and drove toward the mall. "You sure you're okay?"

"I talked to Wes about the drugs."

"Oh. And?"

"He promised he'd quit."

"And you believe him?"

"Yeah. He was sincere."

Hannah looked back to the road. "I hope you're right about Wes…and about Coop."

"I'm right about both of them," Carlotta said. "You'll see."

Hannah nodded, but didn't say anything.

To change the subject, Carlotta said, "So…you and Chance looked cozy."

"Oh, stop."

"What? It's kind of cute in a frat-boy-meets-Elvira kind of way."

"He's good to me, and it's a place to stay for now."

Carlotta frowned. "Why can't you stay at home?"

"Had a falling out with the folks."

Carlotta was stunned. Hannah never talked about her parents, and when Carlotta had probed before about her family, her friend had clammed up tight. "What over?"

Hannah gave a dismissive wave. "It's not important. It's time to get my own place anyway. I should've escaped that zoo a long time ago."

"Zoo?"

"They're not in touch with reality. They don't get me."

She surveyed Hannah's black lipstick, kohl-rimmed eyes, multiple piercings, and visible tattoos. "Well, Hannah, you have to admit…"

Hannah frowned. "What?"

"Uh, nothing." She cleared her throat. "So, you're living with Chance?"

"A toothbrush and a clean pair of thongs at his place does not constitute living together. How long are you planning to stay at Peter's?"

Carlotta bit her lip. "For a little while, until we get the townhouse repaired…or until Peter tosses me out."

"Right. Fat chance. I'm surprised Richie Rich hasn't shackled you in the wine cellar to keep you there. Have you two tried to have sex again?"

"No," she murmured. The first two times she and Peter had tried to consummate their reunion, things had ended…*prematurely.* "We're taking a step back and… enjoying each other."

"What the hell does that mean?"

"Well, tonight we're going to a movie."

Hannah pulled the van into the Lenox Square parking lot and headed toward Neiman Marcus. "Sounds like a barrel of fun."

"Maybe it's a little humdrum," Carlotta admitted. "But with everything else going on in my life, humdrum isn't so bad."

Hannah slowed for a speed bump, then pulled up to the entrance of Neiman's. "Keep saying that. Maybe one of us will believe it."

Carlotta frowned, then climbed out of the van with a wave. She walked into Neiman's, her mind swirling with all the unresolved relationships in her life.

Herb, the security guard hired to keep an eye on her in case Michael Lane showed up, stood next to a rack of flowered capris, resigned to another boring day of watching her dress women who moved in expensive circles.

Carlotta moved through her shift on automatic pilot, waiting on customers with a smile and sales skills that had become second nature to her. But all the while she kept picturing Coop as he'd been yesterday, standing in front of her, inebriated and disheveled, just before the police had shown up and the GBI had slammed him down on her counter, placing him under arrest for murder. She'd flailed in protest, but Jack had shuffled her away.

The scene played over and over in her head until she clocked out at the end of her shift with a stabbing pain behind her eyes. When she removed her purse from her locker in the employee break room, she tossed back Excedrin. Then, as promised, she called Peter to let him know she was finished for the day. His cheerful, calming voice was balm to her frayed nerves. He was just leaving the office. A few minutes later he picked her up and they grabbed a quick bite, then circled back to the mall theater.

Peter, bless him, must have sensed that she'd had a lousy day because he kept the conversation light and bought tickets to a low-key English comedy film. She squeezed his hand and leaned into his shoulder, grateful for the quiet space he gave her.

Still, she couldn't concentrate on the movie. The fact that she was keeping her jailhouse visit with Coop from Peter made guilt simmer in her chest. Meanwhile, her conversation with Coop ran through her head in a continuous loop. She picked it apart, trying to read between the lines and dissect Coop's frame of mind. One bit of dialogue came back to her.

Still living with Peter?

Staying with him, yes.

I'm glad you're safe.

Carlotta lifted her head and her heart sped up. Was that Coop's way of saying The Charmed Killer was still out there? Despite the grim prospect, the possibility cheered her immensely. She was suddenly eager to start looking into the background of the first victim, to hopefully find something that might piece together the identity of the madman stalking the city. And figure out why Coop would be willing to shoulder the blame for such heinous crimes.

When they arrived at Peter's home, a silver two-door Honda Civic rental car sat in the circular driveway.

"It has GPS," Peter said. "And it's yours for as long as you need it. I told my insurance company to slip the key through the mail slot in the front door."

"Thank you," she said, happy to have transportation again. She'd totaled Peter's Porsche without even leaving the driveway. And the pink Vespa he'd bought her had been demolished when she'd been unable to avoid a burned body dumped in her path. A typical day in her life.

When they entered Peter's house, the silence seemed oppressive to Carlotta. She walked through the great room and glanced toward the wide staircase that led to their respective bedrooms. Peter had grown less chatty, as if he, too, felt the awkwardness descend. His expression was a mixture of anxiety and longing.

"I think I'll go ahead and turn in," she said in a rush. "My back is still sore from the accident."

"Okay," he said, sounding relieved. "I think I'll stay up and work a little. Good night."

"Good night." She fled before tension could overtake the moment. Upstairs, she closed the door to the guest room where she'd been staying. Peter had been kind enough to offer her refuge when she'd needed a safe place to stay. But it had come with the expectation that they would work on their relationship. It wasn't too much to ask, Carlotta conceded, but she hadn't anticipated that soon after, Wesley would test positive for drugs, and Coop would be arrested as a serial killer.

And that she would still feel so uncertain about creating a life with Peter.

After washing her face and putting on pajamas, Carlotta climbed under the covers of the bed. She longed for sleep to erase the problems plucking at her. But she was half-afraid to close her eyes, afraid that the morning would bring yet another crisis.

From the nightstand, her cell phone rang. She glanced at the caller ID screen. *Jack.* His call was becoming a nightly ritual.

She connected the call. "Hi, Jack."

"All tucked in by your lonesome again?"

She sighed. "What do you want, Jack? It's been a long day."

"I could come over and rub your—"

"Jack!"

"I was going to say 'feet.'"

"I'm sure Peter would love that," she offered.

"Maybe he's into watching versus doing."

"I'm hanging up."

"Wait. I called to tell you that the GBI agents want you to come in Monday morning to answer more questions."

"About Coop?"

"I'd say that's a safe bet."

"Are you back on The Charmed Killer case?"

"Not officially, but I occasionally hear things."

Pillow talk with Maria? "So when I get the formal request, I'm supposed to act surprised."

"Yeah, you'll have to really stretch yourself because you never lie," he said dryly.

"Acting comes in handy sometimes," she cooed. "A woman never knows when she might have to fake it."

He laughed. "Not with me, sweetheart."

She frowned. He was right, the arrogant man. Unbidden desire whipped through her body, and on the heels of it, a shot of melancholy, because nothing in her life seemed to be in sync. She knew Jack was withholding information from her, and he knew she was withholding information from him.

"Jack…I'm scared."

"Of the dark?"

She smiled. "Yes. I'm scared of the dark."

"Set the phone on your pillow," he said quietly. "I'll wait until you fall asleep before I hang up."

The man was full of surprises. Carlotta set the phone next to her ear and curled onto her side, listening to Jack breathe. She made an effort to outlast him, but she lost that struggle with a smile on her face.

8

Wesley shifted on the uncomfortable chair in the coffee shop, waiting for Meg. He hadn't wanted to crawl out of bed so early, but she'd asked him to meet her outside the office to go over the test data at this godawful hour. So here he was, sneaking a smoke under the table, trying to wake up. He was on his second foamy drink with sprinkles that was some pricey derivative of coffee.

Conscious of his promise to Carlotta, he'd swallowed only half a tablet of Oxy this morning, cutting his normal dose. And he'd hoped the extra caffeine would help to ward off withdrawal. Instead, his head rumbled and his bladder was about to explode, but he wasn't about to carry a damn bouquet of flowers into the john.

He looked at the flowers and hoped Meg didn't notice the brown edges. It was the best bunch the convenience store on the corner had to offer. He picked off a few dying petals, but it left the flowers looking a little bald. He tossed down the rubber-banded bouquet and wiped his hand over his mouth. Like it mattered.

From his backpack, the theme of *The Mickey Mouse Club* sounded. He winced—if Mouse was calling this early in the morning, it couldn't be good. They'd had a lousy collections day yesterday—he probably wanted to work today. Wes cursed under his breath and flipped open the pay-as-you-go phone. "Yeah?"

"Hey, little man, did I wake you up?"

"Nah. What's going on?"

"Bad news. You know that Logan kid you let slip through your fingers yesterday?"

"The Georgia Tech student who owes The Carver ten large? I didn't expect the guy to jump out the window."

"Yeah, well, I just found out the frat boy got kicked out of school. Which means he's probably planning to hightail it back to Cincinnati and skip out on his debt, if he hasn't already."

Wes sighed. "I wasn't planning to work today."

"Change your plans," Mouse said. "The stakes went up when The Carver bought your debt from Father Thom."

Another loan shark he owed...or used to. Now all his markers were with The Carver, the man he was working undercover for in exchange for leniency from the D.A. on a previous charge. To get his foot in the organization, he'd offered to partner with Mouse to collect on "nontraditional" accounts—students whose environments he could infiltrate.

"If this schmuck is still in town, find him," Mouse said.

"And if I can't?"

"The Carver's gonna hold you personally responsible."

The line went dead and Wesley snapped the phone closed. His arm tingled where The Carver had sliced the letters C-A-R into his flesh for a previous infraction, with the promise to finish the job if Wesley stepped out of line again.

Wes lifted the cigarette for a drag.

"You can't smoke in here," the guy at the next table said.

Wesley started to give him the finger, then something in the newspaper the guy was reading caught his eye. *APD Receives Anonymous Note Identifying Headless Man.* "Can I see that?"

"Are you going to put out the cigarette?"

Wesley grabbed the paper out of the guy's hand and took another drag.

"Hey!"

"Relax, dude. Your blood pressure will kill you before my cigarette does."

The guy got up and scurried away. Wes scanned the short article that described the scrap of paper he'd mailed to the APD with three variations of a name scribbled on it. He hoped that one of the names belonged to the headless corpse in the morgue. He was pretty sure Mouse had done the guy in, since the dead man's finger had been in the trunk of Mouse's Town Car. And because Mouse had forced Wes to remove the teeth from the severed head with a pair of pliers.

The APD hopes the person who mailed in the tip will come forward.

"Right," Wesley murmured.

"Hi."

He looked up just as Meg dropped into the seat opposite him. She wore jeans, a striped T-shirt, and rugged sneakers. Her hair was skimmed back into a bouncy ponytail. His heart jerked sideways. "Hi."

"Whatcha reading?" She craned for a look.

"Nothing," he said, setting the paper aside.

"Are those for me?" she asked, nodding to the flowers.

"Uh…yeah." Heat climbed his neck as he snubbed out the half-smoked cigarette.

She picked up the bouquet and brought it to her nose. "Nice. But why?"

Under the table, Wes's leg jumped from the lack of Oxy. "Because I was an ass at the reception. The woman you saw me talking to—she wasn't someone I hooked up with afterward. She's my probation officer. I was embarrassed to tell you."

Meg's pink mouth rounded. "Oh."

"Your dad made me mad, but I shouldn't have left without telling you."

"No, you shouldn't have," she agreed. "Now we'll have to have that first date all over again."

Pleasure coiled through his chest. At the reception, Meg had announced to him that she never put out on the first date. His mind and body had instantly zoomed ahead to the second date, a chance he'd presumed had been lost forever.

She removed a daisy and stuck it in her ponytail. "I'm going to get tea. Do you need anything?"

He stared at her. She made it seem so effortless, being pretty and sexy. She was like a wild animal—natural and carefree and a little scary.

"Wes?"

"Uh, I'm going to hit the head. I'll be right back."

In the bathroom, he splashed his face with water, but nothing seemed to help the excessive sweating. From his pocket he pulled the other half of the Oxy pill he'd swallowed earlier. This half he popped into his mouth and chewed. He needed the quick rush and the relief of his headache if he was going to look at the printouts

Meg had brought. He promised himself he'd cut back on the Oxy again after he left Meg. For now, he needed all his wits about him.

When he returned to the table, Meg was sipping milky tea and already perusing the thick printout of info she'd pulled from the database. The data was arranged in dense columns that would make little sense to anyone just glancing at it. She handed him a yellow highlighter pen when he sat down, then she narrowed her eyes.

"Did you take a hit of something in the bathroom?"

"No," he lied happily. He was starting to feel good.

She looked dubious, then gestured to the page in front of them. "So here are your dad's records. What do you make of them?"

He eagerly scoured the pages, looking for descriptive text, notes from the court reporter, any kind of transcript. But the staccato bits of info he followed with his finger were familiar and useless—his father's name, birthday, the county, the judge's name.

"What were the charges?" Meg asked, her voice tentative.

"Right here. Investment fraud and embezzlement." He scoffed. "What a crock."

She leaned in to look over his shoulder, infusing the air with the scent of strawberries. "What's Mashburn, Tully & Wren?" she asked.

"The name of the firm where he worked."

"He was a partner?"

"Yeah," he said, his chest puffing out a little. "We had a big house. Carlotta and I went to private schools and everything."

"What school did you graduate from? I went to St. Pius."

He squirmed. "I went to Paideia when I was small. After my folks left, I transferred to public school."

She sipped her tea and nodded, but he could tell a public school education made him seem inferior in her eyes.

"Who is Liz Fischer?" she asked, tapping the report.

"My dad's attorney—and mine." He glanced over the rest of the data, then pushed it away with a sigh. "There's nothing here I didn't already know."

"We can keep poking around," Meg offered.

He nodded warily.

"So…did your parents leave in the middle of the night?"

"No," he mumbled, staring into his scummy coffee. "I remember they were dressed up, going out to eat, I think. My mom was wearing a red dress. She always looked and smelled great."

Meg smiled.

"She gave me a kiss goodbye and I stood at the door waving at their car." He took a drink from the cup. "And they never came home."

Meg's smile disappeared. "Just like that?"

He nodded. "Pretty much. Carlotta got me ready for school the next morning. I thought my parents were sick or something. But when we got home from school, I knew something was wrong. Carlotta started making all these phone calls, and I could tell she was scared." He gave a little laugh. "But she kept telling me everything was okay, that Mom and Dad would be home soon."

"And?"

"And…nothing. Carlotta took care of me, and eventually we just stopped talking about our parents."

"So you never heard from them—no phone calls, nothing?"

"They sent a few postcards over the years, to say hi and that they were okay."

"From where?"

"From all over. I guess they stayed on the move."

Her mouth opened and closed. "But you've never… talked to them? You've never seen them in all this time?"

He shook his head.

Meg looked horrified. "But how could they do that to you and your sister?"

Wes could feel his defenses rising. "They knew we'd be okay."

"But to go all this time and not talk to your kids?"

He pushed up his glasses, trying to tamp down his anger.

"What kind of parent does that?"

"Actually…my sister has seen my dad."

Her eyes went wide. "When?"

"A couple of months ago, someone stole Carlotta's identity and jumped off a bridge. For a while, we all thought it was her. The news even reported her death."

"How awful."

"The D.A. asked Carlotta to play dead for a while, hoping it would bring my parents out of hiding."

"And she agreed?"

"Only because the D.A. offered to do something for me, which he later reneged on."

"But the ploy didn't work?"

"My father must have suspected it was a trick. He

showed up in disguise, slipped a note into my sister's pocket."

Her eyes went wide. "What did it say?"

"That he was proud of us, and he would see us soon."

"And have you heard from him since?"

Wes hesitated, but he hated her thinking the worst of his parents. "Dad came up to Carlotta a few weeks ago at a rest area in Florida."

"She'd planned to meet him there?"

"No. He must have been following us. I was there, too, but I was in the car. He just walked up to her at a vending machine. Right under the nose of police." He grinned. "He's got balls."

Meg looked less than convinced. "And then he disappeared again?"

"Yeah. But he said he'd been keeping tabs on us."

"Did he say what they've been doing all this time?"

"He said my mom had been sick some, and that he'd been gathering evidence to prove his innocence."

"So he's going to come back?"

"I think so."

Meg stared at him. "Wow. I can't believe all these things have happened to you."

He shrugged, feeling worldly. "Believe it."

He could almost see the wheels in her head turning, but then she started sucking on the plastic stir stick, and he was totally distracted. She glanced at her watch. "I have to get going."

"Big plans?" he asked casually.

"I'm committed to help out Habitat for Humanity today." She rolled the printout and stuffed it into her shoulder bag. "What about you, are you moving bodies today?"

"I'm on call, so maybe. And I'm trying to locate a guy named Jett Logan. Do you know him?"

She squinted. "Yeah—he's an ATO. Alpha Tau Omega. Big party fraternity. How do you know Jett?"

"Uh…I don't. But I'm trying to get a message to him from a mutual friend."

Meg angled her head. "ATO is having a Hawaiian party tonight. Go with me."

"Do you think Logan will be there?"

"Yes, but more importantly, *I'll* be there."

"Okay," Wes said, his heart beating faster.

She picked up the wilting bouquet of flowers. "I'll be in front of the ATO house, say, at eight?"

He nodded. "Yeah, I'll be there."

She walked to the door, then turned back. "Wes?"

"Yeah?"

"Thanks for the flowers." She bounced out of the coffee shop and into her electric car like a ball of sunshine. He was dismayed at how much he wanted to go after her. But he needed to drop by the morgue and fish around for answers to the questions in The Charmed Killer case he'd promised Carlotta he'd look into. And he needed to do it before the Oxy wore off and left him with another raging headache.

He'd just wheeled into the morgue parking lot and was locking up his bike when his regular cell phone rang. He pulled it out and his stomach clenched at the sight of Liz Fischer's name on the screen.

He flipped up the phone. "Hi, Liz."

"Hi there, handsome. What are you doing tonight?"

He closed his eyes tightly. He wanted to be with Meg…but Liz was a sure thing, and sex might help him deal with the lack of Oxy.

But Meg was also his connection to Jett Logan, and he didn't want to disappoint The Carver.

"Uh, I have a commitment later, but I could come over earlier, around seven?"

"See you then," she said, then ended the call.

Wesley closed the phone and moved toward the morgue, nursing unease. His involvement with Liz made him uncomfortable, especially when he was feeling a strange sense of momentum about his dad's case. Randolph had shown himself to Carlotta twice in the past few months, and now they'd uncovered a bug in the townhouse. If their dad had planted the device, would their absence from the house make him wonder if something was wrong? Would he reappear soon? And if he did, would he reveal himself to Wesley this time?

Wes glanced around the parking lot, alert for any signs of being followed. When he saw no one, he fought disappointment. Then he reminded himself that now would be a crummy time for Randolph to appear, when his name had been mentioned in connection with The Charmed Killer case. Remembering Carlotta's comment about Randolph's possible involvement with one of the victims, Wes hardened his jaw.

He didn't want to believe that Coop had anything to do with those murders. But what if proving Coop's innocence made his father look guilty?

9

Peter looked up from his cereal and newspaper as Carlotta walked into the kitchen, eyeing her pantsuit. "I thought you were off today."

"Uh…Lindy asked me to come in for a trunk show," she lied. Peter would be livid if he knew she'd planned to use her Saturday off to run down leads in The Charmed Killer case.

Disappointment creased his face. "I was hoping we could hang out by the pool."

"Another day," she promised with a smile, stopping at the fridge to pour a glass of orange juice.

"Did you sleep well?"

Her thoughts returned guiltily to Jack's late night tuck-in. She'd slept soundly until the daylight had fallen across her face. "Yes, thank you. You?"

He nodded absently, but the pinched look around his eyes betrayed him. She wondered how much her being in the house, as well as her father's situation, were contributing to his insomnia. On top of her and Peter's awkward attempts to repair their relationship, her father had dragged the poor guy into his mess by calling him a couple of months ago. Randolph had asked Peter for his help in clearing his name at the firm where Randolph had once been a partner and where Peter now worked. Of course Peter had agreed. He'd do anything to get back into her good graces, she realized.

"You look tired," she murmured, caressing his cheek.

"Just a lot on my mind," he said, folding his hand around her fingers and kissing the tips. Then he touched the charm bracelet she wore. "I heard these bracelets were supposed to foretell the future."

"Ha, ha," she said nervously.

"What kind of charms do you have?"

She tried to pull away. "It doesn't matter. It's silly."

"Then show me," he said, turning her wrist. "Does that one say 'aloha'?"

She nodded. "See? It makes no sense."

"I don't know," he murmured. "Hawaii sounds like a romantic place to visit. And the champagne glasses, well…" He grinned. "That could give a man hope."

She blushed.

"And let's see, is that a puzzle piece?"

"I haven't put together a puzzle since Wesley was a kid."

"But you're a puzzle," he said with a smile, then squinted. "Is that…three hearts?"

From his sour expression she could tell he'd done the math and didn't like the bottom line. "See, I told you it's silly." She gently pulled her wrist out of his grasp.

"What's the last charm?"

She gave a wave. "A woman doing yoga. Maybe that's a sign I should start exercising more."

"You look perfect to me."

She gave a little laugh, happy that she didn't have to

reveal the charm of the woman lying down with her arms crossed over her chest, corpselike. "Thank you, Peter."

"I do worry about you. Michael Lane is still out there."

"The store is still providing a security guard to watch over me. And everyone there knows Michael."

He sighed. "Then I guess if you can't be here with me, being at work is the next safest place to be."

"Right," she said with a forced smile. "I'd better get going. Do you have the keys to the rental car?"

Peter pointed to the keyless remote and ignition key lying on the end of the table. "Have you given any more thought to setting a date for our Vegas trip?"

"No, but I will." She picked up the key, then dropped a good kiss on his mouth before walking toward the sliding glass door.

"Can we do something tonight?" he called.

"I'd like that," she said. "I'll call you later. Have a great day!" She waved and closed the door behind her, juggling the cup of juice. Her chest felt tight over the lies. Guilt always seemed to be close at hand when she was around Peter. But if she could help prove Coop wasn't The Charmed Killer, her head would be clear enough to get on with her life. At least that was the story she was sticking with.

To assuage her mind a tiny bit about lying to Peter, she swung by the mall, thinking if Michael Lane was watching her, she'd want to give him the chance to approach her in a public place. Inside the mall, she visited kiosks, jewelry shops, and department stores that sold charms, asking about the people who'd purchased them lately. She showed the sales clerks Michael Lane's picture, hoping to trigger a memory.

"Isn't this the guy who jumped in the Chattahoochee River?" one woman asked.

"Yes," Carlotta admitted. That wasn't the memory she'd been hoping for.

"Haven't seen him, except on TV. Why are you asking questions?"

"I knew one of the victims," Carlotta said, thinking of the prostitute Pepper and the cheeky conversation they'd had only days before the woman had been found stabbed. "I'm simply making my own inquiries. And I knew Michael Lane."

"You think Michael Lane is The Charmed Killer instead of the guy they arrested?" the woman pressed.

"All I know is that with recent budget cuts, the police department is shorthanded," Carlotta offered. "I'm just trying to do some legwork for them."

"Oh, I see."

She knew she could get in a world of trouble for making it sound as if she was working with the APD, but she was desperate. She also knew there were about a thousand places in Atlanta alone that sold charms, not counting the Internet. Add to the mix the fact that some stores had removed their charms from display in deference to the highly publicized rash of killings, while other stores had added them to take advantage of heightened interest, and it was difficult to tell which stores had been selling charms before the serial killer had made the trinkets infamous. The police and the GBI were no doubt working those leads, but she suspected they were taking the angle of proving their prime suspect—Coop—guilty.

As she moved through the mall, she kept looking

over her shoulder for Michael, but she didn't notice anything suspicious. After checking all the possibilities and coming up empty, she returned to the rental car, standing back in the parking lot and making sure no one else was around before she depressed the button on the keyless remote.

When the doors unlocked with a chirp instead of an explosion, she sighed in relief. Jack said he was still trying to find out who had put the bomb underneath her Monte Carlo, but with the device in so many pieces, his investigation to this point had yielded no leads.

After she slid behind the wheel of the Civic, Carlotta reached into her bag for the notebook containing her notes and clippings about the murders. The *Atlanta Journal-Constitution* had featured profiles on each victim. The first victim, Shawna Whitt, had worked at a chain bookstore in midtown, which also doubled as a textbook store to nearby Georgia Tech. Carlotta drove the rental car there next.

The bookstore was relatively empty due to the summer break. Carlotta walked around, jingling her charm bracelet loudly and feigning interest in it every time she got close to a female employee, giving them an opening to make conversation about The Charmed Killer case. No one took the bait. Finally she bought a coffee at the café, allowing her charm bracelet to jangle noisily on the counter while she waited.

"I like your bracelet," the server commented. She wore a name tag that read "Monica."

Carlotta smiled. "Thank you. I stopped wearing it for a while when that serial killer was on the loose."

The woman's face clouded, then she leaned in and

whispered. "A girl who used to work here, Shawna, was one of the victims."

Carlotta gasped. "How awful. Did you know her?"

Monica nodded and handed over the coffee. "Shawna had a bracelet like that one."

Carlotta extended money for the drink and dropped a bill in the tip jar. "Do you know where she got it?"

"She bought it as a birthday gift for herself."

"These bracelets are supposed to be unique. Do you remember the charms that were on your friend's bracelet?"

The woman squinted. "I remember a little phone, and a pair of hands that were locked, like a couple."

Shawna Whitt had mentioned the intertwined hands charm in an entry on The Charmers online community forum that Carlotta had come across after the murder. The site had since been taken down. "What other charms do you remember?"

The woman stopped and looked Carlotta over. "Are you a cop or something?"

"Heavens, no. I work at Neiman's and we sold a lot of these bracelets." She fingered the charms. "The rumor is that the charms tell a person's future. I just wondered if there was anything on your friend's bracelet that…I don't know—spooked her?"

The woman scratched behind her ear. "Let's see, there was a bird of some kind—a chicken, I think."

Carlotta's pulse leaped. The fact that the killer had taken a charm from Shawna's bracelet and put it in her mouth was huge. It proved Coop hadn't added the charm to Shawna Whitt's mouth when he arrived on the scene to move the body. It was all Carlotta could do not to whip out her phone and call Jack on the spot.

"And there was a question-mark charm," Monica continued, "which seemed to fit Shawna because she usually worked the information desk." She snapped her fingers. "Wait. There was a charm that freaked Shawna out a little. It was a woman asleep or something, with her arms crossed over her chest."

Carlotta's mouth went dry. She picked up the corpse-like charm from her own bracelet. "Like this one?"

"That's it! Wow, how creepy that the two of you have the same charm."

"I'm sure there were lots of duplicates," Carlotta murmured, then took a sip from her coffee cup. "The intertwined-hands charm sounds interesting. Did Shawna have a boyfriend?"

"No."

"Are you sure? Maybe someone she knew from online?"

"Not Shawna. She was thinking about joining an online dating service, but she didn't have the chance."

Carlotta poured a packet of creamer into her cup. "I suppose the police came by and asked all kinds of questions."

Monica shrugged. "I heard a detective came in on one of my days off, but I didn't talk to him. I didn't know anything, and I was just so sad, I had to get away from here for a few days."

"Did Shawna mention if any customers made her feel uncomfortable?"

Monica laughed. "If you work retail long enough, you meet your share of weirdos. But I don't remember her saying anyone in particular was bothering her."

Carlotta smiled. "Being a bookstore, you probably get lots of loners."

"Oh, yeah. The guys who can't get a date on weekends put on their toupees and cruise the aisles ogling the help." Monica offered a wry smile, then glanced down the counter to see another customer waiting in front of the pastry case. "Excuse me."

Carlotta nodded and walked away sipping her coffee, thrilled with the information she'd gleaned—information that apparently Jack had missed out on due to bad timing. She walked back through the bookstore to study the information desk—a tall, curved counter with a phone and computer. It was unmanned at the moment. Carlotta imagined the plain, slender woman standing behind the counter, offering up shy smiles to customers. Had she gotten too chatty with a psychopath? Inadvertently ticked him off in some way?

The last two victims, the Georgia State coeds, had been found with book charms in their mouths. Maybe the charms *were* clues to the murderer's identity. Maybe he was an intellectual, or fancied himself to be. If so, it made sense The Charmed Killer would hang out in a bookstore.

But Michael Lane certainly didn't fit that profile.

"May I help you?" a young man asked, stepping up to the information counter.

Carlotta gave him a big smile. "Does your store specialize in a certain type of book? Or is there a unique section that would bring in a particular customer?"

"We sell more textbooks than anything else, mostly to students, of course. But we have lots of professionals come in to buy reference books, too."

"What type of professionals?"

He shrugged. "Engineers, doctors, architects, you name it."

Any one of whom might have latched on to Shawna Whitt. Carlotta pulled out a picture of Michael Lane. "Have you seen this man in here?"

The man squinted. "He looks familiar, but…I don't think so."

Eager to further exonerate Coop by proving he didn't know Shawna Whitt, she pulled out a picture of him taken on their road trip to Florida. In it, Coop looked tanned and happy, a far cry from his disheveled appearance being flashed on television and in newspapers. "How about this man? Have you ever seen him in here?"

The clerk bit his lip, then nodded. "Yeah, that's the white-van guy. He's in here a couple of times a week, checking out the medical books. I figure he's a med student or something."

The breath stalled in her lungs. "How…how do you know he drives a white van?"

"Hard to miss, it's so big. He parks it across the street." The man turned and pointed out the window at the metered street parking. "Are you looking for him?"

She nodded, but the effort was painful. Tears pushed on the backs of her eyeballs. "He's a long-lost friend. Thank you for your time."

She stumbled to a comfortable chair in a seating area to gather herself. So what if Coop came into the store often? It didn't mean he'd known Shawna Whitt.

But if he was a regular customer, wouldn't he have seen her at some point? If so, why hadn't Coop mentioned when they'd arrived to pick up the woman's body that she seemed familiar?

Her palms were sweating against the paper cup of coffee. She opened the notebook and forced herself to write down the details about Shawna and her charm bracelet, but her handwriting was shaky. Carlotta ached to call Hannah or Wesley for support, but she was afraid to give voice to the questions and doubts revolving in her head.

Telling herself that more information about Shawna Whitt might reveal another direction she could follow, Carlotta left the bookstore and drove to the woman's home. She kept an eye on the side mirror, but didn't notice anyone tailing her. Maybe she was all wrong about Michael following her into the ladies' room at Moody's Cigar Bar…or perhaps he'd simply lost interest.

She didn't remember the exact address of Shawna Whitt's Berkley Heights home, so she drove through the older neighborhood until she spotted the little house. Except for the overgrown yard, it was a dream cottage for a single woman—neat and picturesque. Carlotta parked on the street and got out to stretch her legs. She glanced at the neighboring houses. A curtain moved in the window of a bungalow across the street.

Carlotta smiled and headed in that direction. Nosy neighbors could be a treasure trove of information. She cringed, thinking of all the things her neighbor Mrs. Winningham would spill about the Wrens, if given the opportunity.

From the looks of the bungalow, the occupant had lived there for a while. The houses on either side looked updated. Carlotta strode up to the door and knocked. When she didn't get a response, she knocked again.

Finally the door opened a few inches to reveal a woman's wrinkled, wary face. "Yes?"

"Hi," Carlotta said with a smile. "My name is Carlotta Wren. I was wondering if you could answer some questions for me about the lady who lived across the street."

"The one who got murdered?"

"Yes, Shawna Whitt."

"Didn't know her," the woman said.

"That's okay," Carlotta said. "I'll bet you've lived in this neighborhood for a while."

"That's right."

"And you have a nice vantage point to be able to look out for your neighbors. You probably notice things that other people don't."

"Sometimes," the woman admitted.

"Did you see anything strange the day that Shawna Whitt was found in her home?"

The woman's eyes narrowed. "Who are you?"

"I'm working close to the investigation," she hedged. "I was here the night Miss Whitt's body was removed." The woman seemed satisfied with the vague identification. "May I ask your name, ma'am?"

"Audrey Cole."

"Ms. Cole, please try to remember. Did you notice anything out of the ordinary that day?"

"Like what?"

"People in the neighborhood who didn't belong? Strange vehicles?"

"No."

Carlotta pressed her lips together, her mind racing for another approach. "What about the day before?"

"Now that's another matter entirely," the woman declared with a smile. "I noticed a van cruising through the neighborhood. I figured it was the phone company, or Ms. Rosen three doors down getting new carpet. That woman buys new carpet every eighteen months."

Carlotta swallowed. "What color?"

"Same color every time—Sante Fe beige."

"No, I meant what color was the van?"

"Oh. It was white."

Her stomach rolled. "Are you sure?"

"Yes. A long, white van."

"Did the van stop at Shawna's house?"

"No, but it did slow down—once when it went up the street, and again when it came back down. Like the driver was checking for an address."

"Did you happen to see the driver?"

"No. My eyes aren't as good as they used to be."

That made Carlotta smile. "Just one more thing, Ms. Cole. Did you tell the police about the white van?"

"I talked to a big, nice-looking man in a suit, but I didn't tell him about the van."

"Why not?"

"He didn't ask."

Carlotta pursed her mouth. So unless another neighbor had been as attentive as Ms. Cole, neither the APD nor the GBI had this bit of information.

And now that Carlotta had it, what was she going to do with it?

She thanked the woman and made her way back to her car, her mind racing. She needed more info on the case, and no way was she going to get it from Jack or Maria.

On impulse, she opened her phone, pulled up a

number on her contacts list, and connected the call. The phone was answered on the first ring, as Carlotta would've expected from any self-respecting newspaper reporter who was afraid to miss a scoop.

"*Atlanta Journal-Constitution*, Rainie Stephens speaking."

"Rainie, it's Carlotta Wren."

"Hi, Carlotta. What can I do for you?" The woman's tone was equal parts curiosity and suspicion. Since Rainie and Coop had shared some kind of relationship before Carlotta had met either one of them, the reporter had to know why Carlotta was calling.

Carlotta smiled into the phone. "Let me buy you lunch, Rainie."

10

"Salad and water," Rainie Stephens said, handing her menu to the waiter.

Carlotta smiled at the server. "Scratch that. Bring us an appetizer platter and two martinis with lots of olives."

After the man left, the curvy redhead angled her head toward Carlotta. "Are you trying to get me drunk?"

"Are you trying to stop me?"

"Are you kidding? So far, this is the best date I've had all year."

Carlotta laughed, then clasped her hands on the table in front of her. "You and I made a pretty good team recovering Eva McCoy's stolen charm bracelet."

"Glad to help. Although I've spoken to Eva and she's worried sick that all the media she got over her Olympic Lucky Charm Bracelet might have set off this killing spree."

"I can see why she'd be upset, but who knows how or why the charms figure into the murders."

"That's what I told her."

"So…you don't know?" Carlotta probed carefully.

Rainie shook her head. "No."

Carlotta didn't know whether to believe her, but she

backed off a notch. "The Charmed Killer case has been good for the newspaper business."

Rainie nodded. "It's the kind of story that reporters dream of…and it's the most horrendous thing I've ever experienced. I'd give anything if it had never happened. I can't believe that Cooper—" Her voice broke and she fought for composure. "The past couple of days have been a nightmare."

"I know. I went to see Coop in jail."

Rainie leaned forward. "How is he?"

"Not good. But I don't believe he did this, Rainie."

"I don't want to believe it, either."

"Your articles about the The Charmed Killer murders—was Coop your source in the morgue?"

"You know I can't reveal my sources, Carlotta."

"But I need your help, and so does Coop."

Rainie squinted. "Is there…something going on between you and Coop?"

"No." Carlotta shifted on the chair. "I mean, there was a time…a brief window when we might have…" She arched an eyebrow. "Did *you* and Coop have a thing?"

Rainie's smile was coy. "We had our window. I was willing, but Coop was going through a rough time. It was after he'd gotten out of jail, out of rehab—do you know about that?"

Carlotta nodded. "The woman he wrongly pronounced dead on the accident scene?"

"Right. Everything had worked itself out by the time I met him, but he was still…searching. But the Cooper Craft I know couldn't have killed those women."

"So help me."

The waiter brought their drinks and set the platter of

food between them. Carlotta took a healthy swallow from her glass and Rainie followed, then cradled the stem.

"What can I do?"

"Are there any details you can give me, any leads to follow?"

"Why don't you ask Detective Terry? I thought you two were…friends."

"The GBI booted him off the case. You probably know more than he does."

"Such as?"

Carlotta leaned forward. "Dr. Abrams told me the state crime lab was supposed to return DNA from one of the crime scenes. What was it?"

Rainie shook her head. "I don't know."

"Can you find out? And if it matched Coop?"

"I can't make any promises."

"And there's one more thing."

"What?"

"Last week my brother saw Coop at Piedmont Hospital, and followed him to the office of a neurologist. When I asked Coop about it, he went off and basically told me to mind my own business. Can you look into it?"

"Sure. I'll poke around."

"And one more thing…"

The redhead scoffed. "Just one?"

"Can you help me flush out Michael Lane?"

Rainie blinked. "How?"

"I don't know. It would have to be something he'd find irresistible." Carlotta laughed. "Like a sale on Gucci."

"That's actually not a bad idea. Let me give it some thought."

"Oh, and all this needs to be on the Q.T."

"Will I get an exclusive if Lane shows?"

Carlotta lifted her glass. "Absolutely."

Rainie clinked her glass to Carlotta's. "Deal. You have a lot riding on Michael Lane being The Charmed Killer, don't you?"

"Why do you say that?"

The reporter gave her a pointed smile. "Because if Coop didn't kill those women, and if Michael Lane didn't do it, either, then that leaves your father as next best suspect, right?"

Instead of answering, Carlotta picked up a loaded potato skin and took a bite.

Rainie reached for a stuffed mushroom. "Girl, I thought I had man problems. What's up with you and that Ashford guy I saw you with at the country club auction?"

"Peter and I go way back. I'm staying at his place until this all blows over."

"Didn't he win one of the romantic getaway vacations?"

Carlotta nodded.

"I assume for the two of you?"

She nodded again. "He thinks it would be safer if I were out of town."

"Can't say I blame him," Rainie said. "Which means he's not hip to this little fact-finding mission of yours?"

"Right."

"Carlotta, you're a dog with three bones."

She frowned. "What's that supposed to mean?"

"Remember Aesop's fable? A dog with a nice meaty bone is crossing a bridge and looks down to see another dog holding a bone that's even bigger. The dog drops his bone to go after the bigger one and guess what?"

"The dog winds up losing the bone," Carlotta finished.

"Righto."

Carlotta bit her lip. "So who's the nice meaty bone in my mouth?"

Rainie laughed. "You're going to have to figure that one out for yourself."

They finished lunch and Carlotta picked up the tab, then they made their way back to the parking lot to Carlotta's car. She snagged Rainie's arm to hold her back while she unlocked the Civic with the keyless remote. When nothing detonated, Carlotta exhaled and walked forward.

"Do the police think Michael Lane planted the explosive device under your car?" Rainie asked.

"For lack of a better suspect. Detective Marquez said that Michael wants to get rid of me because in his mind, he'll be locked away if I testify against him for the identity-theft murders." Then she shook her head. "Although I can't imagine why Michael would've gone to the trouble of planting a bomb when he could've easily killed me in my bed when he was hiding in our house."

"Maybe he couldn't bring himself to do it up close." Rainie made a face. "But that doesn't mesh with someone who then goes on a killing spree."

Carlotta swung her head to look at the reporter. "It's been suggested that Michael is doing this to *avoid* killing me."

"You mean, an extreme form of projection?"

"Maybe."

"If that's the case, Carlotta, this isn't your fault. Michael Lane is sick and needs to be stopped."

"I know."

"We'll think of a way to draw him out," Rainie promised. "It's Michael Lane who belongs behind bars, not Coop."

Carlotta dropped off Rainie at the *AJC* office and waved goodbye with a heaviness in her stomach that went beyond a self-indulgent lunch. While she felt better knowing that Rainie also believed in Coop's innocence, she wondered if the reporter would change her mind if Carlotta told her about Coop's bookstore connection with the first victim and the sighting of the white van in Shawna Whitt's neighborhood.

Puzzled and apprehensive, Carlotta drove to the Perimeter Mall and spent most of the afternoon flashing Michael Lane's photo to people who worked in shops selling charms, but again with no results. She cruised by the Betsey Johnson and Stuart Weitzman stores for a quick looky-loo at the newest arrivals, and was able to get a walk-in appointment at DASS salon to have her split ends trimmed.

While she was sitting in a chair covered with a poncho and reading *People* magazine, Carlotta felt a prickle of awareness, as if she was being watched. With her senses on alert, she slowly pivoted her head…and found herself in the crosshairs of one Tracey Tully Lowenstein.

Carlotta swallowed a groan. Tracey was the daughter of Walt Tully, her father's former partner at the investment firm. Walt was her and Wesley's godfather, although the man hadn't checked on them a single time after Randolph and Valerie had disappeared. And Tracey, who had gone to the same private girls' school as Carlotta, had done everything in her power to ostracize Carlotta from their social circle. Meanwhile, Tracey had snagged herself a doctor—a creepy OB/GYN—and loved parading him around while sabotaging Carlotta's struggling relationship with Peter because Tracey didn't cotton to hobnobbing with a lowly retail clerk.

Carlotta gave Tracey a tight little smile, then looked back to her magazine and willed the hairdresser to hurry. But as luck would have it, she and Tracey wound up at the checkout counter together.

"Carlotta, I've never seen you in here before."

"First time," Carlotta offered cheerfully.

Tracey surveyed Carlotta's hair. "Next time you should ask for the deep-conditioning treatment. It would help with the frizz."

Carlotta stuck her tongue into her cheek. "Thanks."

"Goodness, you must be so relieved that the police arrested The Charmed Killer."

"I…yes."

"It lets your dad off the hook, doesn't it? Well, at least for this crime."

"Yes," Carlotta murmured, seething.

"I understand the psycho they arrested worked for the morgue. Since you've been moonlighting as a body mover—" she paused to shudder "—you must know him."

"As a matter of fact, I do," Carlotta said evenly.

Tracey *tsk, tsked.* "Honestly, Carlotta, the company you keep. From that Goth-girl to serial killers. Peter must be positively mortified."

Carlotta gritted her teeth. "Peter lets me be my own person."

Tracey leaned in. "But doesn't Peter deserve better? You've really gone to the dogs, Carlotta. Even that red dress you wore to the club auction the other night looked off-the-rack."

"Gee, your husband didn't seem to mind. He practically gave me a pelvic exam with his eyes."

Tracey gasped and recoiled.

Carlotta took advantage of the pause to escape the vile woman's presence. True, Tracey had been friends with Peter's former wife, Angela, so maybe some of Tracey's reaction to Carlotta was out of loyalty to her dead friend. But she didn't have to go out of her way to be so nasty. At the club auction, Tracey had made a big deal out of the fact that her important husband, Dr. Frederick Lowenstein, had to leave the event to deliver a baby. The woman used her husband's position as a social lever, and she wielded her power maliciously. Carlotta wondered if Tracey overcompensated because deep down, she knew her husband was a lecherous cad. Or maybe she was just in complete denial.

Carlotta pursed her mouth. Not that she herself was such a great judge of character—hadn't Michael's gruesome betrayal taught her that? Jack had once told her that everyone was capable of murder, given the right circumstances. Which meant that anyone walking around this mall, the people she came into casual contact with every day, could be harboring horrible, secret compulsions.

She slowed and hugged herself as people passed by her on all sides. Irrational fear seized her. She glanced at their faces, wondering which ones contemplated horrible acts at this very moment, and which ones harbored dark fantasies that might erupt as a result of some random emotional trigger.

And conceding that, according to Jack, there was the tiniest possibility that after years of working with the dead and avoiding the living, Coop's random emotional trigger had somehow been tripped.

11

Wesley parked his bike next to Liz Fischer's garage and slowly walked toward her guest house, where they always met to screw. His balls had their own memory because they tingled with anticipation, but his stomach was tied in knots.

Sure, having sex with Liz guaranteed fifteen minutes of pure physical pleasure. But he kept thinking about Meg and the way she'd fussed over the raggedy flowers he'd bought her and the daisy she'd put in her hair, and it left him feeling…torn. Like he shouldn't sleep with Liz, that he should—he grimaced—*save* himself or something.

Christ, he was turning into a wuss over a girl who probably just felt sorry for him after he'd unloaded his whole sad family saga on her.

It was still early, around seven, but the low-hanging clouds made it seem later. Shadows encroached as he walked up to the French doors of the guest house and knocked. When Liz didn't answer, he peered through the door, but it was dark inside. Then he noticed a note taped to the glass.

Come to the back door of the house.

He frowned, then peeled off the note and headed

across the manicured grass in the direction of the main house. He'd never been inside Liz's home, and he wondered why tonight was any different.

Liz's brown brick house was tucked into an older, expensive community. The dwellings weren't huge, but they were all well-appointed with guest houses and pools, and situated for maximum privacy. Thick trees shielded him—and Liz's other lovers, he presumed—from prying eyes. A curving concrete walk led up to the back door, flanked by tiered planting beds and pots of geraniums. He had trouble picturing Liz getting her hands dirty, but he supposed the woman had a life outside of her job, and gardening was *tres chic* these days.

He stopped at the back door and pressed a button that sent a little buzzing sensation through his finger. The half caplet of Oxy he'd just chewed made everything vivid and experiential—the weight of humid night air on his neck, the shriek of horny crickets in his ears, the sharp scent of evergreen bushes in his nostrils.

The door swung open and Liz stood in the threshold wearing chinos and an untucked button-up white blouse, holding a drink. A pang of disappointment stabbed him that she was dressed at all, but compared to what she typically wore, her outfit was a little dowdy. Her blond hair, commonly coiffed into a French twist, was loose around her shoulders. Her face was free of makeup, making her look softer…and a little old.

Suddenly he relaxed—it was a ploy. Underneath the floppy white shirt, she was probably wearing a latex corset. Or an edible bra.

"Hi, Wes. Come on in."

Her smile was friendly instead of flirtatious, throwing him off a little. Stepping inside, he scanned the room while he closed the door. The kitchen was straight out of *Southern Living,* with white painted cabinetry, black granite countertops, and wood floors. Two lidded pans emitting nice smells sat on top of the commercial-grade stainless steel stove. Through a doorway leading deeper into the house, he saw pale, overstuffed furniture and thick rugs. Elvis Costello's "Allison" sounded from the next room.

Wesley frowned. The setting seemed...cozy.

"Would you like a drink?" she asked.

Conscious of Chance's stern warning not to drink alcohol with the Oxy, he swallowed past a dry throat. "Water would be great."

"Pellegrino okay?" she asked, withdrawing a green bottle from the refrigerator. She topped off her own glass, then looked up.

"Uh, sure," he said, surprised that Liz wasn't having something stronger.

She filled another glass and handed it to him. The heavy musk of her perfume irritated his overstimulated olfactory nerve.

"I'd planned for us to eat in the dining room," she said, "but that seemed so formal. So I set the kitchen table."

Wesley swung his head in the direction she nodded and did a double-take at the two place settings, complete with standing, pleated napkins. "Uh...what's going on?"

She smiled. "I made us dinner."

He felt his eyes grow wide. "Dinner? I thought we were going to—" He swallowed the last word.

"Later," Liz promised. "First, I thought we'd talk."

His balls sagged. "Talk?"

"Yes. Do you like filet?"

"Uh…sure. But I hadn't planned to eat…steak." He glanced at his watch. "I have to be somewhere in less than an hour."

"You have time to eat. Besides, I wanted to chat with you about my newest client."

"Coop?"

"Have a seat and I'll plate the food."

He did as he was told, lowering himself awkwardly onto an elegant chair that was covered in a fancy striped fabric. "Did you ever work in a restaurant?"

She looked back. "I waitressed my way through law school. Why do you ask?"

"You said 'plate the food.' That's a foodie term."

Liz smiled. "And you're a foodie?"

"I watch the Food Network occasionally," he admitted sheepishly.

"You cook?"

"Some. Carlotta is a disaster in the kitchen, so I took over the meals a few years ago."

Liz carried their plates to the table. "I hope my meager skills suffice."

The filet was undercooked, and the mixed vegetables were overcooked, but he appreciated the effort and complimented her. She smiled her thanks, but picked at the food on her plate. Liz seemed nervous, which was so uncharacteristic, it made him nervous.

"Is Coop okay?" he asked.

"It's hard to tell," she said. "He's so…self-deprecating. It's clear to me that he feels like he deserves to be punished for something."

Wes wet his lips. "Do you think Coop is The Charmed Killer?"

She lifted her shoulders in a slow shrug. "I don't know. He doesn't behave like a man who's been wrongly accused. He's not angry, he's not defensive. I have to pull information out of him."

"He's probably going through withdrawal. He's a recovering alcoholic, but Carlotta and I both noticed he'd started drinking again lately."

"I could tell he was coming down from something. I requested that he be kept under observation in the infirmary. Maybe when his health improves, his head will clear."

But she didn't sound optimistic. With a rueful noise, she pushed away her barely touched plate. "So what do you think, Wes? Is this guy a serial killer?"

Wes swallowed a chunk of bloody meat. "No."

Her eyebrows shot up. "That's not exactly a resounding endorsement."

He wiped his mouth with the white napkin. "From what I know of Coop, he wouldn't hurt anyone."

"From what you know," she repeated. "Meaning you don't know him very well?"

"He doesn't talk about his background much. You know the circumstances of him losing his job as Chief M.E.?"

She nodded. "He told me what happened, said it was all his fault, that he'd gotten off easy compared to the woman who was hurt." Liz sighed. "I hope I don't have a client who's willing to take the fall for murder because he thinks he wasn't punished enough for something he did before."

"Is he going to plead not guilty?"

"That's the plan."

"Carlotta mentioned something about DNA evidence?"

Liz nodded slowly. "I can't talk specifics, but it doesn't look good."

"But Coop was on the scene of some of those murders as a body mover. *My* DNA was probably there, as well."

"I know, and if a trial goes forward, his defense attorney will argue just that."

"So you plan to only handle the arraignment."

"As of now, yes. I don't have the litigation experience to try a case like this. I wouldn't mind sitting second chair if my schedule allows. But the hope is there won't be a trial."

"Have you talked to the D.A. yet?"

Liz's mouth thinned. "Numerous times."

"He's out for blood, isn't he?"

"Kelvin Lucas and I aren't exactly friends, but I'd expect him to pull out all the stops on this case since one of his A.D.A.'s was murdered. I don't mind representing a guilty man—everyone deserves counsel. But I don't want a client who's using the legal system to do himself in."

Wes checked his watch. If he didn't leave now, he'd be late. He cut another piece of steak and stuffed it in his mouth. "Carlotta and I are trying to find the real murderer."

Liz frowned. "I don't think that's a good idea. You should leave it up to the GBI."

"But we've got a lot of first-hand information since we were on the scenes. And Carlotta still thinks that psycho Michael Lane is to blame."

Liz leaned forward and crossed her arms. The movement pushed up her boobs, giving him an inadvertent eyeful through the opening in her shirt. Wow, they looked even bigger than usual.

"I hope she's right. The man can't hide forever."

Wes swallowed the half-chewed steak and caught her eye. "Some men can."

She smiled and gave a nod of concession. "Speaking of Randolph, I read in the paper that his name had come up as a suspect in this case."

Wes nodded, remembering what Carlotta had told him about his father's involvement with one of the victims. "They're grasping at straws."

"Have you or Carlotta heard from your dad since he talked to her at the rest area in Florida?"

"No."

"Would you tell me if you had?"

"Probably," he said. "Would you tell me if he'd contacted you?"

"Touché. But he hasn't." She drank more water, then pushed a strand of hair over her ear with a hand that shook slightly.

"Are you okay, Liz? I mean, you didn't sound so good before you left town."

"I wasn't," she said. "I just needed a break from everything, some time to think."

Wes's stomach clenched. In his experience, it was never good when women took time to think.

"What are your plans, Wes?"

He stuffed another bite of steak in his mouth and chewed with purpose. "A friend invited me to a party tonight."

She gave a little laugh. "That's not what I meant. I mean, what are your plans for…your life?"

He blinked. "My life?"

"Are you thinking about going to college, getting a job?"

"I have a job…more than one, remember?"

"I know. But what about when your community service is finished, and the undercover job is over? What do you want to do with your life?"

The *caring* look in her eyes sent a tremor of fear through his chest. "Why are you asking?"

She wet her lips. "No reason. You're just so smart, I'd like to see you make something of yourself."

But her body language made him apprehensive. If he didn't know better, he'd think Liz was hinting that the two of them… No, that was crazy.

She reached forward to stroke his hand. "Are you meeting Meg at this party, the girl whose name you called out when we were together?"

Wes squirmed. "Uh, no. I have to meet up with a guy. It's business for The Carver."

"Well, if it's business, then why don't you come back here afterward? You could spend the night."

At the prospect of an entire night's access to her enormous tits and open thighs, Wesley's body screamed yes. But at the same time his mind sent up warning flags to counter his hardening dick. Spend the night? Since when was Liz willing to risk a neighbor seeing him slip out at an odd hour of the morning? Spending the night was an indication that their relationship had moved beyond the illicit quickie in the guest house. It meant morning breath and awkward exits and…obligation.

His throat convulsed. "Uh…"

She traced little circles on the back of his hand,

sending sensations arrowing to all parts of his body. "I've been thinking that maybe we should start spending more time together, go out once in a while."

His eyebrows practically flew off his head. "Out? In public?"

She gave a little laugh. "I know I'm older than you, but you're very mature for your age, Wes."

"You mean us...as a *couple?*" He choked on the last word.

Liz pouted. "You make it sound like a sentence. We could have a great time, Wes." She reached forward to touch his chest. "We could travel, and I'd pay for you to go to college. I'll bet you could get into Emory without even studying for the entrance exam."

That made him pause. Graduating from Emory University would be cool.

"And we already know the sex is great." She almost looked...pleading. But she must have smelled his panic because her expression softened. "You don't have to answer right away. Give it some thought. Meanwhile, stay with me tonight."

"Uh...I'll think about it," he hedged.

"Good. I'll leave the light on."

He wiped his mouth and stood abruptly. "Gotta run. Thanks for dinner," he added, even though his stomach was already rolling from the too-rare meat and the unpalatable texture of the vegetables.

Liz rubbed herself against him in a full-body goodbye kiss. He pulled back before his cock won the armwrestling match raging in his brain. Then with Liz's offer clanging in his head, Wes fled as if the hounds of hell were chasing him.

12

It was around seven-thirty in the evening when Carlotta left the Perimeter Mall, miraculously, with no shopping bags. And regretfully, with no proof that the silver charms The Charmed Killer had thrust upon his victims had been purchased at any of the stores there.

In the parking lot she looked all around, keeping an eye out for Michael and her hand on her stun baton while unlocking the rental car at a safe distance. She called Peter to arrange to meet him for dinner in an hour and found herself looking forward to it. Then, monitoring her side mirror, she steered the rental car toward Moody's Cigar Bar.

Moody's was a great little slice of old Atlanta, well-situated in a two-story building that retained the architectural charm of the 1920s. A bell tinkled when she walked in, and she was instantly met with the fragrances of tobacco—plum, cherry, and oak. The first floor of the shop was dominated by a black horseshoe-shaped bar that serviced customers buying cigars and accoutrements from glass-fronted cabinets lining the walls. The art-deco fixtures and the piano music wafting over speakers cinched the mood. The shop was crowded with connoisseurs and the merely curious. Carlotta scanned for the owner, June Moody, but she didn't see her.

A stairway in the back led upstairs to a martini bar, with a comfy lounging area for smokers and guests. Carlotta ascended the stairs and waved hello through the crowd to Nathan, the bartender. June, a well-preserved blonde in her fifties, was walking toward her with a tray of empty glasses and full ashtrays. She smiled, then set the tray on the bar and hugged Carlotta.

"I'm so sorry about Coop," Carlotta murmured.

"How could this happen?" June asked, her brow furrowed.

"Jack says jail is the best place for Coop right now," Carlotta said, sidestepping the question. "He'll get sober in a safe place, where he can't harm himself or anyone else."

"That's a good thing," June agreed. "And if that monster, The Charmed Killer, strikes again, everyone will know it wasn't Coop."

"Right."

June squeezed Carlotta's arm. "I feel better knowing you're on Coop's side."

Carlotta hoped her smile wasn't as shaky as it felt. "June, did you know the last two victims, the coeds who were found dead in their car? I'm asking because I know the car was parked not far from here."

"Two blocks away," June supplied, then sighed. "No, I didn't know them, but Nathan turned them away from the bar."

Carlotta's pulse jumped. "That same night?"

"No, not that night, but he thought they'd been in here before with fake IDs. I told the police." Her expression clouded. "I might have made things worse for Coop because the police asked about him coming here, too."

"Don't you worry about it. Coop assured me that everything's going to work out."

June looked past Carlotta's shoulder and smiled at someone approaching. "Mitch."

Carlotta turned to see June's son, Mitchell Moody, a career Army man, striding up to them. He was a big guy, tall and nice-looking, with a shaved head and shrewd, intense eyes. "Hi, Carlotta."

She smiled and dipped her chin. "Sergeant Moody."

"No need to be so formal," he said with a deadly grin.

"Did you get your leave extended?"

"By a few more days. I still have some unfinished business here before I head back to Hawaii."

June averted her gaze, and Carlotta wondered if Mitch was still trying to talk his mother into giving up the bar.

Carlotta glanced around. "Is Eva here?" Mitch had struck up a romance with Olympic runner Eva McCoy after she'd recovered from her ordeal of having her world-famous lucky charm bracelet stolen.

"Not at the moment," he said easily. "I'm going to catch up with her later. Mom, can I have a word with you?"

Something akin to dread passed over June's face, confirming to Carlotta that Mitchell was still pressing her about her "unsuitable" occupation.

"I'll let you two talk," Carlotta said, giving June an encouraging wink before walking back to the bar. She waited until a spot opened, then slid onto a bar stool and smiled at Nathan. "How are you?"

"Good," he said, wiping the counter. "Can I get you something, Carlotta?"

Mindful of the martinis she and Rainie had tossed back at lunch she said, "Just a diet soda."

"Coming up."

"So…June told me you knew the two coeds who were found dead in their car."

He shook his head. "I didn't know them. I just remember them coming in a few nights before, trying to pass off a couple of fake IDs." He sighed noisily, then slid a fountain soda toward her. "If I'd called the police about the IDs, they might be alive."

"You can't think like that. Were they with anyone that night?"

"Nah, they were making the rounds, talking to everyone, probably trying to find someone to buy them a drink."

She pulled a picture of Michael from her bag. "Have you ever seen this guy?"

"Yeah," Nathan said, his voice full of surprise. "Different hair, though. He's blond now."

Her heart thumped in her chest. "Where did you see him?"

"Right here. Last weekend, maybe."

"Last Saturday? When I was here?"

He nodded. "Yeah…maybe. I noticed him because he was so…pristine. Looked a little out of place for this joint. And he was alone."

When she was here a week ago, someone had followed her into the ladies' room. The person hadn't spoken, but she'd noticed the scent of a distinctive, high-end cologne that Michael had liked.

So it *had* been him. Why hadn't he talked to her?

Carlotta swallowed. Or tried to kill her?

"I have to go," she said, glancing at her watch. "If you see this guy again, call the police. His name is Michael Lane, and he's a fugitive."

"The guy who did a swan dive into the Hooch?" he asked, eyes wide. "Yeah, sure, I'll call."

"Don't let him know that you recognize him," she warned. "Michael is…a very dangerous man."

She took a few more sips from the soda, looking all around, expecting to see Michael in every face. Her pulse clicked higher and her palms were moist against the glass. While she hoped Michael would appear and end this torment, she was terrified at the prospect of seeing him again face-to-face. She took advantage of the environment to smoke a cigarette, then another, but she was ever watchful of the crowd reflected by the mirror behind the bar.

After a half hour had passed uneventfully, Carlotta waved to Nathan and climbed off the stool. She walked downstairs to say goodbye to June, who was waiting on customers, but without her usual plucky smile. Carlotta relayed the information about Michael, and showed June his picture.

"We'll keep our eyes open," June said gravely. "Keep me posted on Coop."

"I will. Take care."

Carlotta hurried through the parking lot, partly because of the dim lighting, partly because she was running late to meet Peter for dinner. In her haste, she was almost to the car when she remembered that she should be using the keyless remote at a safe distance. She reached into her purse and backed up.

Into a solid body.

Panic seized her. Michael must have followed her after all. A man's arm reached around her, and she screamed, groping in her purse for the stun baton Jack had given her. Suddenly the man's grip loosened, and the body moved away from hers.

She spun around, stun baton held high. And found Mitchell Moody standing there in the semi-darkness, his hands up.

"Whoa. I didn't mean to startle you, Carlotta, but I think you backed into *me*."

Her chest heaved as she tried to catch her breath. "Sorry…I thought you were someone else."

"Can't be too careful," he agreed. "Are you okay?"

"Yeah."

He waved. "Catch you later."

Mitch veered off toward an SUV with a rental license plate. Feeling silly, Carlotta returned the stun baton to her bag, then unlocked her car with the remote. Still wobbly, she climbed in and locked the doors. On the drive to meet Peter, she called Jack to tell him that the bartender had positively identified Michael—as a blonde.

"You've been sleuthing," he chided.

"Just asking a few questions," she said lightly.

"I'll send a uniform to cruise Moody's, and I'll modify the hair color on the APB. Anything else to report, Nancy Drew?"

The other revelations of the day ran through her mind—the fact that Shawna Whitt had a charm bracelet with a bird charm, Coop's connection to the bookstore where she worked, the sighting of a white van in front of the woman's house, and the fact that she and Rainie were hatching a plot to lure Michael Lane out of hiding.

"No. Nothing else to report, Jack. Bye."

13

When Wes locked up his bike in the parking lot around the corner from the Alpha Tau Omega house, the red phone in his pocket vibrated. That would be Mouse, calling to see if he'd connected with Logan. Again. He ignored the call and followed a stream of students along the sidewalk. Meg was pacing in front of the ATO house under a streetlight, arms crossed. She did not look happy.

"Hey," Wes said, jogging up. When she turned her green eyes on him, his heart went *boing*.

"You're late," she accused.

"Sorry," he said, trying to look contrite. "I was looking for a nice shirt to wear."

Her frown evaporated. "Oh." She uncrossed her arms and nodded at his blue retro-style button-up shirt. "It does look nice on you."

He smiled and pushed up his glasses. "Thanks. You look…wow."

Her blond hair was pulled into a side ponytail, revealing dangling earrings. She wore a black denim miniskirt and a pink Ed Hardy T-shirt that read "Love Kills Slowly."

"Thanks." She seemed pleased with his assessment, which pleased him.

"How did the Habitat for Humanity project go?"

"We made a lot of progress." She held up her thumb, wrapped with a Scooby-Doo Band-Aid. "I missed with the hammer once and nailed myself instead."

He suddenly found it hard to breathe. Meg was the perfect package of smarts and looks and sass. If he wasn't careful, he might fall for her. The kind of fall where a guy might break every bone in his body.

"Oh, wait." Meg reached into her purse to pull out two plastic leis. She lifted one over her head, and held up the other one. "Lean forward."

"What's this?"

"It's a Hawaiian-themed party. If you wear a lei, you're less likely to be tossed out by an ATO. Frat guys aren't keen on having outside bucks around, you know."

He leaned forward. "I guess this is the only lay I'm gonna get tonight."

"Funny," she said, lifting the necklace of plastic flowers over his head. "And true." Then she stopped and sniffed. "Is that perfume?" She pulled back. "Were you with someone else before you came here?"

The girl had the nose of a bloodhound. "No," he said, although his voice came out sounding thin and false. "Uh…it's not what you think."

But of course, it was exactly what she thought and the damage was done. Meg stepped back and lifted her hands. "Hey, it's fine, really. I only asked you to come tonight because you mentioned Jett Logan. It's not like this is a date or anything."

His pride kicked in, straightening his back. "Yeah, right. I feel the same."

He caught the pinched look around her eyes just

before she turned away. "Let's go in. My friends are waiting for me."

Wes followed her miserably. The harder he tried with Meg, the more he seemed to screw things up. Too late he realized he should've said the perfume was Carlotta's, but Meg would never believe that lie now.

He was an idiot for stopping by Liz's first, and probably a bigger idiot for not staying. But he had to find this Logan guy and collect, or face the wrath of The Carver. Although at the moment that seemed preferable to facing the wrath of Meg.

The ATO house practically pulsated with reggae music. Bodies spilling out the doors and milling inside wore wildly flowered shirts, bathing suits, leis, and even the occasional grass skirt in keeping with the island theme. The guy at the door collecting a cover charge, donations to a charity the fraternity supported, looked Wesley over with a frown. "Who are you?"

"He's with me, Charlie," Meg said, stepping up. "Wes is my cousin from out of town."

Charlie gave Meg a leering glance that made Wesley want to punch him. "Hey, Meg, go on in." The guy stared at her ass as she went through the door.

Wesley glared and handed over cash to cover his and Meg's entry, then hurried into the house, trying to keep Meg within sight.

Even though it was relatively early, the air was already thick with the scent of beer and perspiration. Bodies were shoulder to shoulder, with a limbo pole going in the main room and lots of cheering from the sidelines for the girl shimmying underneath. Wes looked around for Meg. The strobe lights in the next room triggered flashes of pain behind his eyes, a sure sign the Oxy was starting to wear off. He cursed under his breath because he knew a blinding headache and various unpleasant side effects weren't far behind.

He had a couple of hits in his pocket, but he was trying like hell to wean himself off, like he'd promised Carlotta.

He grabbed a Pepsi Max from a tub of ice, hoping the heaping dose of caffeine would postpone the worst of the symptoms, and kept weaving his way through the crowded rooms. He felt conspicuous, as if everyone could tell by looking at him that he didn't belong. The guys all looked thick-armed and tanned, wearing sports sandals, their hair full of product. When he spotted Meg, she had her back to him, talking to a knot of people. He walked up to stand next to her.

"Hey, I lost you."

She gave him a pointed look. "You sure did."

Aware that the group was staring at him, he lifted the can to his mouth and took a drink, wishing he was anywhere else. They were probably all Mensa-eligible, destined for think tanks after graduating summa cum lah-de-dah.

"Everyone," Meg said, "meet Wes—my cousin. Wes, this is Paul, Esi, Wendy, and Seung."

"Hey," they chorused with varying levels of enthusiasm.

"Hey," he returned with a nod.

"Are you a Tech student?" Esi asked.

"Uh, no."

"Wes is working for the county morgue until he decides what he's going to do with his life," Meg offered.

Wes ground his jaw. Jesus Christ, two women in one

night pressuring him about his life plans. At the disclosure of his morbid job, he expected to see disgust on the faces of the geniuses around him. Instead, they looked…impressed.

"Cool," Esi said, and the others nodded.

"That'll look good on a med school application," Paul remarked.

"Won't it?" Meg agreed.

"Hey, do you know that sicko who was arrested for killing all those women?" Wendy asked.

"Yeah. Do you know The Charmed Killer?" Paul asked, his eyes wide.

Wes hesitated. His urge to defend Coop warred with his urge to fit in with Meg's friends. "Yeah, I know him. We were both body movers."

They gaped. "Is he creepy?"

"Did you suspect it was him?"

"Is he into doing corpses?"

Wes winced. "What? No. Coop's not a ghoul. In fact, I think the police have the wrong guy."

Esi made a choking noise. "You mean The Charmed Killer is still out there?"

"Yep. It could be anybody." He swept a suspicious glance over the two guys. "Maybe someone you least suspect."

The two girls cast distrustful glances at the guys and shrank back.

"He's teasing," Meg said.

Wes looked at Meg. "Could I talk to you alone, *cuz?*"

"What could we possibly have to talk about?" she asked sweetly. "Uncle Randolph's database records?"

Wes grabbed her elbow and smiled at her friends.

"Excuse us. Meg promised to introduce me to someone I need to talk to."

She rolled her eyes, but allowed him to lead her away. "Did you have to scare my friends to death?"

"They were begging for it," he muttered.

"You need to work on your social skills."

"Jett Logan," he reminded her. He hated to rush things, but his left eye was starting to twitch. The Oxy high was sliding away quickly, and he was hoping to be back at Chance's place, trying to sleep through the worst of the withdrawal. If he could get through the rest of the night without hitting the Oxy tablets in his pocket, it would be a small victory.

"You never really said what you wanted with Jett."

"No, I didn't."

She frowned. "Am I getting in the middle of something?"

"Absolutely not," he said. "You're going to point out the guy, then pretend as if you don't know me."

"Gee, I'm so glad this turned out not to be a date," she said dryly.

Wes swallowed hard. Once he'd told Coop if he liked Carlotta, he needed to do something bold. Considering the hole he'd dug for himself, now seemed like a good time to follow his own advice.

Wesley stopped and walked Meg back a step against the wall. Then he kissed her. She made a startled noise and stiffened for a second, then softened as he plied her mouth with his tongue, and began to kiss him back. Her lips tasted like Cherry Coke and her tongue was a silk ribbon. God, if he had this mouth to kiss any time he wanted, he could be king.

When his lungs threatened to burst, he had to tear his lips from hers and lift his head.

Meg was breathing as hard as he was. "Why...why did you kiss me?"

He shrugged, trying to regain his composure. "To give you something to think about."

She straightened her clothing. "I'm thinking you shouldn't do that again."

"You kissed me back," he countered. The realization buoyed his hope.

"I kiss all my cousins like that."

He laughed. "Right. Admit it, it was good."

"It was good," she said, nodding. "But I'm not looking for a guy who's always in trouble."

"Meg, is this clown bothering you?"

Wes looked up to see the guy he'd once seen out with Meg standing there. Gay Boyfriend had traded his plaid shorts for white pants—nice. Wes set his jaw. Clown?

"No," Meg said quickly. "Mark, this is Wes. You two met at the Vortex once, I think."

"Oh, yeah," Mark said. "You're the one who rides a ten-speed."

Wes returned a little smile. "It's not the horsepower you got between your legs, man. It's what you do with the gearshift."

"Uh, Mark, Wes was just leaving," Meg said, giving Wes a warning glance. "I need to introduce him to someone first, then I'll be back."

"I'll wait for you here," Mark said.

This time she grabbed Wes's elbow and shepherded him down the hall. "That was uncalled for."

"Isn't that dude a little old to be hanging out at frat parties?"

"Mark is an ATO alumnus. He comes back to chaperone."

"A convenient cover for pervs."

"Mark is a successful architect," Meg said. "He's going places."

"I'm happy for him," Wes said.

She made a frustrated noise. "God, you can be such a jerk sometimes."

"So I've been told, by you. Just point out Logan and you can get back to Marky Mark."

Her chin came up, but she didn't respond. Wes swung his head side to side, hoping to catch a glimpse of his target, although all he'd seen of Logan was the guy's back as he'd flung himself out the second floor window of his dorm.

They walked all through the house, then doubled back. Finally, Meg nodded across the room. "That's Jett Logan in the yellow-flowered shirt."

Wes zeroed in on the guy like a laser beam. He had the same general build as the guy who'd gone out the window—short and stocky, and sporting a wrapped ankle that might have been the result of a hard landing. "You're sure that's him?"

"Yeah, that's Jett. I heard he got kicked out of school and he's leaving town. What's going on?"

"I just want to talk to him," Wes said, then looked down at her. "You should go back to your friends."

Her mouth tightened. "You're welcome."

"Thanks," he said. "For the kiss."

Meg gave him a wary look, then turned and walked away.

Wes watched her go, nursing a pang. If things went well with Logan, maybe he'd find Meg again, stay with her and walk her home later. Then he lifted his glasses and massaged the bridge of his nose against the pain mushrooming there. His hand shook, and the eye twitch was getting worse. Who was he kidding? Meg had said she didn't want a guy who was always in trouble. Somehow he doubted she'd be willing to overlook the drugs, the issue with his dad, his massive gambling debt, *and* his undercover work for a loan shark.

He should just let things end here. If he kept pissing her off, she was bound to turn him in for prying into the city databases at work.

Wes positioned himself across the room where he could watch Logan. Jett was a smug little bulldog who carried himself like someone who was entitled to the best. From the rosy glow on the guy's snub face, he'd already had a lot to drink, and the beer in the clear cup he held was down to about an inch. Wes bided his time and shortly, he saw Logan break away from his group and go in search of, presumably, a bathroom.

Wes followed him to the john, managing to get his foot in the door, then wedge himself inside. "Jett Logan?"

"Yeah." The guy stumbled against the opposite wall, hands up. "What the hell, man? I'm not gay."

"I'm not, either," Wesley said. "But I'll settle for happy. You owe The Carver ten grand. I'm here to collect."

Jett's eyes widened. "I don't have it." He gave Wesley the once-over, as if trying to size up whether he could take him in a fight.

"Dude, stop wasting time. I got a headache, and you gotta take a piss. Just pay me and I'm outta here."

"I'll have it tomorrow," Jett said, a pathetic attempt at a bluff.

"Nice try, but The Carver knows you're leaving town." Wes sighed. "Look, man, you can either pay me and walk out of here with your porcelain veneers intact, or you can take your chances with my partner, Mouse, who has about a hundred pounds on me and will be waiting for you with a golf club when you leave."

From his pocket, the red phone vibrated. Wes pulled it out. "See, that's him now. Should I answer and tell him you're being an asshole?"

Jett paled. "No. I'll pay."

"Good decision," Wes said, stowing the phone.

Jett removed a thick wad of money from a back pocket and handed it over. "It's all there."

Wes counted it, then nodded and shoved it into a deep pants pocket. "Dude, if you had the money, why didn't you just pay up? Most of the guys who owe The Carver are flat fucking broke."

Jett sat down on the toilet lid, his head in his hands. "Because I just won it last night. I was going to another card game tonight to double it. Then I was going to pay back The Carver and keep ten for myself."

Wes pursed his mouth. "What kind of card game?"

"Texas Hold 'Em. There's a game going on at a house on the edge of campus, a sure thing."

"Why do you say that?"

"It's a dog track, man, with a bunch of trust fund kids."

Meaning the players were all novices who would bet without regard. Easy pickings.

"You play?" Jett asked.

"Some," Wesley hedged.

"Someone should go," the guy said, gesturing to the door. "It's all yours if you want it." He rattled off the address.

Wes hesitated a split second, then said, "No, thanks," and left the bathroom, his head throbbing like a bass drum.

On the way outside, he looked for Meg and spotted her talking to Mark. They seemed absorbed in each other. He was probably the kind of guy Meg was looking for. Anger coursed through Wesley that things came easy for jerks like Mark. He probably came from family money and used it to catapult himself to success.

One of these days, Wes told himself...

His mind went back to the card game just a few blocks away. He imagined the newbies sitting around a table, with the rank of winning hands printed on an index card as a cheat sheet. A warm sensation swirled in his stomach and chest—a chance like this didn't come around very often. He'd be crazy not to relieve all those rich college boys of their daddies' money.

But he'd promised Carlotta he'd stop gambling. Besides, he didn't have any money.

You have ten grand in your pocket, his mind whispered. He could take a portion of the money and double it. Then he'd give Mouse the ten grand Logan owed The Carver, and keep the rest for himself. A cake walk.

He gave Meg one last glance, then left the house, his heart thumping in anticipation. The last time he'd played, he'd won big, had taken first place in a tournament and split the earnings with Chance. But this time, he could keep all of his winnings, and maybe replace the money that Michael Lane had stolen out of his sock drawer. Carlotta would be so happy to have some extra cash to fix up the townhouse.

The address where the game was being played was a short bike ride away. Wes told himself that he'd simply cruise by and check it out. When he arrived, he told the guy who answered the door that Jett had sent him and he was welcomed into the group. Within a few minutes, he'd sized up the crowd to be just as inexperienced as Logan had suggested.

Only one thing was missing.

In his last card game, he'd been high on Oxy. It had given him a single-minded confidence he'd never known before. Even better, the cards had sailed his way, as if he were calling to them. And he had to get rid of this headache before the cards hit the table.

Before he sat down, he furtively popped a whole Oxy tablet into his mouth, then chewed, nearly groaning with ecstasy as sensations flooded his pleasure centers. When the first hand was dealt, he picked up his pocket cards, and smiled inwardly at the aces winking back.

It was an auspicious beginning to a tragic evening.

Any good pocket cards he got were followed up with ugly community cards. His pair of aces was shot down with three deuces. The idiots at the table didn't know how to bet, which screwed up the pot and messed with his momentum. His irritation led him to make stupid mistakes, like seeing hearts where there were diamonds, kings where there were jacks.

Halfway through the game he was losing money and concentration, so he chewed another hit of Oxy. But instead of returning his pleasant, happy high and laser focus, the dose slowed him down. Everything seemed gluey and distorted. The cards felt thick and unwieldy in his hands. He had problems keeping up with the bets, and couldn't recall if a flush beat a straight. Because he misread tells—body language from other players that hinted at the strength of their hand—he wound up bluffing when he shouldn't, and holding when he should've folded. He played like a rube.

And in under two hours, he lost it all.

When Wesley saw the last of The Carver's money being raked away by some schmuck named Baron wearing a Rolex, he panicked. He'd just lost ten thousand dollars that belonged to a man who'd earned a reputation by cutting people into pieces. He pushed to his feet and stumbled out of the house where he threw up in the bushes.

He sat down on the ground in the shadows of the house and tried to breathe. His mind chugged, desperately searching for a way out. Then he brightened—he could borrow the money from Chance. He dug out his main cell phone while staring at the screen of the dedicated phone that Mouse had given him. Damn, the big man had called three times.

Wes clumsily punched in Chance's number and prayed while the phone rang. "Come on…come on," he pleaded, but Chance didn't answer. Probably banging Hannah.

Wes cursed and held his heavy head in his hands, trying to think. The red phone vibrated, the screen flashing insistently. Wesley groaned and started to press "decline." Then he stopped. Something was working hard to push through the fog in his brain. Finally the thought slid into place.

Mouse didn't know he'd collected the money. Jett was on his way out of town. All he had to do was pretend he hadn't found the guy. The Carver would be upset, but that was better than admitting he'd lost the man's money in a damn card game.

With his mind made up, he connected the call. "Yeah, Mouse?"

"Where you been?"

"Looking for Logan, man. He's Mr. Invisible. I've been all over this campus. He's nowhere. I found a couple of people who know him and they said he's already skipped town."

Mouse uttered a curse questioning Logan's relationship with his mother. "Okay, if he's gone, he's gone."

"I'll keep looking," Wes offered magnanimously.

"Good. Are you okay? You sound high."

"High?" Wes scoffed. "No, man, I'm just tired. From looking for Logan," he added for good measure.

"Okay, let me know if you find the fucker. Otherwise, we'll sort things out Monday."

"Okay," Wes murmured, weak with relief. He ended the call, congratulating himself for talking his way out of a serious jam.

Suddenly fatigue overwhelmed him. His limbs felt like lead. His head was an anvil. His bicycle might as well have been a mile away. Even if he made his way to the bike rack and managed to get it unlocked, he'd never be able to ride it except maybe into a tree. Wes considered the cool ground underneath him, the soft, overgrown grass. He gauged the distance between the foundation of the house and the bushes. There was enough room for a skinny dude to grab a nap. He crawled into the space and pulled a few dry leaves over him to ward off the damp chill.

Damn women trying to convince him he needed to do something with his life. His life was fine, just the way it was. He had everything under control.

14

Sunday morning in the suburbs was depressing, Carlotta decided. In Lindbergh, she was accustomed to hearing neighborhood noise and church bells, something to remind her that people were nearby. Here in Peter's subdivision, there was just this pervasive, profound silence. It was maddening.

She stood on the veranda outside her bedroom, smoking a cigarette. Yesterday's marathon of digging into details surrounding The Charmed Killer case had left her confused and afraid. Every turn had led back to Coop. The tumor of anxiety in her stomach when she thought of him locked away in the city detention center was rivaled only by the sympathy she felt for the victims. To have one's death so horribly showcased— it was abominable.

And it was just the kind of media spectacle that Michael would revel in. But if he was The Charmed Killer, why hadn't he struck again? Had he suspended his killing spree to make Coop look more guilty? Would Michael vanish into thin air, satisfied with getting away with one of the most hideous series of murders the city had ever seen? Or would he wait until Coop was convicted, then kill again to show everyone that he still had the upper hand?

She shivered in the warm morning air, then took another drag on the cigarette. Her hand shook and she felt antsy all over. She needed to *do* something. All this waiting was eating at her.

At a noise below, she walked to the edge of the veranda and looked down. Peter was unrolling a hose, preparing to spray down the stone and concrete surfaces around the pool and the pool house. He wore only swim trunks. He was tall and lean, built like an elegant athlete. The muscles in his tanned chest and back bunched as he moved. His blond hair shone in the morning sun. Her chest expanded with feminine appreciation—he was gorgeous. And he'd been so good to her since he'd come back into her life. But it worried her that they couldn't seem to get back in sync, not the way they'd been when they were younger.

He glanced up and saw her, then grinned and waved. She dropped the hand holding the cigarette behind her and waved with the other. When he looked back to his task, she sneaked another drag, then snubbed out the butt. If Peter was going to be busy for a while, she could use the computer to do more research before she left for work. He'd told her she could help herself to it whenever she wanted, but she knew he'd object to her delving into The Charmed Killer case. Last night over dinner in a nearby restaurant the subject hadn't even come up. Of course, Peter had thought she'd been working all day instead of driving all over town playing Sherlock.

She ducked back inside the house and closed the

door, then grabbed the notebook holding all the details
on the case and jogged downstairs. Her footsteps echoed
through the big, empty house.

Peter's office featured a state-of-the-art desktop computer system with a large hi-res monitor, plus a scanner,
a black-and-white printer, a color printer, and video
equipment. Nearby was another station where Peter
used his laptop. A bookcase full of technical and business reference books lined one side of the room.

A wry smile curved her mouth—Wesley would love
it here. He'd always been such a techno geek. In fact,
he'd made enough money working on other people's
home computers to cobble together a system for himself. But all of his equipment had been confiscated when
he'd been arrested for hacking into the courthouse
records, and terms of his probation prohibited him from
working around computers except as part of his community service.

She shook her head. He'd risked jail to try to get information on Randolph's case. It was more than their
father would do for either one of them.

"Where are you, Dad?" she whispered as she sat
down in front of the monitor. While the machine booted
up, she scanned her notes. Where to start?

She decided to search for recent articles on The
Charmed Killer case, to see if any new details had come
to light. The number of media hits was astronomical, and
after several minutes of tedious skimming, she hadn't
discovered anything new. What she needed was underground info. Wes had once given her tips on using search
engines, advising using more formal language when
searching for sources with legitimacy, and informal lan-

guage for more unofficial sources. She reframed her searches to include words such as "rumor," "gossip" and "leak," and found more interesting fare.

One was a blog maintained by someone who called himself EarToTheGround. He claimed that a source in the Georgia State crime lab reported that latex gloves with fingerprints, hairs, and other personal objects on The Charmed Killer crime scenes were matched to the suspect in custody.

Carlotta murmured a cry of dismay.

"What's wrong?"

She looked up to see Peter standing in the doorway. He had donned a T-shirt, and his cheeks were pink from sun and exertion.

"Nothing," she said, trying to switch the screen to something innocuous, but fumbling over the keyboard.

His gaze fell on the notebook at her elbow. He'd found it once before and chastised her for playing detective. Peter frowned and walked over to the printer, then flipped through the news items she'd printed. He held them up, his expression pinched. "I thought we talked about this, about you not getting involved."

"We did," she murmured. "I'm just…uh, surfing to see if my dad's name has been brought up again in connection with the case."

"Really? Then where were you yesterday?"

She frowned. "What do you mean?"

"I dropped by the store, and you weren't there. Your boss told me you weren't scheduled to work."

Anger spiked through her chest. "You were checking up on me?"

"No." He looked sheepish. "I brought you lunch."

She looked down, contrite. "Why didn't you say anything last night at dinner?"

"I hoped you were doing something with friends, enjoying yourself. But you weren't, were you?"

She pursed her mouth. "I did have lunch with a friend."

"Hannah?"

"No." She wet her lips. "Rainie Stephens."

His mouth tightened. "The *AJC* journalist who happens to be the lead reporter on The Charmed Killer story?"

"Uh…right. And I did go to the mall."

"To shop?"

"Not exactly. I…was hoping to find where the killer might have bought the charms."

He wiped his hand over his mouth. "Carly, why are you doing this? The Charmed Killer is in custody."

"Because I don't believe Coop did it. He told me—" She stopped and her cheeks warmed.

"He told you what?"

"Coop told me he was glad I was here with you, glad that I was safe. He wouldn't have told me that unless he knew The Charmed Killer was still out there."

Peter crossed his arms. "When did he tell you this?"

She hesitated. "When I went to see him in jail."

Peter's head went back, as if he'd been hit. "The authorities just let you in to chat with a serial killer?"

"I…might've fudged a little about my and Coop's… relationship."

He clenched his jaw. "I assume you didn't tell them you were his sister?"

"Uh, no. But it was for a good reason, Peter. I had to talk to him. I had to look in his eyes and see for myself."

"And what did you see?"

"He's wrestling with demons, there's no doubt about it. But I don't believe he did these things, not Coop."

"You trusted Michael Lane, too," he reminded her quietly.

"This is different." She stood and turned off the computer, then took the papers from his hands and shoved them in the notebook. "I'm sorry, Peter, but I have to see this through." She glanced at her watch. "And I have to get to work."

He looked dubious.

"Really," she said. "I have to go to work." She brushed by him, her chest tight with frustration—at him, and at herself. And at the general disarray of her life.

A few minutes later, as she backed the Honda rental out of the garage, she stopped to stare at the remains of the beautiful concrete fountain that had once sent sheets of water cascading down, a lovely centerpiece for the circular driveway. Now it was a broken mass of rock because she'd sideswiped it with Peter's Porsche, which had toppled the entire structure—into his car. In one fell swoop she'd demolished both the fountain and his beloved sports car.

And still he put up with her.

Carlotta drove toward the Lenox Square Mall, racked with guilt. Was she subconsciously testing Peter to see how far he was willing to go to make up for abandoning her when they were younger? He knew she was up to her gapped front teeth in debt. He didn't approve of her body-moving activities. He hated her smoking. She'd asked him to conceal a phone call from her fugitive father from the APD. She'd convinced Peter and herself they had a future in order to keep him from taking a job in New York because she didn't want to risk losing the flimsy connection to her father in case he tried to contact Peter again. And now she'd asked Peter to conceal evidence from the GBI about Randolph's involvement with one of the recent murder victims. And all of this was under the strain of their unsuccessful attempts at lovemaking.

By the time she parked the Civic in the parking garage at the mall, she'd decided to ask Wesley how soon they could move back to the townhouse. Sure the place was in shambles, but the security system worked, so she would feel safe. And with Hannah spending more time at Chance's place, Wes would probably be amenable to coming home and the two of them could work on repairs in their spare time.

On the way into Neiman's, her cell phone rang—it was Hannah.

She connected the call. "Hey, Hannah, what's up?"

"Okay, I feel like a total narc, but I thought you should know."

Carlotta's pulse spiked. "Should know what?"

"Your brother just rolled in looking like he spent the night in a ditch. He's also stoned."

"Oh, no." Carlotta stopped just outside the store entrance and choked back sudden tears. "What should I do?"

"Nothing for now. He's getting ready to make some body runs with that goober Kendall Abrams. Chance has cut off his supply, even if Wes has the money."

"Oh, God, that's a relief."

"But if he has a stash somewhere, it might take a while for him to run out."

"I was just thinking we should both move back to the townhouse soon. I can keep a better eye on him there."

"I'll let you have that conversation with your brother. By the way, Chance and I have a list of those, um, chemical outlets you asked for…and Chance did some drive-by research last night along Ponce de Leon Avenue."

Where a buffet of prostitutes could be found any night of the week. Hopefully one of them had known Pepper.

"I have some information to share, too," Carlotta murmured. Maybe between the four of them, they could think of reasons to explain away the coincidences that incriminated Coop. "I have to talk to the GBI again in the morning. Can we meet at the townhouse at one to discuss what we found?"

"Yeah. I'll make sure Wes knows."

She sighed. "Okay. Thanks, Hannah, for the heads up."

"Ah, well, the shithead's like a brother to me. I don't want him to screw up his sorry life. Later."

"Bye," she said, then ended the call. Carlotta pressed the little phone to her mouth to stem the tide of panic that rose in her throat. If Wesley didn't kick this habit, it would eventually consume him. The information describing OxyContin addiction she'd found online was harrowing. Wesley could die.

"Carlotta, are you okay?"

She turned to see Patricia Alexander walking toward her, wearing a pink Chanel skirt suit and white pumps. Carlotta straightened and dropped the phone into her purse, unwilling to reveal too much about her personal life to Patricia. "I'm fine, thanks. Just getting ready to go inside. Are you on today?"

"Yes, until closing."

"Me, too." Carlotta held open the door for her coworker and followed her inside Neiman's. "Patricia, you should know that Michael Lane was sighted at a cigar bar in town last weekend, and his hair is now blond."

Patricia's eyes widened. "Blond? I'll bet he looks hideous."

Carlotta smiled wryly at the woman's back. "Maybe that'll make him easier to spot."

They walked through the store to the employee break room. "Looks busy today," Patricia remarked, but she seemed distracted.

"Good. That always makes the day go by more quickly."

"And the bills," Patricia said softly as she swiped her employee ID through a card reader to unlock the door to the break room.

Carlotta gave her coworker a sideways glance. Patricia had descended from old, big money, the kind that came with cobwebs and professional oversight. Carlotta had always assumed Patricia only worked because she wanted to, which enabled her to maintain her status in social circles. Employment in a nonprofessional capacity, especially for women, was looked down upon only if one *had* to do it. What kind of bills could someone like Patricia have?

Taped to the front of their lockers was a memo. Patricia groaned. "Inventory starts next Tuesday. I assume you're going to take vacation like most of the old-timers so you can get out of it."

Carlotta frowned. "It's called seniority." Then she grinned. "And yes."

When they stored their purses, Carlotta noticed that Patricia's expression was tight and she seemed nervous.

"I didn't mean to worry you when I told you about Michael," Carlotta offered.

"That's not what's bothering me," the young woman said, then closed her locker with a sigh. "I'm…concerned about Leo."

"Your boyfriend, Leo? What's wrong?"

Patricia fingered the lion charm on her bracelet, which she believed meant she'd been destined to meet Leo. Carlotta didn't put as much faith in the charms as Patricia, but it was hard to argue, especially since the woman's bracelet also featured a tiny baseball mitt and Leo Tennyson played for the Atlanta Braves farm team.

"It's…nothing I can put my finger on." Patricia lifted her gaze. "He just seems…dark. Moody. Maybe a little… I don't know—compulsive."

Unease bubbled in Carlotta's stomach. She'd met Leo Tennyson once, the night of the club auction. Patricia had gushed that they were late because his practice with the Gwinnett Braves had run long. Carlotta's encounter with the man had been brief, but he'd struck her as surly and a bit arrogant. She'd given him the benefit of the doubt, though, since she assumed he was tired, and from the stiff way he'd held himself in the tuxedo, that he was uncomfortable in the posh setting. "Can you be more specific?"

Patricia shrugged. "He flies off the handle at small things…and sometimes he makes comments about other women when we're together."

Carlotta bristled on the blonde's behalf. "Patricia, you shouldn't accept that behavior from someone who's supposed to care about you."

"But we've only been dating for a little while. Maybe I'm expecting too much."

"Don't make excuses for him. This early in your relationship, the man should be using his best manners. If he's disrespectful now, just think how he might be down the road."

Patricia averted her gaze, then looked back. "Have you ever been afraid of a man?"

Carlotta closed her locker door. "Never a man I was in a relationship with."

"Not even Cooper Craft? Rumor has it that you two dated, and he's a serial killer."

"We didn't date," Carlotta corrected. "But the times I was with Coop, no, I was never afraid of him."

"So…I could be wrong about Leo, like you were wrong about this Craft man."

Carlotta shook her head. "I'm not wrong about Coop. I still believe Michael is The Charmed Killer."

"Then why did they arrest someone else?"

"I don't know," Carlotta murmured. "I just know that a woman should almost always trust her instincts." Admittedly, it was the "almost" part that tripped her up.

"You're so lucky, Carlotta. You have Peter." The young woman's eyes got a dreamy look. "And it's clear by the way that man looks at you how he feels."

"Peter is a wonderful man," she agreed.

Patricia sighed. "Oh, well, off to smell stinky feet all day." She plastered on a smile that Carlotta recognized— the one that sales associates mastered to deal with cranky customers on an unending day while a migraine needled the back of their head—and left the break room.

Sympathy barbed through Carlotta's chest. She'd

seen lots of women in Patricia's shoes…and not just in the Shoes department. Dating a man whose actions were just good enough not to break up with him, yet not good enough to sleep well at night, and manic enough to make a woman question her own sanity.

But Patricia was right about Peter, Carlotta thought as she rode the escalator to her department on the second floor. She was lucky to have someone who cared so much about her. Of the three men who'd taken up residence in different corners of her heart recently, only Peter had been there for her throughout. Coop had his own issues, and Jack had to save the world.

She scanned for Herb, the block-shouldered security guy stationed somewhat blatantly in her department, and frowned when she spotted him talking to her boss, Lindy Russell. Herb was studying a sheet of paper that Lindy had presumably given him.

"Hi," Carlotta said, walking up.

"Hi, Carlotta," Lindy said. "I was just showing Herb the updated APB on Michael Lane. Apparently, he's altered his hair color."

"To blond, yes. Did the police fax it to you?"

"Yes, Detective Marquez, I believe. She left me a voice message saying she'd also sent a copy to mall security, and to the company that manages the valet service."

"That was nice of her," Carlotta murmured. But she knew Maria Marquez was only doing her job. No doubt the female detective wanted Michael brought into custody for many reasons, but one of them was probably so she, as a profiler, could pick his brain. So far, Marquez had been wrong about the part where Michael would kill Carlotta if he got the chance. He hadn't.

Yet.

"Herb, would you excuse us for a moment?" Lindy asked.

Herb skedaddled and Carlotta held her breath, waiting to hear what her boss had to say. It could be so many things, ranging from "You're fired" to "Your car blew up in the parking lot again" to "Your wages are being garnished by the city for an unpaid water bill."

Lindy smiled. "Congratulations, your sales are back on top."

Carlotta exhaled. "That's great news, thanks."

Then Lindy's smile wavered. "Carlotta, as much as I would like to, the company can't provide a security guard for you indefinitely."

"I understand. Hopefully Michael will be apprehended soon."

"Yes. I've been authorized to extend the security detail through next Monday. I do, however, have the authority to grant you up to five days of paid leave under extraordinary circumstances, and since inventory starts next Tuesday, I thought it might be a good time to offer it to you."

Carlotta blinked. "Paid leave? Wow…I mean, yes, thank you."

"I'll take care of the paperwork." Lindy walked away, ever aloof and professional. Carlotta marveled again over how many second chances her boss had given her over the years. Mired in the drama of her day-to-day life, it was easy to overlook all the things she should be grateful for.

Like Peter.

As her shift wore on, Peter weighed on her mind even as she waited on customers. She was eager to talk to him and try to put things right between them again. So when he appeared at her station a couple of hours later wearing jeans and a pale yellow short-sleeve button up shirt, she thought for a minute she'd conjured him up.

She smiled wide. "Peter."

"I'm sorry," he said, without preamble.

"I'm sorry, too," she said. "I don't want to keep things from you. We're supposed to be getting to know each other."

"You're right," he said. "And I realize I haven't made it easy for you to share with me, but I can change."

Her heart swelled. "Me, too."

He held up a bag. "I brought you lunch."

She grinned. "Is this yesterday's lunch?"

"No, I ate yesterday's lunch. Today is peanut butter and jelly."

Delighted, Carlotta reached for it. "My favorite."

"With fresh strawberries and dry-roasted peanuts."

"Wow, I can't wait." She pressed her lips together. "Thank you so much, Peter. I've been thinking about you ever since I left the house."

His eyebrows rose. "Oh?"

"I have a proposition for you."

"I'm all ears."

Carlotta moistened her lips, conscious of the big step she was taking. "How about this? We make plans to leave for Vegas next Tuesday for five days, and you don't give me a hard time about looking into The Charmed Killer case between now and then."

A hopeful smile erupted on Peter's face. "I think I can live with that."

15

Carlotta took a deep breath and strode into the lobby of the midtown precinct of the Atlanta Police Department. She'd been in this place so often in the past few months, she knew how many tiles were in the lobby ceiling and that D4 in the vending machine would drop two of whatever snack item happened to be in the slot.

She walked up to the counter and smiled at her friend Brooklyn who dutifully manned the check-in process behind a presumably bulletproof window. "Hi, Brook."

The woman grinned and leaned. "Well, hi, girl. What brings you here?"

"I have an appointment to speak with GBI agents Wick and Green."

Brook checked her computer screen. "About your boyfriend?"

"I'm sorry?"

"McHenry over at City Detention called to get the lowdown on you. Said you were engaged to The Charmed Killer?"

"Uh…well, that was a little misunderstanding."

"Got Jack Terry over there in a hurry, didn't it?"

Carlotta frowned. "Jack is a busybody."

Brooklyn laughed. "Yeah. The man's body has been busy lately, if you know what I mean."

She bit her tongue to keep from asking, but couldn't help it. "With Maria Marquez?"

"That's the rumor." The woman picked up the phone and punched a couple of buttons. "Carlotta Wren is here."

Carlotta wasn't sure why the news bothered her. She'd suspected that Jack and his new partner would hook up eventually. They were both gorgeous, single people who spent a lot of time together in situations where the adrenaline ran high.

Brook hung up the phone. "Don't look so long in the face. Only two ways something like that can end, and you and I know Jack Terry ain't the marrying kind."

"I'm just nervous about the interview," Carlotta murmured.

"Why? You didn't kill all those women."

"Let's just say Agent Wick isn't a fan of mine."

The woman gave a dismissive wave. "Brother ain't so bad. Could use some biscuits and gravy to put a little meat on those long bones of his, though."

Carlotta smiled. "Brooklyn, are you crushing on Agent Wick?"

"Crushin' is right, if I got on top of him," Brook said, giving a hearty laugh that sent her generous curves bouncing. She hit a button to unlock the secure door that led to the administrative area. "Go on back."

Carlotta walked through, surprised to see Jack standing at the coffee station waiting for her. She'd assumed Brook had been talking to one of the GBI agents. Jack looked freshly showered. His collar stood up and his unknotted tie hung around his shoulders. "Hey."

"Hey, yourself." She hoped like hell something had happened overnight to make her interview unnecessary. "Give me some good news, Jack."

He lifted his coffee cup for a sip. "Apple stock is up."

"Very funny. I don't suppose you've heard anything from Michael?"

He frowned. "No. Uniforms are canvasing every motel and hotel in the city, but nothing so far."

"He has to be living somewhere."

"We already know he can break into a house. Maybe he's living in one of the thousands of empty ones that are up for sale in the metro area."

She winced. "That narrows it down."

"Exactly." Then he winked. "Don't worry. We'll get him."

She stepped up to slide his tie around and fashion a knot. He let her. "Sleeping at the office again?"

"Yeah, why?"

"Rumor has it you've been sleeping elsewhere lately."

His mouth twitched. "Don't believe everything you hear. How are *your* sleeping arrangements these days?"

"Separate," she murmured.

"Really? When you didn't answer your phone last night, I wondered if Peter had accidentally stumbled into your bedroom instead of the butler's pantry, looking for Grey Poupon."

She tightened the knot with a bit more force than necessary.

He grunted, then grinned and flipped down his shirt collar.

"Good morning," a honeyed voice sounded behind Carlotta.

She turned her head to see the exotic Maria Marquez heading toward them, ducking a tea bag into a mug. She looked amazing in an off-white pantsuit and peach-colored silk blouse.

"Good morning," Carlotta offered, stifling a stab of envy that the woman was so comfortable in Jack's world.

"Another meeting with the state guys about The Charmed Killer case?" Maria asked.

"Right," Carlotta said. "I'm hoping they'll eventually catch the right guy."

"I'm sorry, Carlotta, but we have the right guy," Maria said, then sipped from her mug.

"Because Coop fits your profile?" Carlotta crossed her arms. "I'd like to see this bulletproof profile you came up with, Detective."

Jack cleared his throat. "That's not going to happen." He nodded toward the hallway that led to the interview rooms. "Come on, Carlotta, I'll take you back."

Carlotta frowned, but followed him. "Whose side are you on?"

"We're all on the same side. We all want justice for the victims. Maria, too."

"I think she wants to make a name for herself."

"Funny, she says the same thing about you."

Carlotta glared. "So, what do you think the state guys want to talk to me about?"

"I don't know. But I will get to listen in this time."

"They're letting you work on the case again?"

"I'm growing on them," Jack said. "At least they're keeping me more informed. Right now, though, I'm focused on finding Lane and trying to figure out who planted the explosive under your car."

"Do you still think they're related?"

"I hope so. It would be nice to kill a flock of birds with one stone." He stopped in front of an interview room. "Don't let them rattle you, darlin'. Remember, you can leave anytime you want to." He rapped on the door and opened it. "Carlotta Wren is here at your request," he said, then stepped aside to let her walk into the interview room.

GBI Agent Wick, tall and slender, had a grim smile for Carlotta. "Good to see you, Ms. Wren." His teeth were white against mahogany skin.

She nodded, then turned toward Agent Green, a stocky white guy who seemed to be relegated to the position of stenographer. "Hello, gentlemen." The last time she'd seen them had been when they'd arrested Coop right in front of her at Neiman's.

"Have a seat," Wick offered.

She took the seat across the table from them. They opened one folder, then another, murmuring back and forth between themselves for a few seconds. Finally, Wick looked up.

"How are you, Ms. Wren?"

"Better than the last time you saw me."

"Yes, well, that was an unfortunate scene, but necessary. I understand you visited our suspect—" He checked his notes. "Friday."

"That's right."

"What did you talk about?"

"Why don't you listen to the tape?"

He smiled. "Actually, we have. I was just seeing if you would lie to us…again."

At the reference to her failed polygraph, she shifted in her chair.

Wick gestured to Green, who handed him a printout. "Speaking of which, we have the polygraph examiner's report right here. Deception indicated on questions six, seven, and nine," he read, then looked up. "Question six was about having a romantic relationship with Detective Terry."

She didn't respond.

"You denied having one."

"I remember what I said."

"Would you like to change your answer?"

"No. Detective Terry and I don't have a romantic relationship." With Jack, it was all about sex.

The agent frowned. "Okay, moving on. Question seven—when asked if you knew the whereabouts of your father, you said no."

"Correct."

"But according to this report, you were lying."

She shrugged. "I guess I thought of the postcards we've received over the years from different states. But I don't know where Randolph is now. If I did, believe me, I'd drag him back to Atlanta myself."

Wick's eyebrows rose. "Still nursing animosity toward your parents for abandoning you and your brother?"

"Yes," she admitted. In fact, she could feel her blood pressure rising now. When Randolph disappeared, he'd put her in the position of having to defend him, of having to make excuses for him. Wesley had made up outlandish stories of international espionage to explain away their father's absence, but she hadn't possessed the imagination and optimism of a nine-year-old. Ten years later, she was still covering for Randolph.

"But you're still claiming you don't know where your father is."

Inside, she kicked and screamed. "That's right."

Wick sighed noisily, then looked back to his report. "Question nine was about the identity of the person known as The Charmed Killer. You said you didn't know who had committed these crimes, but the polygraph indicates that you do." He dropped the report and looked at her expectantly.

"I believe Michael Lane is responsible," she said. "But I responded no because I'm not positive."

Wick leaned toward his partner. "I think she knows her buddy Cooper Craft is responsible."

Under the table Carlotta clasped her hands. "Coop isn't a monster."

"But he's a drunk." Wick continued talking to Green, as if they were having a private conversation. "A drunk who put a woman in a body bag while she was still alive."

Her throat convulsed. "He paid for his mistake."

"Yeah, he lost everything—his title, his job, and his ability to practice medicine. That would really work on a man, make him crazy…maybe even homicidal."

She shook her head. "You're wrong. Coop was happy with his life."

"He got lonely," Wick said to Green, ignoring her. "But women aren't exactly clamoring to go out with a guy who spends more time with dead women than live ones, you know what I mean?"

Green nodded, absorbed in the story.

Carlotta sighed. "Is this going somewhere? I thought I was here to help you get to the bottom of these murders."

"Hang on, I'm getting to the best part," Wick said. "So

Dr. Craft meets a woman and falls head over heels for her. But, not surprisingly, the woman doesn't feel the same about him. So, he starts to obsess over her…and he back-slides into the bottle…and then he starts to hate her."

Green's eyes grew larger. "And then what?"

Wick frowned at his partner. "And then he decides if he can't kill her, he'll kill someone else—another woman…and then another…and then another."

Wick looked back to Carlotta. "Now what do you think of my story?"

"I think you've been spending a lot of time with our resident profiler."

"So would you be surprised to learn that Craft had a picture of you on his refrigerator?"

She hesitated, realizing how that must look. "I gave him that picture. And I saw it on his fridge when I was at his place. But that doesn't mean anything. I'm sure he had other pictures of friends around his place."

Wick shook his head. "Nope. Just the one of you. Did Dr. Craft ever make any romantic overtures toward you?"

Under the table, Carlotta wiped her wet palms on her slacks. "Coop let me know that he was interested in me romantically, yes."

"So the two of you were involved?"

"No, we only worked together occasionally. And I went on a road trip with Coop a few weeks ago to pick up a VIP body."

"Oh?"

"My brother Wesley went with us."

"Let me be more specific. Did you and Craft ever sleep together?"

Carlotta slid her gaze to the mirrored window, half

wondering if Jack had put Wick up to asking that particular question. "It's no one's business, but no, Coop and I were never intimate. I consider him to be a good friend."

"So you rejected him?"

She wet her lips. "That's not what I said. It was a mutual agreement that we wouldn't pursue a romantic relationship. There were no harsh words, there was no argument."

"Did he stalk you?"

"What? No!" Carlotta leaned forward. "But guess who *is* stalking me, Agent Wick? Michael Lane. *He's* the man you should be looking for."

"The good men and women of the Atlanta Police Department are handling that case."

"It's the same case," she said through gritted teeth.

Agent Wick studied her. "You should know that we've been able to prove Dr. Craft frequented the same places as many of the victims. He purchased books from the bookstore where Shawna Whitt worked, he belonged to the same gym as Cheryl Meriwether, he shopped at the grocery store where Marna Collins shopped. And from your statement, we know he knew where the prostitute Pam Witcomb hung out." The man angled his head at her. "What do you have to say about that?"

Still trying to process the information, Carlotta swallowed hard. "Coincidence."

The agent's expression hardened. "Ms. Wren, we found charms in Dr. Craft's home."

Panic blipped in her stomach. "Charms?"

"All kinds of charms. Now why would a single adult man have a stash of charms?"

Her mind raced, then her shoulders dropped in relief. "They're for his dioramas."

"Beg your pardon?"

"It's Coop's hobby. He recreates scenes in miniature in cigar boxes. He uses charms as pieces in the scenes. He built one for June Moody, the owner of Moody's Cigar Bar. It's a complete replica of her store in one little box. It's amazing."

Wick exchanged a glance with Green. "Sounds like a very strange hobby."

Green nodded in agreement.

"He said it helped him quit drinking, that it kept his hands busy," Carlotta said. "When I was at his place, he showed me the one he's working on now—it's a miniature library."

"And the charms found in the mouths of the last two victims were books. Now that *is* quite a coincidence."

When she realized she was only reinforcing Wick's case, frustration sent her lunging to her feet. "Coop didn't do this. I don't care what you found in his home, or what kind of DNA you have."

The man leaned back in his chair and clasped his hands behind his head. "Did I say we had DNA?"

She frowned. "I have my sources, too, Agent. And DNA can be planted."

The agent laughed. "So…you think someone framed him?"

Her chin went up. "Maybe. Or maybe you quit looking when you came across a suspect who was easy to apprehend."

"Back to Michael Lane again?"

Carlotta averted her gaze, then turned and walked away from the two men, away from the mirrored window. They were obviously unconvinced that

Michael was their man. She was torn. She had information about Coop's connection to the first victim that would further cement him in the minds of the GBI agents as The Charmed Killer. On the other hand, she had a piece of information that could send them off on another tangent that might buy Coop a little time. She rubbed the back of her neck to combat the tension vibrating through her body. The fact that she was hesitant to divulge something distasteful her father had done made her even more angry toward Randolph. He didn't deserve her loyalty.

"Ms. Wren, is there something you'd like to share?"

Randolph hadn't been there for her for the past ten years, but he could be useful to her—useful to someone who meant a great deal to her—right now, at this moment.

She turned to face the agents. "You asked me in the last interview if I knew that the second victim, Alicia Sills, worked in the same office building as my father. Or if I'd ever heard Randolph mention her name."

Wick dropped his hands—she had his attention. "And you said no."

She nodded. "Right. And that was the truth. But since then, it's come to my attention that my father knew Alicia Sills and, in fact…they might have had a relationship."

Wick blinked. "How did this piece of information come to your attention?"

She hugged herself. "My, um, boyfriend, Peter Ashford, remembered going to work with my father once, years ago when he was in high school. A woman delivering mail came into Randolph's office. Peter said it was obvious that Randolph and this woman…knew each other well. Peter looked into old employment records and determined it was Alicia Sills."

She could tell Wick hadn't expected the curve. "Are you now saying that you think your father might be involved in these murders?"

"No. I'm just correcting information I gave you before about a connection between my father and one of the victims."

"Peter Ashford," Wick muttered. "That name sounds familiar."

"He works at Mashburn and Tully. You interviewed the employees there and asked them about my father?"

"Right," Wick said, gesturing for Green to check their notes. "So why didn't Mr. Ashford let us know himself?"

"I asked him not to. I didn't think it was relevant."

"And now you do?"

"Now I'm just trying to demonstrate that you shouldn't lock in on Cooper Craft based on circumstantial evidence."

"You needn't involve yourself with the procedures of this case, Ms. Wren. We've got that under control."

Carlotta leaned forward, hands on the table. "If you've got it under control, Agent Wick, then why am I telling you things you don't know?" She reached for her purse. "Unless you have more questions, I'm leaving." She started toward the door.

"Ms. Wren."

She turned back.

Wick wore a constipated expression, as if she'd messed up his plans for the day. "You need to let us know if you're planning to leave town."

"As a matter of fact, Agent, I am. Peter Ashford and I leave for Vegas next Tuesday."

"We'll need to talk to Mr. Ashford again before then."

"I'll tell him." She turned and walked out the door, then headed for the exit.

"Carlotta, wait."

She closed her eyes briefly, then turned to see Jack striding up to her. He pulled his hand down over his face. "That was...revealing."

"That was my last voluntary interview, Jack. I'm done."

"Fair enough. You've been a big help."

She frowned. "And what are *you* doing to help Coop?"

"Hoping he isn't granted bail when he's arraigned today."

Her eyes widened. "You hope he doesn't get bail?"

"Carlotta, if Coop is innocent, there's a good chance The Charmed Killer is going to strike again. When that happens, the best alibi for Coop is jail."

She knew that, but still, the thought of him in that place...

Then Jack crossed his arms. "So...Vegas, huh?"

"Vegas," she confirmed with a nod.

"Just be careful. A lot of people get out there in that overoxygenated air and go crazy, wind up doing stupid things, like...getting married."

She angled her head. "You were the one who told me I should marry Peter."

He picked up a strand of her hair and rubbed it between two fingers. "Since when do you listen to me?"

The thickness of his voice made Carlotta's heart thud in her chest. "Jack, can you give me a reason I shouldn't go away with Peter?"

He studied the dark hair for several long seconds, then suddenly released it. "No, I can't." Then he turned around and walked away.

16

Carlotta walked to her rental car in the parking garage adjacent to the police station and unlocked it from a safe distance. She looked around, wondering if Michael would be careless enough to follow her, but apparently not. She slid into the driver's seat, then scrolled through the directory on her phone until she reached Fischer, Liz. After connecting the call, she drummed her fingers on the steering wheel, waiting for the woman to answer.

"Liz Fischer."

Carlotta flinched. Even the woman's voice grated on her nerves. "Liz, it's Carlotta Wren."

"Hi, Carlotta. I hope this isn't about Wesley."

"No, I don't get involved in Wesley's personal life."

"Pardon me?"

"You don't have to play dumb, Liz. I know you and Wes have a thing, but he's old enough to make his own mistakes. Heaven knows you won't be his last."

"Was there a point to this call?" Liz chirped.

"Actually, I'm calling about Dad. You know, the other Wren man you slept with?"

"What about Randolph?"

She told Liz about his connection to Alicia Sills. "I just

informed the GBI this morning and I thought it might help you in Coop's arraignment. Between Michael Lane and now this link to my dad, the D.A. has to know there would be reasonable doubt if the case against Coop goes to trial. It might at least help Coop get bail."

"Carlotta, I'm going to fight like hell for bail, but D.A. Lucas is going to come in like a sledgehammer."

"But think about it, Liz. Who does Lucas want as much as The Charmed Killer?"

"Randolph Wren," Liz relented.

"Imagine if Lucas thought that Randolph might *be* The Charmed Killer."

A conceding noise sounded over the line. "It might rattle Lucas a little. My plan is to point out to the judge that the prosecution has only a circumstantial case against Dr. Craft. At the moment, the jail is overcrowded, so that will work in our favor. And we might get lucky and draw a sympathetic judge. Of course, the judge might set a bail so high that Dr. Craft can't cover it."

"When is the arraignment?"

"Sometime early afternoon."

"I'll keep an ear to the news. Good luck."

"Carlotta?"

"Yes."

"I do care for Wesley."

"So do I, Liz. Goodbye."

She disconnected the call, feeling marginally optimistic about Coop, but less confident when it came to Wes. She hoped he hadn't gotten in over his head with Liz, although she understood the attraction. He obviously liked Meg, but in some respects a physical relationship was easier to deal with than an emotional one.

Which was probably why she was so drawn to Jack.

Carlotta spent the rest of the morning driving from jewelry store to jewelry store, "pretending" that she was doing legwork for the police and asking if they'd sold charms to anyone suspicious. She presented Michael's picture, explaining he might be blond, but very few retail outlets reported any male customers buying charms at all. And none of them had aroused suspicion.

"Pretty girl like you should have a great big diamond on your finger," a stooped, white-haired salesman told her with a wink.

Carlotta's thoughts went to the Cartier ring Peter was holding for her. "I'm not quite ready for marriage yet."

The man grinned. "Who said anything about marriage? An engagement ring is just something nice to wear while you make up your mind."

She rubbed her empty ring finger and considered his words, then thanked him for his time. At the moment, she had another type of jewelry on her mind. All morning her attention kept returning to the charm bracelet she wore, and to whether the charms it came with held special meaning. And if the charms the serial killer used held special meaning.

After he'd killed Shawna Whitt, he'd taken a charm from her bracelet and placed it in her mouth. Had her bracelet broken during a struggle? Had the charm simply become a spontaneous signature, with no particular meaning other than accessibility?

And after Shawna Whitt, had the killer continued with the signature simply out of compulsion? Since none of the other charms that Shawna's coworker had described from her bracelet had been left at subsequent crime scenes, it seemed as if the jewelry had been chosen deliberately. Or maybe the charms had significance in the killer's mad mind but would be nonsensical to anyone else.

On the drive to the townhouse, Carlotta conceded she was looking for a needle in a haystack. In at least the first case, he'd taken a charm from the victim's own bracelet. After that, he could've obtained more of them anywhere—from the victims' jewelry boxes, through an online store or auction, at a flea market. The charms could've belonged to someone in his home—a mother, or a sister…or a wife. Or he could've stolen them. A man who would murder women for sport would certainly think nothing of shoplifting a few trinkets.

Her mood was decidedly morose when she pulled into the weedy driveway of the townhouse. Hannah's van and Wes's bike were already there. She wondered wryly if Chance was going to join them, then chastised herself. If Hannah was happy dating the schlubby guy with the questionable revenue stream, then who was she to judge? After all, Hannah wasn't exactly nuts about Peter, yet she managed to keep her hostility to a minimum.

Sort of.

Carlotta climbed out of the rental car, pulled accumulated mail from the box, and made her way to the front steps, hoping to get inside without drawing the attention of Mrs. Winningham.

No such luck.

"Carlotta! Yoo-hoo!"

She winced, then turned toward the fence that kept the Wrens out of their neighbor's manicured yard. "Hello, Mrs. Winningham."

The dour-faced woman stood there holding a ruffled pink parasol over her dog, Toofers. "I want to talk to you."

"About the fire ants—"

"How did you get rid of them?"

Carlotta squinted. "Excuse me?"

The woman gestured to the areas in the yard where she'd previously pointed out the offending sandy hills allegedly brimming with dog-eating ants. "They're gone. What product did you use?"

"I...don't know," Carlotta said, impressed that Wesley had taken care of the pests. He was obviously trying to compensate for his other mistakes. "But I'll ask Wes to let you know. Goodbye, Mrs. Winningham." She jogged up the steps and pushed open the door to the sound of raised voices.

Wes was facing Hannah and Chance. "Both of you get off my back!"

Carlotta pulled the door closed with a bang. They turned to look at her, then all of them shifted awkwardly.

Carlotta shot Wes a pointed look. "Why would Hannah and Chance be on your back?"

Wes straightened and tried to look nonchalant. "No reason."

Anger whipped through her. "Stop bullshitting me, Wesley Wren! I don't need it today."

He shifted from foot to foot. "I messed up last night and got high. But I'm getting clean, Sis, I promise."

Carlotta stared at him, feeling very close to losing it. She gripped the strap of her purse for dear life, then reached inside and pulled out a cigarette, breaking her rule of not smoking in the house. Her hand was shaking so badly as she lit the tip, the lighter's flame bobbed. She inhaled on the cigarette until her eyeballs bulged, then exhaled noisily. She could feel everyone's eyes trained on her, as if they were waiting for her to flip out. Carlotta took two more powerful drags before lifting her gaze to Wes. To his credit, he looked scared.

"Are you okay, Sis?"

"We'll talk about this later," she promised. "Let's get down to business."

Wordlessly, Hannah and Chance headed for the kitchen. Carlotta thought about the listening device imbedded in the wall over the window, then decided it was a moot point. On the remote chance someone was listening, she couldn't imagine they'd be interested in The Charmed Killer case. Most likely, whoever had planted it had given up listening long ago. For all they knew, it could've been in the house before the Wrens had moved in.

She followed the trio into the kitchen and snubbed out her cigarette before taking a place at the table. Without preamble, she pulled out her notebook and opened it. "Okay, Hannah, you said you and Chance had some information?"

Hannah looked at her warily. "Carlotta, we don't have to do this now."

"Coop is supposed to be arraigned today," Carlotta said carefully. "If you found something helpful, tell me."

Hannah looked dubious, but handed over a folder. "It's not hard to get cyanide if you want it. Pharmacists can get it, and chemists. Plus people in the pest control business, and jewelers. Cyanide is also used in some photographic and printing processes. And if a person doesn't have access to it through their job, all they need is a friend who does."

Carlotta sighed. "That doesn't exactly narrow it down."

"Those are only the legal ways," Chance offered. "I made two phone calls to my, um...*alternative* contacts, and I was told as long as I had cash, I could have as much as I wanted."

Carlotta's shoulders fell. "So anyone can get it."

"But that's a good thing, right?" Hannah asked. "That will help Coop."

"I suppose. But I was hoping it would lead us to a smaller group of suspects." She looked at Chance. "Hannah said you'd talked to some people who knew Pepper?"

He nodded. "Two of her friends said Pepper was having trouble with a guy."

"Who was he?"

"A customer. They didn't have a name, but they said he was a doctor."

Carlotta's pulse raced. "Did anyone see this guy?"

"No. She just complained about him a couple of times, said he gave her the creeps."

"Do they know if she was supposed to meet this person the night she was killed?"

"No, they didn't see her the night she died."

"Did they say if this man ever gave her jewelry? Or did she have a nickname for him?"

Chance snapped his fat fingers. "She called the guy Doc."

Carlotta pursed her mouth. "So he could've been a doctor, or someone who said he was a doctor, or Dr. Doolittle?"

Chance frowned. "Who?"

"Never mind," Hannah said, patting his hand. "You did good."

Carlotta sighed, feeling contrite. "Yes, Chance, thank you. Do you have the names of the two friends you talked to?"

"It was Whisper and Tambourine. They hang out at the donut place on Ponce."

Carlotta wrote down the names and the nickname "Doc," but even as she did, she realized she would only be giving the authorities more reason to suspect Coop. With tempered optimism, she looked up to Wes. "Have you seen Liz?"

"Yeah."

"Spare me the sordid details," she said, holding up her hand. "Did you find out anything about Coop?"

Wes frowned. "Nothing good. Liz says that Coop doesn't act like an innocent man. She's worried."

"That's all she said?"

"She asked me if *I* thought he was The Charmed Killer."

Panic began to bubble in Carlotta's stomach. If Coop's attorney thought he was guilty, things were looking bleak. "What did you tell her?"

"I told her the Coop I knew couldn't do it."

The Coop they knew. Carlotta felt queasy. Was there a side of Coop they didn't know?

"You said you came across some new info?" Hannah asked Carlotta.

Carlotta reluctantly relayed what Shawna Whitt's coworker had revealed—that Shawna had worn a bracelet and one of the charms had been a chicken, and that the guy at the information desk had ID'd Coop as a frequent customer. She also told them about the white van Shawna's neighbor had seen the day before her body was found. When she finished, she wet her lips and glanced around the table. "So I need theories to help explain the coincidences. Anybody?"

They all stared back at her.

"I'm waiting," she said, tapping her pen on her notebook.

Chance scratched his chin. "Uh...everybody's lying?"

Carlotta frowned.

"Okay," Hannah said, leaning forward. "When we last talked, we said there were two ways to tackle this. We could either disprove it's Coop, or prove it's someone else. Carlotta, do you still think Michael Lane is The Charmed Killer?"

"Yes. By the way, he's blond now. A bartender at Moody's confirmed that Michael was in the bar last weekend when I was there."

Wesley looked concerned. "You didn't see him?"

"No, but someone followed me into the ladies' room. The person didn't talk, but I smelled cologne that seemed familiar. It wasn't until later that it occurred to me it might've been Michael. The fact that the bartender ID'd him confirms it."

"But Lane is still unaccounted for?" Hannah asked.

Carlotta nodded. "Jack's working on it now since the GBI is keeping him away from The Charmed Killer case. I met with a reporter for the *AJC* yesterday and she agreed to help me think of something that might flush Michael out of hiding."

Wes made a strangled noise. "You're going to taunt this guy?"

"I still have a security detail at the store, and the stun baton Jack gave me. I'll be careful."

"That lunatic probably blew up your car!"

"I appreciate the concern, Wes, but let me handle this. You've got your own problems," she added with a meaningful look.

"How was your interview with the GBI this morning?" Hannah asked.

Carlotta sighed. "Predictable. They're stuck on Coop, even though I pointed out there were other suspects."

"Are there others besides Michael Lane?"

Carlotta exchanged a look with Wesley. "Our father's name came up in the investigation."

"But it was spit out as part of a profile, wasn't it?" Hannah asked.

"Right." Carlotta frowned. "I think the APD's new profiler is eager to get her picture in the paper."

"I saw her picture," Chance offered. "She's smoking hot."

Hannah whacked him on the arm.

"But she's nothing compared to you, babe," he added obediently.

Hannah looked smug, then glanced back to Carlotta. "So they don't have anything else on your father, right?"

"I...told the police that he gave me a charm bracelet when I was fourteen. Jack asked for it, and I gave it to them."

"That's a pretty thin thread," Hannah said.

She doodled in the margin of her notebook. "And as it turns out, Randolph knew the second victim, Alicia Sills."

"The lady we thought fell off the stepladder?" Hannah asked.

Carlotta nodded. "The two of them used to work together and...maybe more."

Wesley lurched forward. "You didn't tell the GBI, did you?"

She caught his gaze, then nodded. "I told them this morning."

"Why?" he demanded.

"To plant doubts and maybe buy Coop some time."

Wes stood and paced away from the table. Carlotta wasn't sure how much of his agitation was with her and how much was due to the Oxy. He shoved his hands in his pockets, probably to hide the tremors, she realized. When he got to the wall, he banged his palm against it, then strode back.

"I was at the morgue yesterday," he blurted. "The burned body is still unidentified. But Kendall Abrams told me the charm pulled out of the victim's mouth is a bottle."

Carlotta turned to the page where she'd made notations about the charms. "Any particular kind of bottle?"

"No...just a bottle."

But something in his tone made her look up. "Is there something you aren't telling me?"

He wiped his hand over his mouth. "I was thinking about all the charms that had been left behind, trying to figure out if they had something in common."

Carlotta leaned on her elbows. "And?"

"The first charm was a chicken, right?"

She nodded.

"Chicken...coop."

She scoffed. "That's a stretch."

"The second charm was a cigar," Wes continued. "And Coop hangs out at Moody's. Plus he collects cigar boxes—I've seen them in his van."

"But those are for a hobby of his," Carlotta said. "I explained it all to the GBI this morning. That's why they found charms in his house—he uses them to create miniature scenes in cigar boxes. Coop showed me the tiny library he's working on now."

Hannah averted her gaze.

"What was the third charm?" Wes persisted.

Carlotta checked the list. "A car."

"Coop is a car buff. Look at that primo classic Corvette he drives. What was the fourth charm?"

"A gun."

"Coop has a handgun. We saw it when we were in Florida, when those guys started firing at the rest area. Coop pulled out his pistol and shot back, remember?"

Carlotta remembered. Because of his record, Coop wasn't allowed to own a gun. Jack had covered for him after the shooting incident.

"What was the next charm?" Wes prompted.

She looked down at her notes and blinked rapidly to focus on her own writing. "Handcuffs."

"We all known Coop's worn those before," Wes offered. "And the next charm?"

"A keg…maybe a barrel," Carlotta murmured.

"A barrel maker is called a cooper," Wes said, then waited a beat for the info to sink in. "Are you starting to see the pattern, Sis?"

Carlotta pushed to her feet. "No…it doesn't mean anything."

"The charm left in the next victim's mouth was a

bottle," Wes said. "That's pretty self-explanatory. And the last two charms were books. Coop is an egghead, and you said he was working on a miniature library."

She nodded, numb.

"So what if…" Wesley trailed off, then lifted his hands. "What if Coop was using those last charms to steer the police back to the bookstore where he met the first victim?"

Carlotta shook her head. "I don't believe it…I can't believe it."

"You don't *want* to believe it," Wes said. "None of us do, Carlotta. But you have to face facts. It's starting to look as if Coop really is The Charmed Killer."

Carlotta blinked back tears. She'd had doubts herself, hadn't she? Hadn't she opened her mind to the sliver of possibility that Coop's proximity to death had driven him to indulge in horrific urges? That it was so contrary to his normal personality that he was able to keep that side of himself hidden from others?

But she'd seen other sides of Coop that the people in this room hadn't seen. She'd seen him in tender, vulnerable moments during their walks on the beach in Florida, when he was matter-of-fact about his problem with alcohol. And later, when they'd almost made love before Wes had interrupted them with an emergency. Coop had been warm and funny and romantic. How could she believe that mere weeks later, he would embark on a killing spree?

Carlotta lifted her chin. "There's nothing you can say to convince me that Coop is The Charmed Killer."

Wes shook his head, then gripped the back of a chair. "Since you told the GBI about Dad being acquainted with one of the victims, I assume you told them about everything else—what you learned at the bookstore about Coop? And about the van spotted in the victim's neighborhood?"

"No," she murmured.

He threw up his hands. "You're in denial, Sis." He reached for his backpack. "I gotta go to work."

"Me, too," Hannah said apologetically, pushing to her feet. Chance followed, sending wary looks in Carlotta's direction, as if he thought she might be losing her mind.

"Thanks for your help, both of you," Carlotta said. "I'll keep you posted."

Hannah and Chance nodded, but she could read in their expressions that from here on out, she was on her own.

"Wesley," she called before he could get away. He said goodbye to Hannah and Chance, then came back.

"What?" A muscle worked in his jaw.

She studied his face, ticking off the physical symptoms of Oxy abuse he was showing against the list she'd memorized from the Internet: bloodshot, twitchy eyes… blotchy skin…parched lips. He needed a kick in the pants, but she'd always spoiled him. Perhaps she'd loved him too much.

She stood to face him. "Wes…if you don't take care of this drug habit of yours, I'll turn you in myself."

Wesley's lips parted. "You'd send me to jail?"

"Yes, I would."

Anger darkened his expression and his body shook. "Of course you would. You've thrown Dad under the bus. Why not me, too?" He turned around and stormed toward the door.

"Wes—wait!"

But he was gone. The second man who'd walked away from her today. And it wasn't until he'd disappeared that she remembered she'd forgotten to ask him how he'd gotten rid of the fire ants.

17

"Thanks for the ride," Wes muttered to Mouse as the Town Car pulled into the parking lot of the county morgue.

"No problem," Mouse said. "You okay, little man? You kicked ass today collecting, but you've been in a bad mood all afternoon."

Wes just wanted to get out of the car. This morning at work, Meg had treated him like a paperweight. Then Carlotta not only refused to believe the mounting evidence against Coop, but had offered up their father as a diversion to the GBI. Top that with being a nervous wreck that Mouse would somehow find out about the money he'd collected from Jett Logan and then lost, and Wes had been glad to have an outlet for his nervous energy.

Although he harbored a bit of remorse for swinging the baseball bat—and connecting—more than usual, the result had been impressively higher collections.

"I just have a headache," he assured Mouse.

"Maybe it's from all those little white pills you're taking."

"Dude, I told you—I got it under control."

"Really? You're as moody as my wife. Your hands shake like an old man's. And you're jumpy as hell."

"I just got a lot on my mind."

"Did you ever find out who planted the bug in the wall of your place?"

"No. I'll probably just drywall over it."

"Not a bad idea," Mouse agreed.

"Listen, since we had a good collections day, would you mind if we skipped tomorrow?" He jerked his thumb over his shoulder. "Things are busy at the morgue, and I've been asked to put in some extra hours."

Mouse pursed his mouth. "Yeah, that's okay. It'll give me a chance to do some things around the house my wife has been bitching about."

"Pick me up after my probation meeting Wednesday?"

"Yeah, sure. Hey, I keep meaning to ask you about something."

Wes's pulse hammered. "What?"

"There was something in the paper over the weekend about a tip on the identity of the guy you de-toothed. Do you know anything about that?"

Wes blinked, not sure what surprised him more—the fact that Mouse thought he was the tipster, or the fact that Mouse read the newspaper. "How could it be me? I don't even know who the guy is—er, *was*."

"Right." The big man chewed his lip, nodding. "Okay, see you Wednesday. And hey, don't worry about letting Jett Logan get away from you. I'll fix things with the boss."

Wes swallowed. "Thanks."

He retrieved his bike from the trunk, then watched the black Town Car roll away. His knees felt rubbery as he locked up his bike. A cannon was going off in his head. He had promised himself he'd start weaning himself off the Oxy today, but there was just too much going on.

Tomorrow, he promised as he tossed another capsule into his mouth. Tomorrow he would kick the O for good.

He made his way into the morgue and stopped at the front desk to sign in. He had offered to meet Kendall Abrams to help clean the vans and do some routine pickups. And he was still trolling for information. On the way down the hall, he passed M.E. Pennyman, who had worked at the morgue for a while.

"Hey, Wes. Haven't seen you around here lately."

"I'm holding down two other jobs. And I worked primarily with Coop."

"Oh. Right. Did you hear the news?"

"I guess not. What's going on?"

"The judge granted Coop bail."

Wes blinked. "Really? Did the D.A. reduce the charges?"

"It's still murder, but only one count, in the case where DNA was recovered. I guess the D.A. is waiting for more evidence to link the other killings."

"What kind of DNA was recovered in the one case?"

"I can't be specific, but the killer left items at the scene."

"Which victim?"

"Wanda Alderman."

Inside his pockets, Wes fisted his hands. "That was a bad scene."

"I remember," Pennyman said, nodding. "Didn't the woman's son find her?"

"Yeah." In his mind, Wesley could still see the stricken look on the kid's face. It was similar to the way he'd felt when he realized his parents weren't coming home. But at least he'd had Carlotta. Suddenly, like a big sissy, moisture pooled in his eyes.

"You okay, man?" Pennyman asked.

Wes lifted his glasses to rub his eyes. "This new lens prescription is going to take some getting used to. So, Coop is out of jail?"

"Not yet. The bail was like a million dollars. And he has to wear a GPS ankle bracelet, so I guess that'll take a day or two to get worked out. But a lot of people aren't happy about it."

"I can imagine," Wes said. After all, even *he* was starting to believe he'd been all wrong about Coop. "Dude, has the burnt body been identified?"

"Not yet. We're still waiting for results from the state crime lab."

"There was another Doe in the crypt, a John Doe, no head. Has that body been ID'd yet?"

"Not yet, but the APD passed us a tip on the man's name." Pennyman made a rueful noise. "The kicker is that Coop was working on the case. Now, it could sit for months."

With a sinking sensation, Wes watched Pennyman walk away. At this rate, the headless man would never be identified. The man's family would never know what had happened to him.

Wes caught up with Kendall Abrams in the garage, spraying down the morgue vans. Kendall was intent on his job, his thick brows furrowed. Once again, Wesley wondered whether the guy could live up to his uncle's expectations. Kendall was studying to be an M.E., but so far he'd demonstrated an incredible insensitivity to the deceased, treating them much like the roadkill he'd cleaned up in his previous job with the Department of Transportation. Still, Kendall seemed eager to learn, and even more eager to please his over-worked uncle.

"What's on the schedule today?" Wes yelled over the noise.

"Hey," Kendall shouted, then turned off the water hose. "Boring stuff—hospital pickups."

"Ready to go?"

"Yeah, let's get out of here."

Wes climbed into the passenger seat. "Where to first?"

Kendall checked a clipboard. "Piedmont Hospital. They got five bodies waitin' for us."

Wes's mind jumped ahead. The last time he was at Piedmont Hospital was when he'd pretended to be a doctor and crashed Meg's father's lecture. It was also the day he'd followed Coop to the neurologist's office. Maybe he could snoop around for answers while he was there.

Kendall yammered on like a yodel-head—the guy was a total redneck. "...and iffen the animal happened to be in pretty good shape, I'd put it in a cooler and take it to my friend Danny, who's a taxidermist, and he'd stuff it for me...got a whole wall full of deer head... course they all look a little startled..."

When they arrived at the hospital morgue entrance, Wesley climbed out and coordinated the transfer of the five bodies from the crypt drawers to the shelves in the van that resembled bunks. Kendall seemed happy to do what he was told.

When they were finished, Wes said, "Do me a favor, man, and hang out here for a few minutes. I need to look in on a friend who's recuperating."

"Okay, sure." Kendall pulled a half-eaten sandwich

out of his pocket and settled on a stool in front of a monitor showing an autopsy in progress.

Wes left the morgue and entered the main part of the hospital. From there, he rode the elevator to the floor where he'd followed Coop. After he stepped off the elevator, it took him a while to get his bearings, but he managed to retrace his steps back to the neurologist's office where he'd seen Coop sitting in the waiting room. The place was studded with patients, a few of them clearly in some stage of radiation or chemotherapy. His throat convulsed. Some people got dealt a shitty hand.

He walked up to the receptionist's desk and gave the young woman there his best sad smile. "Hi. My last name is Craft. I've forgotten when my next appointment is. I was hoping you could look it up for me?"

She smiled. "No problem. Who's your doctor?"

Wesley glanced down at the stack of business cards on the counter, but the names of at least five doctors were listed for the practice.

He touched his forehead and squinted. "I'm sorry— this is so embarrassing. My memory is completely shot. I guess that's why I forgot my appointment."

"That's okay, sir. What's your date of birth?"

He could guess at the year Coop was born, but didn't have a clue about the date. "Uh...I don't know."

"It would be on your driver's license," said a male voice behind him.

Wesley turned to see Meg's father, Dr. Harold Vincent, standing a few feet away. Wes almost swallowed his tongue. "Um...I don't have a driver's license."

"Mr. Craft forgot the date of his next appointment," the young woman told the older man, then tapped her forehead in what Wesley presumed was supposed to be a discreet gesture.

Dr. Vincent stepped forward to pass the receptionist a thick stack of files, then looked back to Wesley with a smirk. "So today it's Mr. Craft?"

"I, uh…actually was asking for a friend. How are you, Dr. Vincent?"

The man ignored his greeting. "This hospital doesn't give out personal information on any of its patients. So unless you have business of your own here, you should leave."

Wesley frowned. "I'm at the hospital on business for the county morgue."

"Oh, yes…the body moving. I believe I saw that on a resume."

"You mean on a background check, don't you?"

The man's mouth pinched. "The last time I looked, Wren, the morgue was in the basement. If I see you around here again trying to pull another con, I'll call the police."

"You're just trying to keep me away from Meg."

The doctor squinted, then looked into Wes's eyes. "Oh, and you're high on something, too. Figures."

Wes pulled back, assuming his pupils were dilated. "I took a couple of pain pills for a migraine."

"Right." Dr. Vincent made a rueful noise. "The point is, I don't have to do anything to keep you away from Meg. Punks like you implode on your own. It's just a matter of time before my daughter figures you out."

Dr. Vincent turned to the receptionist and pointed to Wesley. "He's leaving now. If he shows his face in here again, call security."

Then the man strode away, leaving Wes feeling like a…punk. If Meg Vincent had ever been within his reach, she had just slipped a little farther away.

18

Carlotta juggled her cell phone while she pulled the strap of the slingback sandal over her heel. "So it looks like Coop will be out of jail by morning," she said to Hannah, the words tumbling out in a rush. "Technically, he could've been released after the arraignment yesterday except there was some glitch in the system that monitors the GPS ankle bracelets." She hopped across the bedroom into the bathroom, putting on the other sandal in the process. "But all that matters is he's getting out of that horrible place."

Silence rang across the line.

Carlotta frowned at her phone, then tapped the microphone. "Hannah, are you there?"

"I'm here."

"What's wrong with you? This is great news!"

Hannah sighed. "Carlotta, maybe Coop belongs in jail."

She stopped. "Don't tell me you actually believe Coop is The Charmed Killer."

"Okay, let's just put that aside for now. Have you considered for even a moment that Coop might be in danger when he's out—from the public, or from...himself?"

Carlotta dropped into a vanity chair. "No. I don't think Coop would hurt himself. Do you?"

Tension vibrated over the line. "Sweetie, you need to accept the fact that Coop might've undergone some sort of personality change. Maybe he suffered a nervous breakdown or some kind of posttraumatic disorder from all his years of seeing the worst of what can happen to people. Or maybe he really is sick. Maybe there's more to him being at that neurologist's office than he wants anyone to know."

Carlotta pressed her lips together and picked at the hem of her skirt. "Rainie Stephens said she'd try to find out about the neurologist. Meanwhile, can't you let me be optimistic? The prosecutor's case isn't rock solid if Liz Fischer was able to convince the judge to give Coop bail. That has to be a good sign."

"Bail was set at a million bucks. That's not exactly a vote of confidence. I'm wondering if the judge assumed that Coop couldn't make that kind of bail. Not many people could," Hannah added in a suspicious tone.

"He probably put up a property bond," Carlotta said. "No doubt his building in Castleberry Hill is worth a nice sum."

"Still."

From downstairs, Peter called her name. Carlotta turned her head. "I gotta run."

"Big plans tonight?"

"Peter is taking me to dinner at the new tapas place in midtown."

"You mean Morsels?"

"Right. Have you eaten there?"

"Yeah. You might want to take a snack with you. The portions are minuscule."

Carlotta laughed. "It's supposed to be the hottest

restaurant in town. Peter had to pull strings to get us reservations."

"I'll add string-puller to his list of good qualities," Hannah muttered.

"Do you and Dough Boy have plans?" Carlotta asked sweetly.

"Are you and Peter going to have a *quickie* before you go?"

Carlotta frowned. "I'm hanging up."

"Me, too."

Carlotta stabbed a button to end the call, irritated. Hannah's comment reminded her of all the sex she wasn't having with Peter, and how awkward things had become between them in the intimacy department. Both of them seemed content not to force the issue.

But she knew it was one of the reasons Peter had pushed for setting a date to go to Vegas. A change of venue would be good for both of them, to get away from the stress and ghosts plaguing both of them here.

"Carly," Peter called up the stairs again. "We need to leave soon if we're going to make our reservation."

"Two minutes," she called back, then pushed to her feet and reached for her makeup bag. She added blush to her cheeks and stroked on red lipstick, then ran a brush through her hair in broad strokes, opting to leave it loose around her shoulders.

She considered changing purses to something smaller, but she'd promised Jack she would keep the stun baton with her at all times. So she dropped her cell phone into her shoulder bag and went downstairs. Peter waited at the bottom, smiling up at her. Her heart squeezed with affection.

"Sorry to keep you waiting."

"It was worth the wait," he said, reaching up to clasp her hand.

It was a beautiful summer night. Carlotta felt a pang for the absence of the Porsche convertible, but the sunroof in Peter's luxury SUV let in the stars. A few minutes into the drive, Peter's cell phone rang.

He picked it up and frowned. "It's Brody Jones, I have to take this."

"Of course," she murmured, instantly anxious. Brody Jones was chief legal counsel for Mashburn & Tully. From the side of the conversation she could hear, she knew the topic was the connection between her father and Alicia Sills.

When Peter ended the call, his face was creased. "Brody wants to go with me when I talk to the GBI tomorrow."

"Why? You're not under suspicion."

"Brody is concerned that the GBI or the D.A.'s office will use this as an excuse to look into the company's records."

"Look for what?"

He hesitated. "Evidence that your father has been corresponding with someone in the building over the years."

She scoffed. "With Alicia Sills? That's ridiculous."

"Probably," he conceded. "But Brody is concerned that even if Randolph has nothing to do with The Charmed Killer case, the D.A. will see this as an opportunity to nose around for information that might be relevant in your father's fraud case." His mouth flattened. "And after all, your father did contact me."

Her pulse jumped. "Have you told anyone?"

"No. But if the company's phone records are sub-poenaed, I'd have to think they'd be looking closely at mine."

"Because of our relationship?"

He nodded.

She closed her eyes briefly. "I'm so sorry Randolph got you involved. If you want to tell the GBI about the phone call when you talk to them tomorrow, you should."

"It's not relevant to the case they're working on."

"I know, but I don't want this to blow up in your face, Peter. You can't risk the appearance that you're aiding and abetting my father."

He gave her a reassuring smile. "Don't worry."

She smiled back, but anxiety still gnawed at her as Peter held open the door for her at the restaurant.

Morsels was tucked into a large former single-family residence on Juniper Street, one block off Peachtree. True to its reputation, the place was packed. The inside had been gutted, with only the beamed ceilings bearing testament to the original interior design. The lighting was dim and lively piano music sounded from a far corner. Their table wasn't ready yet, so they stepped into the bar area to order a drink.

"How about champagne?" Peter asked.

Her thoughts immediately went to the charm on her bracelet of the two flutes touching, overflowing with bubbly, celebrating...something. "Champagne makes me a little headachy. Would you mind if we had wine instead?"

"Of course not. Whatever you want."

She chastised herself for being superstitious. But right now, she didn't want to risk doing something that might rip a hole in the fabric of the universe.

While the piano tinkled in the background, they sipped a buttery white burgundy wine and made small talk.

"Someone is coming out to repair the fountain Saturday," Peter said.

A flush warmed her neck. "Have I apologized today for demolishing the fountain and your car?"

He winked. "It was an accident. Insurance will take care of everything. Just think of it as…a contribution to the economy."

She laughed. "When are you getting a new Porsche?"

"Soon," he said, toying with the stem of his glass. "Or maybe not."

"But you loved that car."

"Yes, but it's not very practical."

"That's not really the point of owning a sports car, is it?"

"No. But I'm at a different point in my life than when I bought the Porsche. Then it was just me and Angie, and we didn't plan to have a family."

Carlotta nearly choked on her wine.

Peter gave her a little smile. "So I think I'll hold off for now."

She was saved from responding by the hostess arriving to say their table was available. As they were led to their seats, Carlotta did a double-take when she recognized the couple seated at an adjacent table—Jack…

And Maria.

And the way their heads were together, they weren't discussing blood-spatter patterns.

"Hello," Carlotta said, unable to keep the surprise out of her voice.

They looked up and separated guiltily. "Hi, Carlotta,"

Jack said stiffly. Then he stood and extended his hand to Peter. "Small world."

"Yes," Carlotta murmured in agreement.

Maria hid her reaction by taking a sip from her water glass.

"Peter, you remember Detective Maria Marquez," Carlotta said.

"Good to see you again," Peter said.

"Yes, you look well," Maria said, referring to the last time she'd seen him—stretched out on Carlotta's couch recovering from an accidental zap from Carlotta's stun baton. Maria nodded to Carlotta. "Enjoy your dinner."

Dismissed, Carlotta moved woodenly to her seat. Peter held out her chair and murmured in her ear, "Do you want to get another table?"

"Don't be silly," she whispered back. It wasn't as if their tables were close enough to hear each other's conversations.

Darn it.

From where she was sitting, she had a perfect view of the couple, just over Peter's shoulder. Their server gave them menus. Carlotta pretended to study the small plate items while reeling inside—and peeking over the top. Maria wore a clingy brown sleeveless dress and strappy sandals. Jack wore tan slacks and a black collarless dress shirt. It was clear they hadn't just left the office and dropped in for a beer before going home.

"What looks good?" Peter asked.

She jerked her gaze back to the menu. "Um…everything. You pick."

"Why don't we start with an olive tray?"

"Uh…sure." She glanced back to the table next to theirs, noting the couple seemed to be concentrating on eating.

"Carly."

She looked back to Peter. "Yes?"

"Are you going to be distracted by Jack and his girl-friend all evening?"

She frowned. "I'm not distracted. I was looking at what they ordered." She turned her head and nodded to a saucer of colorful food the couple on the other side of them was sharing. "Is that paella? It looks good."

Peter gave her a pointed look, then nodded to her glass. "Finish your wine."

She lifted her glass for an obligatory sip. "Do you think I have time to go to the ladies' room before they bring the appetizers?"

"Probably."

"I'll be right back," she promised, then shouldered her bag and walked past Jack and Maria's table. Once she was out of Peter's sight, she stopped a server. "Is there somewhere I can step outside to smoke?"

The waiter nodded. "There's a covered stoop through that door at the end of the hall."

Carlotta hurried down the hall, then pushed open the door to step out onto a small concrete pad. Hemmed with a thin metal railing, the stoop faced a line of trees about ten yards away. Light from the house on the other side filtered through the shadows of the thick foliage.

She slid out a cigarette and lit it quickly. The first drag soothed her frayed nerves a bit, but as she chewed a thumbnail, the hurt she'd been keeping at bay descended, swamping her chest. When Jack hadn't pursued a relationship with her beyond their few trysts, she'd assumed he wasn't looking for a relationship, period. Yet here he was, on a date with Maria, in a nice restaurant Carlotta would've sworn he wouldn't be caught dead in.

Obviously he was making exceptions for the new woman in his life that surpassed simply dressing better.

She took another drag on the cigarette, irritated with herself that seeing Jack with Maria bothered her so much. She had Peter. She'd been living in his house for a couple of weeks now, and was planning to go to Vegas with him next week. Why should she care who Jack slept with?

She gave a little laugh—that was it. When she'd thought he was only sleeping with Maria, it wasn't so bad. But dating Maria? Taking her to nice places and being seen in public? That signaled…commitment.

From inside her purse, Carlotta's phone rang. She removed it and glanced at the caller ID screen to see Rainie Stephens's name appear. Curious, she connected the call. "Hi, Rainie."

"Hi, Carlotta. Is this a bad time?"

"It's fine, but I only have a couple of minutes. Great news about Coop getting bail, huh?"

"Yeah. That means the D.A. doesn't have a slam-dunk case even in the one murder they charged him for, the Alderman woman."

"I wasn't on that scene," Carlotta said, taking another puff on the cigarette. "But I remember my brother talking about it."

"I was able to get my hands on what kind of DNA was recovered at the scene. It was a pair of latex gloves with Coop's fingerprints on the inside, plus saliva on a paper cup found in the kitchen trash."

Carlotta scoffed. "Both of those things could've been planted."

"I know. I'm just telling you what the D.A. has."

"Were you able to find out anything about Coop's visit to the neurologist?"

"Not yet, still checking. But I did think of something we could do that might flush out Michael Lane."

Carlotta took another drag. "What?"

"How do you think he'd react to a story in the paper announcing that you'd agreed to write an expose on him for a tabloid? You know, air his dirty laundry?"

"I think he'd be furious. Michael could be flamboyant, but he didn't like other people knowing his business."

"I noticed that on the profile, which is why I suggested it."

"Profile?"

"Yeah. I got my hands on a report that a profiler with the APD used to analyze suspects and compare them to the one created for The Charmed Killer."

Carlotta smirked. "Really? Tell me about the profile for The Charmed Killer."

The sound of papers being shuffled sounded in the background. "UNSUB is male, aged twenty-five to fifty, probably Caucasian. He probably has a dysfunctional relationship with his mother. He's a loner who struggles with authority. He holds a job that he feels is inferior. Feels wronged by society. Has above-average intelligence, is admired by peers and coworkers. Is well-read and compelled to achieve, but tends to misrepresent ability. Craves approval, but is private and paranoid. Narcissistic, not a joiner. Could be a physician or someone in the medical field. Has a credible, non-threatening appearance to gain trust of victims. Physically fit. Probable scouting, military, or police background, or otherwise trained in killing methods."

"Military?" Carlotta repeated.

"Does that mean something to you?"

Her mind scrolled back over her interaction with Sergeant Mitchell Moody. He had exhibited stalking behavior toward Eva McCoy when she had been engaged to another man.

"I have to think about it," she murmured. "The murdered prostitute's friends said she was having trouble with a client she called Doc. If the killer *is* a doctor of some kind, it would help explain why Coop fits some aspects of the profile. Doctors can be so arrogant." Inexplicably, her mind went to Frederick Lowenstein. And when she recalled that she'd been with him on the nights when two of the murders had occurred, her heart thudded in her chest.

The night that Tracey and her doctor husband had crashed her and Peter's blanket at the Screen on the Green event in Piedmont Park, she'd left with Wesley for a pickup that had turned out to be Alicia Sills, victim number two. The Chief Medical Examiner later determined she had died not of a fall from a stepladder, but of blunt force trauma. Frederick Lowenstein had arrived late to the event with Tracey, not long before Carlotta had left to move the body…at an address within a mile of the park.

And the night of the auction at the country club, Freddy had left early after receiving a page, not long before she and Hannah had left to join Wes on a body-moving job that had turned out be Marna Collins, victim number five, poisoned with cyanide.

Not far from the country club.

Doctors could get cyanide. And Freddy Lowenstein had always given her the willies…

"Carlotta, are you there?"

"Rainie, will you do me a favor?"

"If I can."

She squinted to remember the words that Dr. Lowenstein had said before he left the auction that night. *Looks like the Lindelhoff baby decided to come early.* "Check to see if a baby with the last name of Lindelhoff was born at Piedmont Hospital the night of the auction at Bedford Manor."

"Do you want to tell me what this is about?"

"Just a hunch…it might be nothing."

"Lindelhoff? Okay, I'll check."

"Does the profile say anything about the meaning of the charms?"

"Says here that since none of the victims were sexually assaulted, leaving a charm in the victim's mouth could signify the sex act. Or the charm could demonstrate the killer's remorse afterward. It's undetermined whether the charms belonged to the victims. One charm, the gun, coincided with cause of death. The two victims found together had the same charm, indicating he may have planned ahead to kill two victims. The charms could be clues to the killer's identity or motive. They could have belonged to another woman in UNSUB's life. Or they could be completely random."

"Meaning, no one knows."

Rainie sighed. "Right. That's why they were so eager to make an arrest, just to quiet things down. And since they couldn't find Michael Lane—"

"Coop was the next best suspect."

"Looks like it. So what do you think about running the fake piece saying you're going to reveal all concerning Michael Lane?"

Carlotta exhaled, nodding to herself. "I think it might work. Play up the fact that I know his deep, dark secrets, that I want everyone to know the real Michael."

"Okay. It'll run as soon as I can wrangle good placement—probably this weekend, but I'll let you know. Meanwhile, I'll inform APD. If this works and Lane comes out of hiding, I don't want to see you get hurt again."

Carlotta glanced at her watch. "Don't worry about it—I'll talk to Jack Terry. Thanks for calling, Rainie. I gotta run."

"Talk soon," Rainie said, then hung up.

Carlotta stowed the phone and took one more wistful drag on the half-spent cigarette. But at the sound of twigs snapping in the direction of the tree line, she froze. She couldn't make out anything in the darkness. Conversely she felt like a sitting duck standing on the stoop with uplights shining on her knees. She swallowed hard, her gaze darting all around. She reached into the bottom of her bag and rummaged for the stun baton.

Behind her a scraping noise startled her so badly, she almost swallowed her cigarette.

But it was only the door to the restaurant opening. And to her dismay, Maria Marquez stepped out.

Frankly, Carlotta mused, she would've rather faced a stalker.

19

"I had to have a smoke, too," Maria said with a wry smile.

Carlotta managed a nod in response, and moved over to share the stoop. Upon closer inspection, Maria's brown dress was Diane von Furstenberg, her sandals, Sergio Rossi. The woman had exquisite taste.

Maria pulled out her cigarettes and withdrew one to light. She inhaled deeply, then exhaled before speaking. "Nice place, huh?"

"Seems like it."

"I suppose you're wondering what Jack and I are doing here together."

Carlotta raised a hand. "It's none of my business."

"It's not what you think."

She considered the woman's words, then caved to the curiosity gnawing at her. "So what is it?"

"It's…something else," Maria offered. "Don't make any knee-jerk decisions based on what you see."

"I don't know what you mean."

"I was with Jack watching your interview with the GBI agents. I heard you say you were going to Vegas with Peter."

"That's right."

Maria took a deep drag off her cigarette. "I also heard Jack make a sound as if he'd been stabbed."

A little shiver of satisfaction ran over Carlotta's shoulders, then she remembered Jack's response afterward when she'd asked him to give her a reason not to go. He'd walked away. "Maria, Jack doesn't want me."

"He doesn't want anyone else to have you—isn't that the same thing?"

"I don't think so."

"So you're with Peter now?"

"I'm staying with Peter until The Charmed Killer is caught," Carlotta said evasively.

Maria exhaled a spiral of smoke. "We got him. You can go back home any time you want."

Carlotta pressed her lips together. "Coop isn't a serial killer, Maria. The fact that he's getting out on bail tomorrow means that the case against him isn't as strong as you want everyone to believe."

"No, it means that the jails here are overcrowded and Dr. Craft was clever enough not to leave more evidence at the crime scenes." She tapped her cigarette on the railing to rid it of ash. "Watch yourself, Carlotta. You're putting your faith in the wrong guy, and I know what that's like."

"And I know what Coop is like," Carlotta countered. "Michael Lane is responsible for killing those women. Or someone else is."

From the tree line came the sound of crackling twigs, the brush of leaves. Carlotta's head swung around. "Did you hear that?" she whispered.

"Yes," Maria murmured, alert.

"I thought I heard someone just before you came out."

The flash of a metal disc broke the blackness—a necklace? A watch? Carlotta sucked in a sharp breath as alarm seized her.

Maria dropped her cigarette and stepped on it while reaching into her bag. She pulled out a pistol and held it down to her side while she scanned the tree line. "Carlotta, go back inside," she ordered. *"Now."*

"I'll get Jack."

"No…I can handle this. Get out of here."

Carlotta hurriedly snubbed out her cigarette, then pulled on the door and scurried inside. Handle, shmandle. If Michael Lane was out there, he'd already killed a morgue full of women, including an A.D.A. He'd have no compunction killing Maria. Carlotta practically ran back to the table where Jack sat frowning at the tiny plate of food sitting in front of him. He looked up and instantly his body tensed.

"Jack, Maria's outside. Someone was watching us from the trees."

He was on his feet before she finished her sentence. He hurried down the hallway, with Carlotta trotting behind. But just as he reached the door, it opened and Maria stepped inside.

"It was just a dog," Maria said with a reassuring smile.

"But I saw a flash of something," Carlotta said.

"From the tag on the collar," Maria supplied. "Nothing to worry about."

Carlotta exhaled in relief as they walked back toward their tables, but couldn't help watching Maria and Jack, the way their bodies moved in tandem. Their stride was even the same. Maria's denial that something was going on between them fell flat when one observed their natural chemistry. And while Maria's body language seemed self-conscious, obviously no one had told Jack they weren't on a date. He held out Maria's chair and when she was seated, scooted her closer to the table. Then he leaned down and murmured something in Maria's ear that made her smile.

Carlotta forced her feet to keep moving toward the table where Peter sat fingering his napkin. His shoulders were slumped, his expression drawn. Remorse washed over her. Peter, the dear man, deserved her full attention. She slid into her chair and he looked up, having missed the commotion unfolding behind his back. "I was getting ready to send out a rescue team."

"Sorry...I got a phone call from Rainie Stephens."

His mouth twitched downward.

She lifted her finger. "We have a deal."

He nodded. "I know." He picked up a black olive from the petite plate that had been delivered in her absence. "I hear that Craft is getting out on bail tomorrow."

"That's what I've been told, yes."

He chewed the olive, then swallowed. "Word around the office is that someone put up his bail."

Carlotta blinked. "Really? Who?"

"I don't know. A family member, maybe?"

"I wouldn't know. Coop has never talked to me about his family."

He took another sip of his wine. "I thought maybe the two of you got...*close* while you were in Florida."

"You thought wrong," she said softly, then reached across the table to squeeze his fingers. "Let's enjoy our dinner."

She could feel the presence of Jack and Maria only a glance away, but resisted looking, instead concentrating on Peter and his conversation…or trying to. And mostly succeeding.

The food was exquisite, but in bite-size portions. It was fun tasting several gourmet dishes, from black forbidden rice to crab with coconut milk to white anchovies, but throughout, her mind wandered to Jack—she couldn't see him filling up on this frou-frou food. And while Peter tried to entertain her by mentioning a funny incident from the office, she incubated the possibilities of either Mitchell Moody or Frederick Lowenstein being The Charmed Killer. Her money was still on Michael, but if not, since she'd been targeted to literally run over the body that had been dropped into the road in front of her, she had to assume it was someone she knew.

Or at least someone who knew her.

"Are you looking forward to Vegas?" Peter asked. Her hand was palm up and he was stroking it softly.

Remembering his reference earlier to them someday having a family, she managed a shaky smile and nodded. "I've never been to Vegas. You've probably seen it lots of times, haven't you?"

"A few. But being there with you, it'll be like experiencing it all again for the first time. We'll have fun, I promise."

A big, broad-shouldered shadow fell across their table. Carlotta looked up to see Jack standing there, flanked by Maria.

"Just wanted to say good-night," Jack offered. "Peter, I understand you're coming in to talk to the state guys tomorrow."

Peter tightened his grip on Carlotta's hand. "That's right."

"If you have any concerns, I'll be around."

Peter nodded. "Thanks."

Jack flicked his gaze over their hands, then turned to Carlotta. "Keep that stun baton handy. You never know when you're going to need it."

She gave him a private, withering look—just when she thought he was being mature. "Good night, Jack. Goodnight, Maria."

"Good night," Maria murmured, although her mind seemed elsewhere.

On how the night might end? Carlotta tamped down an irrational flash of envy. Her own sexual encounters with Jack had been accidental, spontaneous. At the time, she'd found it exciting…thrilling. But in hindsight, she realized she'd been a cheap date. Jack hadn't gotten dressed up for her, hadn't held out her chair.

Carlotta watched them walk away, then turned her attention back to Peter and lifted her wineglass for another drink. They lingered over shared dessert, then left and drove back to Peter's home. Talking companionably about their respective schedules for the following day, they walked up the stairs. At the landing, Peter gave her a nice, long kiss. But, as always, when things started to warm up between them, he pulled back.

"I'm really looking forward to Vegas," he said.

"Me, too," she murmured, hoping the trip would be a turning point for their relationship, one way or another.

They parted and went into their separate bedrooms. Carlotta closed her door, then covered her face with her hands. Her mind raced with so many details, she was practically dizzy. After donning pj's and washing her face, she turned on the TV and reached for her notebook. The national and local news were consumed with The Charmed Killer case, flashing Coop's picture and announcing that he was being released on bail. Roving reporters talked to victims' advocate groups and random Atlanta residents who expressed alarm and anger that "a cold-blooded murderer would be let back out on the street."

Carlotta bit her lip. Maybe Hannah had a point about Coop's safety.

She turned down the TV volume and recorded in the notebook the info Rainie had given her about the DNA found on the Alderman murder scene, and about the profile Maria had developed. And she noted her own suspicions about Dr. Lowenstein and, more reluctantly, Mitchell Moody. Detective Marquez hadn't been in the frame of mind to hear about alternate suspects when they'd chatted earlier on the stoop, but Carlotta made a mental note to talk to Jack tomorrow.

Her cell phone rang.

Or tonight.

She picked up her phone and confirmed it was him before she answered. She connected the call and laid her head back on the comfy upholstered chair where she sat. "Hi, Jack."

"Did I wake you?"

From the background noise, she deduced he was in his car. "No, I was up."

"Good," he said. "Listen…about tonight at the res-taurant—Maria asked *me* out."

"You don't have to explain anything to me, Jack. I

was there on a date, you were there on a date. It's what adults do."

"Uh, yeah. I guess."

"Your evening ended early," she ventured, bemused that he wasn't sleeping over at Maria's.

"Uh-huh," he mumbled thickly.

She frowned. "Are you eating?"

"Yeah, sorry. The portions at that restaurant wouldn't keep a damn cricket alive. I swung by The Varsity to get a sack of burgers."

She smiled. So the restaurant wasn't his kind of place after all. "Jack, I need to throw something out there regarding the case. Mind you, I'm just thinking out loud."

He sighed. "What now?"

"June Moody's son, Mitchell, fits the profile Maria created."

He made an exasperated noise. "How do you know about Marquez's profile?"

"Never mind. Mitchell Moody is a career army man. He arrived in town on leave from Hawaii just before the murders began, and he's still here."

"Is that all? He was in Atlanta when the killings began? Because so were six million other people."

"He doesn't have a good relationship with his mother, which also matches the profile. And although he's seeing the Olympian Eva McCoy now, before she was available, I saw footage of him on TV standing vigil in front of her house with the paparazzi. Plus he's been hanging out at Moody's, and two of the victims were found near there." She decided not to add that the "aloha" charm on her bracelet inexplicably heightened her suspicion, as if a cosmic finger was pointing to the man.

"But Michael Lane was at the cigar bar, too. And we *know* he's killed before. Have you changed your mind about Lane being The Charmed Killer?"

"No...I've just been thinking of other people... around me...who give me the creeps."

"There are others?"

"Dr. Frederick Lowenstein, he's an OB/GYN at Piedmont. I saw him at events on the same nights two of the victims were killed—Alicia Sills and Marna Collins. And both events were in close proximity to the crime scenes. He was late arriving at one event, and the other one he left early."

"He delivers babies, Carlotta. His schedule is probably pretty frantic."

"Humor me, Jack. Run a background check on him and Mitchell Moody. What would it hurt?"

"Okay," he mumbled between chewing. "Anything else you need to tell me?"

Her pulse blipped. Had Rainie called Jack to tell him about the fabricated piece in the paper meant to incite Michael Lane? "Uh...not that I can think of. Thanks for offering to help Peter out with the GBI."

"Glad to help." He cleared his throat. "I'm sure you know that Coop is getting out of jail tomorrow."

"Yes, that's a good sign, isn't it?"

"Don't read too much into it. Just because the D.A. doesn't have a truckload of evidence doesn't mean Coop is innocent."

"Jack, how many times do I have to tell you? Coop didn't do this."

He was quiet for a few seconds. "I'll say one thing. If I were in trouble, I'd want you on my side."

Warmth infused her chest. "I can't imagine you being in trouble, Jack."

He grunted. "Just don't go getting any ideas about trying to see Coop, do you understand? It could make things worse for him, especially if the GBI is still trying to prove that he did these things because he's hung up on you."

"I'm just happy that he'll be free on bail."

"Coop won't be free on bail," Jack corrected. "He'll be under house arrest—big difference. He can't leave his home, his calls will be monitored, and with that GPS bracelet on his ankle, the GBI will know when he goes to the john."

"But he'll be home."

"And if he has a stash of liquor on hand, he'll be able to drink himself into oblivion."

"But he'll be home," she insisted.

"Yeah," he said with a tired sigh. "Home sounds good right now."

She guessed that meant he was sleeping at the station again. "Home sounds good to me, too," she murmured, suddenly missing her childish white bed and the sound of Wesley whistling as he made breakfast in their cramped kitchen.

"Hang in there, darlin'. I'm still on the job."

"I know. And I know deep down, Jack, you believe The Charmed Killer is still out there. Otherwise, you'd have given back my red panties," she added lightly.

"You don't think I'd give them back before you go to Vegas, do you?"

"You'd rather I go without?"

A strangled noise sounded over the line. "I gotta go. My burgers are getting cold."

"Good night, Jack."

20

Double vision, Wesley decided, wasn't so bad if he could look at Meg all the time. She sat on one foot at their grubby shared workstation, bobbing her head to the music on her iPod. The tip of her ponytail swung in the air as she looked back and forth between her monitor and the printouts on her desk. His blurred vision exaggerated her movements and the bright colors she wore. He wanted to frame her.

Meg lifted her head from her work, looked at him and removed her earbuds. "What?"

"I didn't say anything."

"You're staring at me."

"Maybe I like staring at you."

She rolled her eyes. "Maybe you're stoned."

"I'm getting clean." And he felt like living hell. He'd been tasked to read a manual on database design, reading that would've blinded him on a good day, but was impossible with the sludge in his brain. As the hour approached noon, his body screamed for Oxy.

Meg gave him a wry smile. "Well, talk to me when you *get* clean."

"Go out with me tonight," he said impulsively. He

wouldn't be in top form, but he couldn't get her off his mind. And he was afraid if he sat on his hands much longer, Mark the Metrosexual would plant his flag.

Meg frowned. "You're seeing someone else—who reeks of bad perfume, by the way."

A headache landed between his eyes like an axe. He grimaced, but forced himself to talk through the pain. "I'm...not...seeing...anyone. I stopped to see my attorney before I came to the party."

"On a Saturday?"

"It's complicated. She was my father's attorney, so she's more like a...friend of the family."

"Liz Fischer. I remember her name from the court records data we went over."

"Right. She asked me to come by because she's representing my buddy Cooper Craft."

"You mean, The Charmed Killer?"

He couldn't bring himself to think about what Coop had done. "Whatever. Anyway, she wanted to ask me some questions about him. That's why I was late."

Meg angled her head. "So how did her perfume get on you?"

"She hugged me before I left. Like I said, Liz is a friend of the family."

"Why didn't you say so the night of the party?"

"Because I already had to explain about my probation officer. I was afraid you'd find it kind of...seedy. I know your father already doesn't like me."

She pursed her mouth and conceded his remark with a nod. "Lucky for you, I'm not my father."

His heart lifted with hope, but she narrowed her eyes. "If you think you're getting laid, Wren, you're not.

If I decide to give you another chance, it'll be starting over with a first date, seeing as how you abandoned me at my father's reception, and the frat party was a bust."

"Right," he agreed, nodding like a trained dog.

"So about going out tonight—were you planning to pick me up on your bicycle?"

He flushed and pushed up his glasses. "Uh, I guess I didn't think it through."

"It's okay," she said with a sigh, then leveled her gaze on him. "I'm going to see an Italian film tonight at Landmark Theater, seven-thirty. If you can handle subtitles, I'll meet you there."

He blinked. "Yeah, I'll be there."

Meg glanced at her watch then stood and grabbed her purse. She leaned over as she walked by and murmured, "Bring a kiss."

Her words lit him up like a bulb. He wanted to follow her out, but he wasn't sure how his legs would perform once he stood. So he waited until the sound of her footsteps faded, then gingerly pushed to his feet and picked up his backpack. The effort had him sweating profusely, and his vision was still blurred. No way would he make it to his probation meeting with E. without driving his bike into the path of something much bigger and much faster.

He pulled out the empty ink pen where he stored his stash of Oxy. His hands shook so badly, he dropped the pills on the floor and had to scramble to recover them, losing one down the hole of an outlet. He was so rattled, he impulsively chewed an entire tablet, effectively blowing the tapering program he'd had himself on for the past two days. Carlotta's threat reverberated in his head. His sister had been a lenient guardian for the most part, but he knew when she meant business.

He would start tapering again after his probation meeting, he promised himself, but gave thanks as the sweet, sweet drug zapped his headache instantly and stilled his trembling hands. He double-checked to make sure he had a packet of urine screen to dump into a sample if E. asked for one at the meeting, and by the time he exited the building and unlocked his bike, he was feeling good. Amazing, even. And the promise of seeing Meg that night had him humming dopey rock ballads on the ride to the probation office.

He didn't even mind the sourpuss at the check-in desk, or the stale odor of the waiting room. He laid his head back and smiled to himself. Oxy was a panacea. The drug gave everything a rosy hue…made him feel as if everything in his life would work out. He'd get to be with Meg, someday play in the World Series of Poker, and his parents would come home. Coop would beat his murder rap, get his job back, and someday marry Carlotta.

It could happen.

"Wren!" the woman at the desk crowed. "You're up."

He sauntered back to E. Jones's office, then rapped on her door.

"Come in," she called.

When he walked in, E. was standing at a file cabinet. She flashed a quick smile over her shoulder. "Have a seat, Wes. I'll be right with you."

He swung into a chair, then straightened, reminding himself that E. had an eagle eye, so he needed to be on his best behavior.

She closed the file drawer and sat down at her desk. Her red hair was pulled back into a tight bun. E.'s movements were jerky and her eyes were red-rimmed. With a start, he also noticed her left hand was bare. Had she given Leonard's ring back?

"How are you?" she asked with forced cheer.

"Good."

"How's your job?"

"My community service job? It's fine."

She looked up from the form she was writing on. "I meant your courier job."

His cover for the work he was doing for the D.A. in The Carver's organization—even E. didn't know about it, which was all the better since the lughead she was engaged to also worked for the loan shark. "Oh…the courier job is fine, too."

She looked over the papers in front of her. "I still need a note from your employer to put in your file. Can you bring it next Wednesday, please?"

He nodded, thinking Jack Terry could probably forge something that looked believable. "I noticed you're not wearing your engagement ring."

E. glanced at her finger, then moved her hand to her lap. "It's being cleaned. So, I hear that your former boss, Dr. Craft, is getting out on bail?"

He nodded. "He was supposed to be released this morning, last I heard."

E. set down her pen. "How has all this affected you, Wes? Someone you looked up to being charged with such terrible crimes."

"I…don't like it. I thought I knew Coop, but I guess I was wrong."

She looked sympathetic. "We can all be wrong about people." Then she angled her head and her eyes narrowed. "Wes, are you…on something?"

"No," he blurted.

"Take off your glasses."

"Why?" he asked, stalling.

Her gazed was locked on him, her jaw firm. "Because I said so."

He shifted in the chair, then took off his glasses.

"Look at me," she demanded.

He lifted his gaze to hers. "I can pee in a cup if you want."

She gave him a flat smile. "That won't be necessary."

He exhaled in relief.

E. picked up the phone on her desk and punched a couple of buttons. "Kathleen, I need you in my office with a kit. Thanks."

Wesley started to get a bad vibe. "What was that all about?"

"Just sit tight," she said, making more notes on his file. "Did you and Leonard have an argument?"

E. didn't look up, but her mouth tightened. "This isn't a two-way street, Wesley. My personal life is none of your business."

The door opened and a thin older woman wearing a scrub top walked in carrying a small bag. She nodded at Wesley. "Roll up your sleeve, please."

Wes looked back to E. "What's this?"

"Nurse Kathleen is going to draw blood for a drug test."

He panicked. "I told you I'd leave a urine sample."

"This is more accurate," E. said. "Roll up your sleeve."

Wes's mind raced. He was sunk.

E. stood and crossed her arms. "Wesley, roll up your sleeve, or I'll summon an officer to take you into custody. It's your choice."

Wes slowly unbuttoned and rolled up his sleeve, revealing the angry red scars left behind when The Carver had whittled the first three letters of his name into Wes's flesh.

E. gasped. "What happened to your arm?"

"Paper cuts," Wes muttered.

As he watched his blood going into the vial, he imagined it shimmering with the drug that made him feel like Superman…and would send him back to jail. Sweat trickled down his back. It was beyond dumb to have dosed before his meeting. After the nurse left, he slowly unrolled his sleeve.

"How soon will you have the results?" His high was plummeting.

"In a few days," E. said, her mouth contracting downward. "I hope you haven't been lying to me, Wes."

He swallowed hard. "Are we finished?"

"Yes. I'll see you next Wednesday…if not before."

He got the hell out of there, bursting through the door of the building and into the sunshine to gulp fresh air. Except the summer air was hot and sticky, catching in his throat. He had to lean over to grasp his knees. His mind galloped.

Carlotta would be devastated if he went to jail…and Meg would never speak to him again. His date with her tonight might be the last time he'd get to spend with her—he'd better make the most of it.

"Hey, shithead!"

He turned to see the black Town Car sitting at the curb, with Mouse calling through the window.

"Get in."

Wesley straightened, then trudged over to unlock his bike. By the time he made it back to the car, Mouse had popped the trunk. Wes stowed the bike inside, then walked around to the passenger side and climbed in.

Mouse grunted and steered the car away from the curb. The big man seemed to be nursing a bad mood, driving for several long minutes in silence. With no fast-food bags in sight, Wes wondered if he was on a diet and cranky from the lack of carbs. Meanwhile, Wes wiped at the sweat on his forehead, already craving another hit of Oxy, and feeling a little light-headed from the blood loss.

"Something wrong?" Mouse snapped, breaking the silence.

Giving in to the panic, Wes put his head down, his elbows on his knees. "Man, I'm screwed."

"You're going to have to be more specific."

"My probation officer just drew blood for a drug test."

"And?"

"And when it comes back positive, my probation will be revoked and my ass is going to jail."

Mouse made a rueful noise. "Told you drugs would mess you up. What are you on?"

"Oxy," Wes said. "But I'm trying to quit."

"Too late for that shit."

"I guess so," Wesley said forlornly.

"Besides…you got bigger things to worry about."

Wesley turned his head. "What?"

Mouse wiped his hand over his jowly face. "Jett Logan came to see The Carver."

Wesley felt his blood drain to his feet. "I…I thought Logan left town."

"Changed his mind."

Panic wrapped around Wes's lungs and squeezed like a vise. "What did he say about the money he owes?"

Mouse put on his blinker to make a turn, taking his time to respond. Finally, he swung his fat head around to look at Wesley. "Funny thing—he said you tracked him down last Saturday and got it. All ten gees."

Wesley thought he was going to be sick.

"And then he said he told you about a card game he'd been planning to play in. Said he even gave you the address."

Wes wet his lips. "I can explain."

"How much did you lose?"

He wanted to cry. "All of it."

Mouse spewed a creative combination of curse words that questioned Wesley's parentage, wisdom, and longevity.

"I'll pay it all back," Wes said.

"That's a given," Mouse said. "But why the fuck did you lie to me?"

"I didn't want to look like a screwup. I was high and played like an idiot."

Mouse backhanded him across the face so hard Wes's ears rang. "When you lie to me, it looks like I'm lying to The Carver. Now I look like the screwup."

Holding his head, Wes glanced around and recognized his surroundings with a stabbing fear. The arm bearing The Carver's scars twinged, reminding Wes of the last time he'd been in this part of town. Like a buffoon, he'd ridden right up to The Carver's warehouse and offered to turn over a memory chip with incriminating photographs of The Carver that Wes had set up with a transvestite, in return for the loan shark not killing him.

The Carver hadn't killed him, but he'd held him hostage for twenty-five thousand dollars, and carved a letter in Wesley's arm for every call he had to make to raise the money—Chance, then Liz, then Peter Ashford. Chance hadn't been able to get his hands on that much cash within the allotted time, and Liz had refused to be dragged into something unlawful. Peter had come through, though, because he was eager to cozy up to Carlotta's family.

It had been their secret. Peter had agreed not to tell Carlotta if Wes would help to smooth the way for Peter and Carlotta to get back together. Wes had kept up his end of the deal, interfering when Coop and Carlotta had taken a road trip together, and telling Jack Terry to step back because he couldn't make his sister happy. The fact that Carlotta had moved in with Peter meant that he'd done a pretty decent job.

But Wes suspected that Peter wouldn't be able to buy his way out of this one.

To his credit, Mouse looked ill as he pulled into the parking lot of the warehouse. Wes panicked and reached for the door handle to escape.

But the handle had been removed.

"I was afraid you might try to run," Mouse said with a heavy sigh. "I'm really sorry it has to be like this." He parked the car, then heaved his big body out and came around to the passenger side.

Resigned to his fate, Wesley sat there sweating, knowing he was powerless to do anything to escape. And if he did manage to get away, he was only postponing the inevitable.

Mouse opened the door and the look on his face was almost parental—part anger, part disappointment. "Let's go, little man. Where are your phones?"

"In my backpack."

"Leave it."

Too late, he remembered the GPS chip that Jack had inserted in the phone that Mouse had given to Wes, just in case he was ever in trouble. At least they'd be able to find his backpack, he thought hysterically. Maybe they'd put it in his coffin when they couldn't find anything left of his body to bury.

Wes climbed out of the car, feeling drained. He knew The Carver's knife waited for him, knew it would be worse this time than last, more creatively cruel.

Mouse patted him down, then grasped his arm in an iron grip and walked him toward the warehouse. The big man unlocked the door and opened it, then shoved Wes inside. It was pitch black, with no windows. Mouse flipped a couple of breakers on a box just inside the door and rows of fluorescent lights came on in grids. The scent of building materials infiltrated Wes's lungs, along with other sour smells.

He remembered vomiting in the room where The Carver had had him tied to a chair, a room with lots of rust-colored stains on the concrete floor. It had been the drain in the floor that had scared him most, knowing that he could be killed and bled in that room, like an animal, his carcass then cut up and discarded. The Carver didn't like to be crossed. Wes couldn't imagine a scenario in which the man would let him live.

The walls were mostly studs, with a sheet of plywood and insulation here and there. A couple of rooms remained from some long ago use. The warehouse seemed to be empty, like the first time Mouse had brought him there. And once again, the big man led Wesley to a cramped little bathroom in the bowels of the building and shoved him inside. The door closed, then the deadbolt turned.

Wes slammed into a wall, then got his bearings and found a light switch. A naked bulb in the ceiling sent a dim glow over the hideous green bathroom. The rickety toilet and leaning sink were sickeningly familiar. Everything was corroded with dirt, and the place reeked of human waste. He lowered himself to the ledge of the nasty bathtub and put his head in his hands. He had no Oxy, no phone, no way out.

And worse, he was going to miss his date tonight with Meg.

21

Peter's rueful sigh sounded over the phone. "I'm afraid Brody was right. During the questioning, I got the feeling the GBI wasn't nearly as interested in your father's connection to Alicia Sills as the APD was interested in discovering whether your father had maintained contact with her or someone else over the years."

Carlotta, who had ducked behind a clothing rack to take the call, put a hand to her head. "Was Jack there?"

"Oh, yeah. Jack was the lead interrogator. So much for his offer to help."

Anger barbed through her. Since Jack had been relegated to the periphery of The Charmed Killer case, his presence there proved the police were more interested in finding a way to apprehend Randolph, than proving him a serial killer. "Did you tell them that Dad called you?"

"No. But Jack did say the D.A.'s office would be asking for a subpoena of the company's phone records, so they're suspicious. Of course, all of this is under the guise of investigating your father's involvement with Alicia Sills."

"What did Brody say?"

"He told Jack the firm's offer of a one hundred

thousand dollar reward for Randolph's return negated the possibility that anyone there was working with your dad. Brody insisted they wanted him found as much as anyone…which played right into Jack's hands because he asked for open access to company records."

"How did it end?"

"Brody walked the public relations line, but told them they would need that subpoena."

She sighed. "I'm just so sorry you got dragged into this. And it took your entire afternoon."

"I did it to myself when I dug through those old employment records."

"Still…I know you did it for me, to get to the truth."

"I'm just afraid this renewed interest might impede our plans to look into your father's case from inside the firm like we'd planned."

Carlotta closed her eyes briefly, forcing herself to compartmentalize her problems. If she thought about everything pressing on her, she might unravel.

Peter must have sensed her anguish because he made a comforting sound. "Let's just take it one day at a time."

"You're right," she agreed with a sigh. "I should go. I'm not supposed to use my phone on the sales floor."

"Okay, I'll see you later tonight."

She ended the call and stowed her phone in her jacket pocket, then checked her watch for the hundredth time. All day long she'd been antsy, thinking about Peter's interview and knowing that Coop was out on bail.

She longed to see Coop, to reassure herself he was okay, but Jack's warning to stay away remained vivid in her mind. She didn't want to give the GBI more ammunition against Coop. Just knowing he was out of the detention center—out of that jumpsuit, out of the shackles—had made her feel better...at first.

When she'd taken her lunch break, she'd joined others in the employee locker room who gathered around the TV set to watch CNN. The prime suspect in The Charmed Killer case being granted bail was big news. District Attorney Kelvin Lucas was catching hell from reporters for what was perceived as a failure in the prosecutor's office. Lucas announced that no stone would go unturned by the legion of police officers assigned to check and double-check leads in the case, but surprisingly, the odious man hadn't appeared ruffled by Coop's release.

In fact, Lucas seemed to go out of his way to repeat several times that Dr. Cooper Craft would be under house arrest in his single-family home in Castleberry Hill. It was as if he were inviting every vigilante in the area to Google-Maps Coop and take the law into their own hands. She'd wondered if Lucas hadn't opposed bail as vigorously as expected, hoping that Coop might be slain before a trail was even convened. If the evidence wasn't overwhelming enough to convict, a dead defendant would let the D.A. off the hook.

Carlotta conceded that maybe everyone else was right—maybe Coop did belong in jail, if only for his own safety.

She chewed on her thumbnail as the minutes ticked toward the end of her shift, then retrieved her purse and chatted with her personal bodyguard, Herb, as he walked her to her car. She'd grown accustomed to parking in a far corner of the garage and using her keyless remote to unlock the rental car from a distance when no one else was around. But so far, whoever had left the explosive under the Monte Carlo hadn't revisited their crime.

Although her heart still raced every time she turned over the ignition.

She pulled out of the parking garage, pushing away Jack's suggestion that Coop could've planted the bomb. He hadn't—period.

She steered toward Peter's house, glad the workday was over and looking forward to the evening. Peter had a business dinner, so she'd invited Hannah to come over to hang out in the hot tub. She knew her friend would help to take her mind off things for a few hours, and she was eager to smooth the tensions between them. The Charmed Killer case had affected them all.

She was sitting in traffic on Peachtree when her phone rang, displaying the name Rainie Stephens. Carlotta smiled and connected the call. She felt a kinship with Rainie, especially where Coop was concerned. "Hi, Rainie."

"Hi, Carlotta. You got a minute?"

"Yeah, I'm stuck behind a fender bender. What's up?"

"I thought you'd like to know I checked the births for the night of the country club auction and there were no babies born with the last name of Lindelhoff that entire week at Piedmont, nor at any other metro hospital. Does that answer your question?"

Carlotta's heartbeat sped up. "Yes."

"Now are you going to tell me what's going on?"

She told Rainie her suspicions about Tracey's husband, Dr. Lowenstein, his coincidental absences and proximity to two crime scenes. "Jack agreed to do a background check. I don't know if it'll turn into anything concrete, but I thought it was worth mentioning."

"If the man was lying, he could just be having an affair."

"True," Carlotta said, conceding a pang of sympathy for Tracey if that was the case.

"On another note, I wasn't able to directly connect Coop to any neurologist in the city."

"But that's good news."

"There's more. An obituary came over the wire a couple of hours ago, and the name tickled the back of my mind—Sarah Edlow."

"I don't recognize the name."

"Sarah Edlow," Rainie said, her voice poignant, "is the woman whom Coop pronounced dead on the scene of a car accident."

A shiver traveled over Carlotta's arms. "I heard she had serious complications because she didn't receive immediate care."

"That's right, although she eventually recovered."

"What did she die from?"

"A brain tumor. And she was being treated by a neurologist at Piedmont Hospital."

"So Coop must have known and was somehow involved in her treatment?"

"That seems likely."

"And it explains Coop's sudden personality change, and why he started drinking again. Finding out about the Edlow woman's terminal illness must have dredged up too much guilt for him to handle." Carlotta heaved a sigh of relief that at least a few pieces of the puzzle were falling into place. "So when Coop told me that his being at the neurologist's office had nothing to do with this case, he was telling the truth. When did she pass away?"

"This morning, at hospice," Rainie said. "It's so sad—she was only in her forties."

Carlotta made a rueful noise. "I wonder if Coop knows."

"I don't know. It's going to be a blow to him, I'm sure. I called his attorney and tried to arrange an interview for the paper, but she shut me down. Frankly, I just wanted to see for myself that he was okay."

It was evident from Rainie's tone that she still had feelings for Coop. Or maybe the case had resurrected those feelings. There was something very powerful about the sensation of having let something good get away...

"Coop is strong," Carlotta said, as much for herself as for Rainie. "He'll survive this, too."

"Keep those good thoughts coming." Rainie emitted a slow, harried sigh. "So, are you still agreeable to the article running about you giving the tabloids an exclusive on Michael Lane?"

"Absolutely."

"It's slated for Friday. Do you have something to protect yourself?"

Her gaze slid to her purse that held the stun baton. "Yes, Jack made sure of that."

"I thought he might. Gotta run."

"Okay, talk soon."

Carlotta ended the call, her mind swirling with new developments. Within a few minutes the accident had been moved to the far lane and traffic began to move again. When she pulled into Peter's driveway, she reached automatically to press the remote control on the visor to open the garage door. She knew exactly how to angle the car to give her plenty of room on either side, knew exactly how far to pull up before cutting off the engine. The garage door lowered behind her. She got out and entered the house, punching in the security system code to disable the motion detectors on the first floor. As she walked through the mud room and into the main part of the house, she realized how comfortable she'd become with the routine of living in Peter's house.

She stood in the center of the great room and turned a full circle, taking in the opulence of the life that could be hers for the asking. Beautiful address, beautiful things, beautiful children. So why was she terrified at the thought of making what should be such an easy decision?

She turned on lights and walked through the shiny, luxurious kitchen, suddenly homesick for the gaudy red kitchen of the townhouse. On impulse, she rooted her phone from her purse and called Wesley. They hadn't talked in two days, not since she'd given him the ultimatum about getting clean. He'd accused her of turning on him, of turning on Randolph. Just the memory of it brought moisture to her eyes—she couldn't seem to do anything right where the men in her life were concerned.

Wes didn't answer his phone, so she left him a quick, upbeat message to call her sometime. Everyone kept reminding her that at nineteen, Wesley was an adult. But she couldn't help feeling responsible for him, not after everything they'd been through together.

The ringing of the house's land line broke into her thoughts, startling her. She glanced at the main console and saw the call was coming from the callbox at the security gate. She turned the small flat-screen TV to the monitoring channel and smiled at Hannah's mug staring into the camera, then picked up the ringing phone.

"Hi."

"This is way too much trouble just for a goddamn soak in a hot tub. I passed a fucking rest area on the way here."

Carlotta smiled to herself. "I'll buzz you in."

22

Carlotta punched in Peter's security code for the gate, and a few minutes later, she heard the sound of Hannah's van pulling into the circular driveway. She walked to the front door to greet her friend, who looked more cheerful than usual in tall black boots, a red short pleated skirt and white T-shirt that read "Go Away."

"Hi," Carlotta offered. "Did you bring a suit?"

Hannah frowned. "A suit? I thought it was just us."

"Never mind. Peter told me there are extra suits in the pool house."

"You wouldn't be so modest if you'd grown up with sisters." Hannah clomped past her, and Carlotta noticed that once again, her friend took pains not to acknowledge the lavishness of the house. Hannah ignored and/or mocked Peter's wealth at every opportunity.

Carlotta closed the door. "You have more than one sister?"

"Yeah."

"Tell me about them."

"They hate me. Got any snacks?"

Classic Hannah, deflecting personal questions. "Sure. Raid the pantry while I grab my suit."

She jogged up the stairs to her bedroom, pulled a one-piece swimsuit from a drawer and changed quickly, shoving her feet into flip-flops. By the time she got downstairs, Hannah had grilled them sandwiches and brewed a pitcher of pinkish tea.

"How do you do that?" Carlotta asked.

"There are two things I'm good at," Hannah said, lifting a laden tray. "Cooking and screwing."

"And on that up note, let's retire to the patio, shall we?" Carlotta grabbed her cell phone in case Wes called back.

A sliding glass door off the casual eating corner led to the pool area that was accented with beautiful stonework. The centerpiece was the aquamarine pool, its surface still and glistening in the early evening light. The pool was flanked by a waterfall and hot tub. Past the al fresco kitchen, which also featured a bar, was the shuttered pool house. Carlotta directed Hannah to set their food on the bar, then she produced a key ring she'd snagged from the kitchen and unlocked the door to the tiny building.

"Isn't this where Peter's wife turned tricks?" Hannah asked.

Carlotta frowned. "Allegedly."

She pushed opened the door. Since the windows were shuttered, the little house was dark. She felt for a light switch and flipped it up to illuminate a small but elegant tiled sitting room furnished with a couch and two chairs upholstered with a tropical-print fabric, all of it custom, Carlotta was sure, down to the leaf-shaped green area rugs. Against one wall an entertainment center included a wet bar, small refrigerator and microwave.

The room to the left was a bedroom with a cozy

bathroom and shower. Carlotta couldn't help but stare at the queen-size bed, imagining Peter's wife servicing well-to-do johns. Angela had been part of a high-end call-girl ring, the extent of which was still unknown, although Carlotta had a feeling that Angela's friends at the Bedford Manor Country Club knew more about the goings-on than they'd revealed to police.

Hannah stuck her head inside the room. "Do you think she did it because Peter couldn't deliver in the sack?"

Carlotta frowned. "Angela was responsible for her own behavior." Resisting the urge to snoop in the closet for lingerie and props, she retraced her steps back through the living room to the room on the other side. The changing room had two individual booths against the far wall. There was also a mirrored vanity, and an armoire full of bathing suits, wraps, hats, and sandals.

"Take your pick," Carlotta said.

Hannah pulled out a nautical-themed one-piece and frowned. "You're kidding, right?"

Carlotta laughed and selected a mustard-colored halter bikini. "How about this?"

Hannah considered it for a minute, then shrugged. "That's not so bad, I guess."

"Hurry. Our sandwiches are getting cold."

While Hannah changed, Carlotta looked around, hugging herself. The place gave her the creeps, no doubt because of what had gone on here. Had Angela entertained men while Peter was only steps away in the house? Her respect for Peter ballooned, knowing he'd forgiven his wife for the sordid things she'd done in their own home.

Especially since Carlotta couldn't even forgive Peter for leaving her all those years ago…

With a start she realized it was true. She was still withholding part of herself from Peter to punish him. What did that say about her?

"Let's eat," Hannah said, emerging from the changing room.

Carlotta smiled at her statuesque friend. The suit flattered her athletic figure and revealed her body art. "That looks great on you."

"Whatever."

Carlotta followed her outside where they dived into the sandwiches and the pitcher of tea.

"How's my brother?" Carlotta asked.

"Scarce."

"Gawd, he's probably staying with Liz Fischer."

"Chance is holding strong on not letting him have anymore Oxy."

"That's good. I called Wes a few minutes ago, but he didn't answer. I don't think he wants to talk to me."

"He'll come around."

"I hope so."

They made small talk, but Carlotta still felt the underlying tension of their disagreement about Coop's guilt because they both so scrupulously avoided talking about it. By the time they finished eating, dusk had settled enough for the outside lights to kick on.

They eased into the hot tub and Carlotta moaned with pleasure as the warm, bubbly water encased her body. She admired the addition to Hannah's back tattoo. "Is that the one Chance bought so you'd go out with him?"

"We're not going out," Hannah said flatly. "We're fuck buddies, that's all."

"Does he know that? I saw the way he looked at you when we met at the townhouse. I think he's in love."

Hannah scoffed. "In love with my pussy, maybe."

"And you don't have feelings for him?" Carlotta fished.

"No, but the fat man can give head for hours, so I'm in as long as his tongue holds out."

Carlotta looked off in the distance.

"Whose tongue are you thinking about?" Hannah asked dryly.

A flush burned her neck. "Nobody's." Damn Jack.

"If Peter can't keep it up long enough to have sex, the least he can do is go spelunking."

"Enough, okay? We're...waiting."

"For what, a Beatles reunion?"

"We're going to Vegas next week."

Hannah's eyebrows went up. "Really. For how long?"

"Five days."

Hannah gave a dry laugh. "Maybe that'll give Richie Rich time to get to third base."

"This is serious, Hannah. I can't keep stringing Peter along. He's talking about us having kids, for heaven's sake."

"Is he planning to hire someone to impregnate you?"

From the table Carlotta's phone rang. She gave Hannah a chastising look, then climbed out of the hot tub and padded over, wrapping a towel around her. The number was local, but she didn't recognize it. Frowning, she connected the call. "Hello?"

"Is this Carlotta?"

Her mind raced to identify the man's thick country accent. "Yes."

"This is Kendall Abrams."

The Chief M.E.'s hick nephew. "Yes, Kendall, what can I do for you?"

"I'm trying to reach Wes, but he's not answering his phone."

"I'm sorry, but I don't know where he is."

The young man emitted a groan and she pictured him hitting himself on the head. "We're really short-handed at the morgue. I'm on a commercial pickup now, but I have a residential job after this one, and those are the ones my uncle says I suck at. Can you try to find Wes for me?"

Carlotta pursed her mouth and glanced across the patio to Hannah, who looked bored to death. "My friend Hannah and I could give you a hand."

From the silence on the other end, she could tell that wasn't Kendall's first—or second—choice.

"Or not," she sang. "You probably have other experienced body movers who are available at a moment's notice."

Kendall sighed. "Okay. I'll meet you there." He gave her an address in west Atlanta. "It's a blue house. Iffen you get there first, tell my uncle I'm on my way."

Hannah needed no coaxing. They were out of their suits and into dry clothes in a matter of minutes. Carlotta left a note for Peter in case he came home before they returned, then they clambered into Hannah's van and sped off. It took them thirty minutes to pick their way across town through traffic, but once they got into the newly developed neighborhood, they found the house easily, due to the number of flashing lights and official vehicles.

"Oh, shit," Carlotta muttered. "This looks serious. There's a GBI van...and Jack's car."

"Did the goober nephew tell you what had happened?"

"No, and I didn't think to ask."

Hannah glanced at her side mirror. "There's a TV news van behind us."

Carlotta's heart sped up. "Maybe The Charmed Killer has struck again. God, I hope not. But if so, it's good for Coop since he's home under surveillance."

Hannah pulled up to the police-car perimeter, and they presented their morgue IDs. Carlotta recognized the uniformed officer as the same cop who'd spilled his guts while she'd borrowed a light from him on a former murder scene. He recognized her, too, and waved them in. The news van behind them wasn't afforded the same treatment.

The tidy blue house was lit up like a torch. As soon as Hannah brought the van to a halt, Carlotta slid out and approached the residence, looking for a familiar face. Suddenly a man appeared in the open front door— Jack. From the haggard look on his face, she knew The Charmed Killer had taken another victim. He moved woodenly down the steps of the home. She hurried toward him. "Jack?"

He looked up and when he saw her, pain descended on his face.

"Jack, what happened?"

His jaw hardened and he seemed to be struggling to maintain control. "It's Maria. She's dead."

Horror knifed through Carlotta's heart as she realized this was Detective Marquez's home. She covered her mouth. "Oh, no. Jack…how?"

His face contorted. "That sick bastard. He drowned her in the bathtub. Held her down by her neck."

"The Charmed Killer?"

He nodded, his expression bleak.

She put her hand on his arm. "Jack, I'm so sorry."

His phone rang and he strode away a few steps to answer it.

Carlotta felt nauseous. Her mind raced, trying to make sense of a senseless act. Had The Charmed Killer targeted Maria because she had profiled him? Other than the Assistant District Attorney, no one else had been associated with the case, and the A.D.A.'s only distant connection had been that she was an officer of the court. All the other victims had seemed random. Was The Charmed Killer changing his pattern?

Chief Medical Examiner Bruce Abrams and M.E. Pennyman stood at the top of the steps conversing. Pennyman held up a small clear plastic bag under a light. From her vantage point, it looked like an evidence bag. Suddenly a gust of summer wind tore it out of his hand. Both men lunged for the bag, but it tumbled down the steps and landed practically at Carlotta's feet. As she picked it up, she identified the contents—a silver charm, probably the one taken from Maria Marquez's mouth. Through the plastic she saw it was a tiny lipstick.

The bag was plucked out of her hands and when she looked up, Dr. Abrams was standing there, a frown on his pinched face. "Why are you here? Where's my nephew?"

Carlotta drew back at the man's sharp tone, but reasoned everyone was under a tremendous amount of stress, and having key evidence blowing around the crime scene would make anyone testy.

"Kendall called me, saying he needed a hand," she

explained. "He was on another call and asked me to tell you he'd be here shortly."

Dr. Abrams made an exasperated noise, then gave her a curt nod and rejoined Pennyman at the top of the steps.

At the sound of Jack's raised voice, she glanced in his direction. He jammed his hand into his hair, obviously distraught, then he snapped the phone closed and stood stock still.

"Jack?" She approached him slowly. "What now?"

The raw emotion on his face tore through her. "Coop is missing."

Denial exploded in her brain. "How's that possible? He's wearing a GPS ankle bracelet."

"There's a crowd demonstrating outside his place. A uniform stopped by to check in and found the GPS bracelet attached to a damned robotic vacuum. It was programmed to move around, so no one realized he was gone." Jack fisted his big hands. "He killed Maria, and now he's gone again."

Carlotta shook her head, but she couldn't summon the words to defend Coop because she knew Jack didn't want to hear them. And deep in her heart, she wondered if Coop had learned about the death of Sarah Edlow, and if the news had sent him over the edge.

23

Wes lay in the filthy green bathtub, wracked with pain. The scent of his own sweat and vomit permeated his nostrils. He wanted to scream, but didn't have the energy. Merely blinking his eyes sent avalanches of agony through his head. His body needed Oxy... demanded it. And in the back of his mind, he knew the real torture hadn't even begun.

He didn't know how much time had passed when the bathroom door opened, was barely conscious of being picked up and dragged. He was limp, unable to resist. He thought he was drooling because his mouth felt wet...but maybe he was crying.

When he stopped moving, he became distantly aware of lying prone on a hard surface—the floor, maybe. And then, someone was pulling at him, tearing off his clothes. He was naked...freezing...his body shook violently. He had the sense of hours passing, or it could've been minutes.

At some point he was picked up and set in a chair, then strapped down. He remembered the chair. It was where Mouse had held him while The Carver sliced his initials in Wesley's arm. The pain was worse this time.

He was stabbed again and again. Inside he screamed, but he wasn't sure if he made a sound. Mercifully, he finally passed out.

When he woke, he was being held under water. He clawed at the hands holding him and finally got his face above the surface. He choked, dragging air into his lungs, then was stabbed in the arm again. As he slid into unconsciousness, he came to the realization that he was probably being gutted in the bathtub. When the plug was pulled, his blood would go down the drain with the water. Then he'd be easier to cut up and dispose of.

Carlotta would never know what happened to him. She'd think he simply abandoned her, like their father.

And Meg… Oh, Meg…

24

The memorial service for Maria was held Friday afternoon. Carlotta went through the motions like an automaton. She was numb, afraid to let herself absorb too much of what was going on around her.

The manhunt for Coop had gone nationwide. Rainie Stephens had come forth with the information she'd uncovered about Sarah Edlow's terminal brain tumor and subsequent death, as well as the woman's connection to Coop. With a possible trigger for his killing spree revealed, Coop had already been tried and convicted in the public's eye. And since he wasn't around to defend himself, it was getting harder for Carlotta to hang on to her faith in him.

Just like with Randolph.

Meanwhile, the fake article designed to smoke out Michael Lane had been cut, confirming to Carlotta that even Rainie was now convinced that Coop was their man and suggesting that Michael's crimes weren't shocking enough in the scheme of things to warrant attention. Granted, though, nearly every column inch of the *Atlanta Journal-Constitution* was devoted to covering the horrific new developments in The Charmed Killer case.

The memorial service was solemn and inspirational. The minister spoke lovely words about Maria being a beautiful person inside and out. But Carlotta kept replaying in her mind the spiteful things she'd said to the woman to her face and behind her back. Maria hadn't done anything except save Carlotta's ungrateful butt a time or two, encourage her to get to know her friends better, and warn her about putting her trust in the wrong man. In fact, Maria's only offense was looking better than any woman with a gun should, and turning Jack's thick head.

The casket was pearlized ivory with silver hardware—stunning. But when Carlotta looked at it, all she saw was Maria lying in her bathtub, dressed in a modest white cotton nightshirt, still wearing one fuzzy house shoe. The other shoe had been dislodged during the struggle, along with the shower curtain. The woman had been brushing her teeth when she was attacked. She had put up a fight, even broken two fingers defending herself. But with the element of surprise, and what appeared to be a considerable amount of strength, the killer had overpowered her.

Carlotta sat in the balcony of the cathedral. The floor level was a sea of blue uniforms—hundreds of fellow police officers from all over the country had come to pay respects for their slain comrade. The visibility of the case coupled with the fact that now Coop had been labeled a cop killer pretty much guaranteed he would be shot on sight.

Jack was sitting in the front row in his dress uniform, his back straight. His head never moved. She suspected he'd chosen a spot on the opposite wall to stare at during the ceremony, holding his gaze with laser focus. He hadn't called when she'd returned home that awful night, nor last night. And she didn't expect him to call tonight, either. He needed time alone to grieve and to beat himself up properly. Because regardless of what Maria had meant to him personally, Carlotta knew enough about Jack to know he was broken inside that he hadn't protected his partner.

The fact that he blamed Coop, someone he had once held in esteem, for Maria's death undoubtedly only cut deeper.

Near the end of the service, a tall dark-haired man dressed in a decorated police uniform walked to the casket and placed a single red rose on top. He looked grief-stricken, his shoulders bowed. He leaned over to kiss the casket and his sobbing could be heard throughout the cathedral.

Carlotta assumed he was Maria's ex-husband, Rueben Garza. She glanced at the In Memoriam card she'd taken from the stack at the entrance.

In Memoriam, Maria Elena Marquez,
a brave public servant, a loving companion
Maria, full you are of grace
Rueben Garza

As far as she could tell, there were no other members of Maria's family present.

Was Rueben the man Carlotta had once overheard Maria talking to on the phone? Maria had told the person never to call her again. When Carlotta had asked Maria why she had moved to Atlanta, the detective had said she'd wanted a fresh start. Had Maria been trying to escape a bad situation? If so, how profoundly sad that the job she'd taken to save her had led to her death.

A hand on Carlotta's knee startled her, then she remembered with a mental shake that Peter had come with her. He gave her a reassuring smile and she moved closer to him.

After the service, they filtered out of the church and walked hand in hand toward the parking lot. Since Wesley was still avoiding her, Peter had offered to take her by Chance's to see if she could catch Wes and try to patch things up. But when she and Peter reached his SUV, to her surprise, Jack was waiting for them.

He looked taller and broader in his uniform. His face was drawn in the afternoon sun and she wondered if he'd slept since Wednesday. He nodded to Peter. "Thank you both for coming."

"It was a nice service, Jack," Carlotta offered quietly.

"Yes, it was," he agreed, then settled his gaze on her. "A word, Carlotta?"

After a few tense seconds, Peter released her hand and gestured to the vehicle. "I'll wait for you in the car."

Carlotta's heart thumped against her breastbone. She waited until the SUV door closed with a *thunk* before lifting her gaze to Jack's.

"Did you think I wouldn't find out?" he asked.

She swallowed. "About what?" There were just so many things he could be referring to.

His mouth tightened. "This morning I went back to the bookstore where the first victim worked. Imagine my surprise when I interviewed the girl in the coffee shop and she told me about a woman with long, dark hair who came in last Saturday asking questions about the very same thing."

Her mouth went dry. "Jack, there are lots of women in this city with long, dark hair."

"And a gap between their front teeth?"

She tongued the gap that had always plagued her. Darn it, she should've worn her retainer.

"I can describe the shoes you were wearing if you want."

She pressed her lips together.

Jack looked murderous. "Carlotta, I'm not in the mood to play games. Start talking."

She sighed. "Okay, so I went in and asked a few questions."

"And?"

"And, I'm sure the girl told you what she told me— that Shawna Whitt had a bracelet with a charm on it shaped like a chicken. She said that Shawna was planning to join an online dating site, but didn't have the chance. And she said that she hadn't mentioned anyone bothering her."

"What else?"

She closed her eyes briefly. "A guy at the information desk told me that Coop came into the store a couple of times a week. He identified his picture, and his white van."

"What else?"

"That's all."

A vein in his temple jumped. "Why didn't you tell me this earlier?"

"Because—"

"Because it incriminated Coop?"

She nodded.

"Meanwhile, you ask me to run background checks on two random guys who give you the creeps? Which turned up nothing, by the way." He crossed his arms and she had the feeling it was to keep from shaking her. "Do you realize that you withheld evidence we could've used? Now we know the Whitt woman had a charm bracelet, which wasn't found in her home, and that the charm in her mouth came from her bracelet. That's big. And we can prove that she and Coop had many opportunities to cross paths."

Carlotta remained silent.

He gritted his teeth. "I should arrest you for obstruction of justice."

Carlotta scoffed, outraged. "Last time I looked, Jack, I don't work for the APD. I was a citizen asking questions on my own behalf. I wasn't obligated to give you the information I uncovered."

"But if you had, maybe we could've connected more of the dots before the bail hearing. Maybe Coop wouldn't have been released." His jaw hardened. "And maybe Maria would still be alive."

Carlotta blinked back sudden tears. "You're blaming me for her death?"

Jack looked away and expelled a noisy sigh. When he glanced back, he seemed more calm. "No, I'm blaming Coop. But if you hadn't been trying to protect him, things could've gone differently." He leaned in closer. "Maria was right. You play detective to make up for the fact that your life is so screwed up. Why don't you stop trying to fix everything else and get your own affairs in order? And I do mean affairs."

Carlotta felt as if she'd been slapped.

Jack straightened and remorse flashed in his eyes for a split second, then disappeared. He turned to go.

"Jack."

He turned back and sighed. "What?"

Her shoulders fell. "There's something else I didn't tell you." She haltingly described visiting Shawna Whitt's neighbor, telling him what the woman had said about seeing a white van in the neighborhood the day before Shawna had been found dead. "The neighbor's name is Audrey Cole."

"Wait a minute—I talked to her."

"I know. But she said you didn't ask the right questions."

Jack scowled. "Anything else?"

She took a deep breath. "The prostitute Pepper told two of her friends that she was having trouble with one of her clients, a guy she called Doc. And…all of the charms up to Maria link back to Coop in some way." She ticked them off on her fingers. "Chicken coop, he smokes cigars, he's into cars, he has a gun, he's been in handcuffs, a barrel maker is a cooper, he's a drinker, and he likes books." She lifted her hands. "I don't know how the lipstick fits in. Also, the charms weren't purchased at any store in the Lenox Square Mall, the Perimeter Mall, or any jewelry store in the Buckhead zip code."

Jack seemed to have been struck speechless.

The door to the SUV opened and Peter stepped out. "Sorry to interrupt, but Carlotta, Hannah's on the phone. She says that Wesley is missing."

Carlotta's heart jumped. "What?"

"She's called all around. He hasn't been to work in two days. When he left his meeting with his probation officer Wednesday, someone saw him get into a black Town Car. No one's seen him since."

Carlotta frowned. "That's doesn't make sense." Then she gasped and turned to Jack. "Do you think this has anything to do with Coop?"

Jack massaged the bridge of his nose. "Actually…no. I might know what this is about. Let me make some phone calls." He looked at Peter. "Take Carlotta home. And tie her to something."

25

"So, what did Jack want back there?" Peter asked as they drove home.

Carlotta chewed on her thumbnail as Jack's accusations whirled in her head. *If you hadn't been trying to protect Coop, things could've gone differently...maybe Maria would still be alive... Why don't you stop trying to fix everything else and get your own affairs in order?* Even now, his words cut to the bone.

"He's a little upset that I've been poking around asking questions."

"I can understand why. He just lost his partner to this maniac. He doesn't want another death on his conscience."

"I'm just trying to help," she murmured.

"I know," he said, reaching over to stroke her arm. "And Jack knows, too."

"Why would Wesley just disappear?"

"He wouldn't. I'm sure there's an explanation." Peter winked. "He's probably with a girl."

"He's been sleeping with Liz Fischer, you know."

"His attorney? Wow."

She slugged him in the arm.

"I'm not saying I approve, it's just that...isn't he like, nineteen?"

"Yeah, and she's like fortysomething. She was my dad's attorney."

"Yeah, I seem to remember that."

"Liz was also my dad's mistress."

"Okay, that sounds...complicated."

Carlotta scoffed. "That's putting it nicely."

"What about the girl we saw with Wes at Screen on the Green? She looked to be his age."

"Meg. Yeah, I think he likes her, but I'm not sure he knows what to do about it."

He laughed. "The age-old question."

She was quiet for a few minutes, studying her ragged nails. She used to pride herself on perfect salon manicures, but lately she'd fallen into the habit of nibbling them down to the quick. The last time Wes had "disappeared," Peter had brought him home. It had taken some prying, but she'd finally gotten out of Wesley that The Carver had held him and tortured him. "Do you think that animal The Carver has him again?"

"Let's hope not," Peter said carefully.

"The other time...did you see the place where they held him?"

"No. I picked him up at a gas station in east Atlanta."

"That's not a very good part of town."

"Generally, no," he agreed. "But Jack seemed to have some inside information, so let's let him do his job."

She clasped her hands in her lap, brooding over a topic they'd never discussed because Peter had danced around it...and she hadn't really wanted to know. "The last time Wes was in trouble, he was able to call you.

So the man must've wanted something in return for re-leasing Wes."

Peter squirmed.

"It was money, wasn't it?"

"Carly, that's between me and Wes."

"But you did it because he's my brother."

"Okay, yes, I helped him out of jam because he's your brother. I happen to love you, and I know you love him. I didn't think twice."

"How much did you have to pay?"

"Please, don't ask."

"Five thousand?" she pressed.

"Carly—"

"More? Ten thousand?"

"I'm not—"

"Omigod, *more?* Twenty thousand?"

He pressed his lips together.

Carlotta gasped. "Twenty-five thousand?"

Peter swung his head to look at her. "It's just money."

She covered her mouth. "Oh, Peter…I had no idea. How can we ever pay you back?"

"It wasn't a loan, it was a gift." He dipped his chin. "And I don't want to hear any more about it."

Carlotta sat back, her mind reeling. She was over-whelmed at the lengths Peter was willing to go for her family…for her. And no matter what he said about the ransom being a gift, she felt obligated to pay him back…somehow.

When they arrived at Peter's home, he suggested they take a swim to relax. But she resisted, still melan-choly over Maria's death and worried sick about Wesley.

And Coop.

"I'm going to rest a while, then we can cook dinner together," she said.

He nodded and kissed her. "Don't worry. Wes will be fine."

She climbed the stairs to her bedroom and turned on the news to watch while she changed out of the somber mourning clothes. Coop's picture was plastered across the screen with a bold graphic "Charmed Killer on the Run" running across the bottom. A photograph of Maria Marquez in uniform flashed while the newscaster reminded viewers that Dr. Cooper Craft was considered armed and dangerous.

"Coop, where are you?" she whispered.

She retrieved her cell phone, pulled up Liz's number and connected the call. She expected to leave a message, but Liz answered.

"Hi, Carlotta."

"Liz, have you seen Wes?"

"Not since last Saturday," she said in a tone that indicated she was irritated with him. "Why?"

"No one seems to know where he is. If you hear from him, will you have him call me?"

"Sure thing."

"I don't suppose there's any news about Coop."

Liz sighed. "Nothing good. The best possible scenario is Cooper calls me and I negotiate his surrender."

Carlotta could spin the worst-case scenarios on her own—and she'd been doing so since Jack had told her Coop was on the run.

"I won't tie up your line," Carlotta said. "I just thought you might know where Wes is. Sorry to bother you."

"No trouble. If you talk to Wes before I do, ask him to call me. It's…important."

"Okay. Bye, Liz."

Carlotta ended the call and wondered if Wesley had broken things off with Liz. He'd said he'd only slept with her to steal the confidential work-product file for Randolph. Now that they had it, maybe he'd decided to end his relationship with Liz to pursue Meg.

She could only hope.

Carlotta removed her cigarettes and lighter from her purse and walked out onto the veranda for a smoke. She lit one, then another for good measure and put both cigarettes in her mouth for a deep inhale.

It was late afternoon on a cloudless summer day—a beautiful day to be buried. Detective Marquez's casket was probably underground by now. She'd read somewhere that Maria was to be interred in Atlanta, in deference to her commitment to the city and to its people. Tears filled Carlotta's eyes. Life wasn't fair. People weren't supposed to be cut down in the prime of their lives.

Like the women Michael Lane had murdered. And all the victims of The Charmed Killer, whoever he was.

Coop, where are you?

She drew deeply on both cigarettes, sighing in relief as nicotine sped through her system, taking the edge off her anxiety. Pacing along the edge of the veranda, she watched Peter as he used a long-handled net to skim leaves off the surface of the pool. Her heart welled with affection—to think that he'd handed over all that money to save Wesley's life. The fact that he hadn't told her endeared her to him even more.

The sound of a car pulling into the front circular

driveway caught her attention. She walked to the other side of the veranda and looked down. Jack climbed out of the driver's side of his dark sedan, then walked around to the trunk and removed a bike—Wesley's bike. Her heart skipped a beat.

After setting aside the bike, he walked back to the rear passenger door, opened it, and helped Wesley out. Her spirits buoyed, but even from this distance she could see her brother was in bad shape—he looked dazed and was having trouble walking. She raced back into her bedroom, snubbed out the cigarettes, and hurried downstairs to throw open the front door.

Jack, still in his dress uniform, had his arm around Wesley's shoulders. Wes looked pale and gaunt, his eyes bloodshot and unfocused. His hair stuck up at all angles, and his jaw was scruffy with beard growth. His clothes were disheveled and filthy, and he smelled of urine and vomit.

She was ready to crumble when she met Jack's gaze over Wes's head. His look telegraphed that she needed to be strong—and useful.

"Grab his bag," he said.

She dashed to the car and pulled the backpack from the floorboard. "Bring him inside."

"He needs a bed."

Thinking it would be easier to get him downstairs than up, she said, "Take him to the bedroom in the basement."

She walked in front of them, opening doors and turning on lights. The basement of Peter's house held a wine cellar, a home theater, and a bedroom suite with high-end furnishings that rivaled any room in the main part of the house. Jack helped Wes sit on the bed. When

Wes lay down, his eyes instantly closed and he rolled into a fetal position with a groan.

Carlotta started to go to him, but Jack pulled her back into the hall and closed the door.

"What's going on?" she demanded.

"He's going through detox."

"What? Where did you find him?"

His mouth flattened. "Don't ask."

She crossed her arms. "I'm asking, Jack. Where did you find him?"

He considered her silently, then seemed to relent. "With a man who works for Hollis Carver."

"I'm confused."

"Apparently this guy was helping Wes detox from Oxy. He had him in a place where he could take care of him. Did you know Wes was hooked?"

She closed her eyes and nodded. "I gave him an ultimatum earlier this week about getting clean. But who is this guy and why would he care?"

Jack averted his gaze.

"Wait a minute. How did you know where to find Wes?"

After much foot shuffling, he looked back to her. "As part of his plea agreement for the body-snatching incident, Wes agreed to snoop around in The Carver's organization."

Her eyes widened. "He's spying on a loan shark?"

"Relax. He's just riding along on collections and keeping his eyes open. He's on the payroll, so he's working down his debt, too. It was a good deal for Wes, all the way around." He sighed. "But to be on the safe side, I had a GPS chip installed in the phone they gave him. I tracked it to his backpack in a car sitting outside a building, and I found them inside."

Her mind whirled. "So…Wes isn't working for a courier?"

"Only in the loosest interpretation."

"So he's been lying to me."

"He had to," Jack said. "That was part of the deal with the D.A.—no one could know except Liz and me. You can't say anything, Carlotta. I know that's like telling a cut not to bleed, but I'm telling you anyway."

"But it's dangerous."

"So is jail," he snapped. "Your brother got a break here. And the guy he works with obviously gives a damn about him to take this on. Detox is not pretty. You should be grateful."

All the fight drained out of her and she nodded. "You're right. And I am grateful. What can I do?"

"Apparently he's through the worst of it." Jack dug in his pocket. "Here—the guy who was taking care of him wrote down a few things. He's say right now, Wes feels like he has the worst imaginable case of the flu."

She glanced at the list written in a masculine scribble.

Valium to sleep
Hot baths for muscle aches
Imodium for the runs
Strong mineral supplement
B6 vitamins
Gradual exercise
Soft, bland food
He should be fine in 24 hours.

Her heart squeezed in appreciation for the person who had the knowledge and the patience to help Wes through what must have been an awful ordeal. "I can take it from here," she said, then put her hand on Jack's arm. "Thank you for finding him and bringing him to me."

His expression softened. "You're welcome."

She stared into his gold-colored eyes, wishing she knew what made him tick.

"I should go," he said, turning to head toward the steps. She followed him upstairs and as they walked into the kitchen, the sliding glass door to the pool area opened. Peter stepped in and blinked when he saw Jack.

"Jack brought Wesley home," Carlotta explained. "I put him downstairs."

"Is he okay?"

She nodded. "I'll walk Jack out, then I'll fill you in."

She followed Jack to his car, brimming with emotion. "This has been a terrible day for you, Jack, and here you are taking time out to do something for me."

"I need to stay busy," he said, then tried to smile. "Luckily with you around, that's not a problem."

She stepped forward and hugged him, pressing her face against his blue coat. "I'm so sorry about Maria." She choked on the woman's name.

"I know. Me, too." He put his arms around her waist and pulled her closer.

After a long, warm moment, she stepped back and wiped the corners of her eyes.

Jack cleared his throat, obviously struggling to maintain control. "Try to stay out of trouble," he said gruffly, then climbed into this car and drove off.

Carlotta went back into the house and relayed to Peter what had happened. "Is it okay if Wes stays here for a couple of days?"

"He's welcome to stay as long as he wants," Peter said. "What can I do to help?"

She smiled up at him, thinking how lucky she was to have him. "Can you loan him some clothes?"

"Let's go pick out a few things," Peter said and they jogged up the stairs together. Carlotta ducked back into her room to turn off the television, but stopped when she saw a picture of an attractive blond woman flash on the screen. Something about her seemed familiar.

She turned up the volume in time to hear the newscaster say, "Breaking news just in from the Fulton County Morgue in Atlanta. A positive ID has been made on the only unidentified victim of The Charmed Killer that was burned beyond recognition. The victim's name is Casey Renee Sutcliffe from Jonesboro, Georgia. Twenty-seven-year-old Sutcliffe had not been reported missing—her family said she was between jobs, and she lived alone. They believed her to be fine until they received the call today from Chief Medical Examiner Bruce Abrams. Very sad news indeed."

Carlotta stared at the woman's smiling face, and then recognition hit her hard, stealing her breath.

One of the last times she'd seen Coop was at Moody's Cigar Bar. He'd been drinking and behaving out of character, with a slinky woman draped over him.

Casey Renee Sutcliffe.

26

Wes opened his eyes and groaned, then waited for the pain to barrel through his head. When it didn't, he wondered if he was dead.

If so, hell had a pretty comfy mattress.

He turned his head, but didn't recognize the dark room. Yellow light peeked in around the edges of a curtain. He pushed himself up gingerly and sucked in a breath at the overall soreness of his body. He felt as if he'd been turned inside out, and his memory was like Swiss cheese. He limped to the window and pulled aside the curtain. The sunlight blinded him. When he finally blinked the scene into focus, he was still confused. The window was level with the ground and he was looking out onto what appeared to be a side yard.

He turned back to the room and searched for a light. He was in the basement of a house, but whose?

The light revealed a nice, if boring, room that he'd never seen. He was wearing gray sweats and a T-shirt he didn't recognize, and he was barefoot. His glasses were on a table next to the bed. He jammed them on to check the clock—9:37. In the morning, apparently.

He went to the bathroom and found his backpack

sitting in a corner. Both of his phones were dead, so he plugged in the charger and connected his main cell. When it powered up, the message on the screen said he'd missed twenty-seven calls.

Christ, what day was it?

His throat was parched and his eyeballs felt dry. He filled a glass on the vanity with water from the sink and downed it, then washed his face. He found mouthwash and a comb in the medicine cabinet. He was so weak, he leaned into the vanity as he attempted to tame his hair that had dried sticking up.

The water gurgled in his empty stomach. Damn, he was raw as hell. He had a faint recollection of violently expelling fluid from both ends. He felt utterly purged. And while the idea of popping an Oxy was mildly entertaining, his body wasn't screaming for it.

He still wasn't sure what had transpired, but he felt better than he'd felt in weeks.

After taking a whiz, he poked around the other rooms—a wine cellar and a home entertainment theater—and suddenly realized he was at Peter's.

He winced. That meant Carlotta was around somewhere, waiting with a sermon. He had no recollection of coming here, so this should be interesting.

With the help of the handrail, he climbed the stairs and pushed open the door at the top, trying to piece together the fragments of his memory. He remembered Mouse taking him to The Carver's warehouse and locking him in the bathroom. After that, things were sketchy. He recalled pain and convulsions…and being stabbed. He rubbed his arm under the T-shirt sleeve, noting no new gashes, but the muscle under one red spot was tender—as if he'd received a shot…or more than one.

The kitchen was big and luxurious and empty. He listened for signs of life, but heard only the sound of distant pounding—like hammer meeting rock. He walked through the kitchen and into a combination sitting room/eating area. "Sis? Peter?" His throat was scratchy.

The sliding glass door opened and Carlotta stepped inside. His heart thudded in his chest—she must hate him.

When she saw him, though, her face lit up. "Hi. Nice to see you up and around."

He exhaled in abject relief that she wasn't angry. "I'm still a little foggy. What day is it?"

"Saturday."

His last recollection was of Wednesday. "What happened exactly?"

"Are you hungry?"

"Yeah."

"Sit and we'll talk."

While she scrambled eggs and made toast, she told him the story that she'd cobbled together. Wes filled in the blanks silently with mounting incredulity. Apparently Mouse had taken him to the warehouse not to fillet him, but to get him off the Oxy.

"I'm glad you're clean," she said, "but I wish you'd told someone you were going to detox. We were all worried sick about you."

"It was a last-minute decision," he mumbled.

"Your friend even gave Jack notes so we could take care of you," she said, pushing a piece of paper in his direction.

He glanced at the list. His memory of being strapped

to a chair and stabbed was probably Mouse shooting him up with enough Valium to knock him out. He'd stripped him no doubt to make the puking and the diarrhea easier to deal with. And instead of holding him under water to drown him, he'd forced him into hot baths to alleviate the muscle cramps.

The man was a fucking saint.

"Sounds like I grossed everyone out," Wes offered.

"Obviously the worst of it was over by the time Jack brought you here yesterday. Peter got you in a hot shower and into clean clothes. I gave you a tablet of Valium and you fell back to sleep." She pushed a plate of eggs toward him and poured a glass of orange Gatorade. "So…how do you feel?"

He shoveled the eggs into his mouth and within a few bites, he could feel his energy returning. The drug had released its hold on him. "I'm good," he said, stuffing buttered toast in his mouth. "Got any jelly?"

She smiled and retrieved a jar of strawberry preserves from the refrigerator. "So…did it stick?"

"What?"

"The detox," she said, wearing her mom face. "Have you quit Oxy for good?"

Wes swallowed the food in his mouth, then took another drink and set down the glass. When he considered how lucky he was to have people around him who cared about him—maybe more than he cared about himself—he started to choke up. He cleared his throat and thumped his fist on his chest to regain his composure. Then he lifted his gaze to Carlotta's and said, "Sis, I swear, I'll never do drugs again. That stuff will eat your brain—I was stupid on Oxy."

She smiled and reached across the bar to hug his neck. "I love you."

He made a face. "I love you, too."

Carlotta laughed. "I know that hurt, but thanks. It's good to have you back."

He dove back into his breakfast with gusto. "So what did I miss?"

From the way Carlotta's face blanched, he knew something bad had happened. With brimming tears, she told him about Maria Marquez's murder and Coop's disappearance. When she told him that the burned body had been identified and also linked to Coop by several eyewitnesses—her included—his heart sank.

"So Coop really is The Charmed Killer?" he said.

Carlotta didn't respond, just busied herself cleaning up the kitchen. He could tell the stress of worrying about Coop was wearing on her.

"Coop has dug his own grave," Wes said. "You gotta let it go, Sis."

She raked the remnants of his plate into the sink disposal with jerky motions. "I know." She turned on the machine, and a few seconds later when she flipped it off, she seemed to have pushed aside the dark thoughts for the moment. "Liz wants you to call her. She said it was important."

"Okay." But inside he was wincing. He hadn't spoken to Liz since fleeing from her offer to sleep over last weekend. She was probably pissed, but she'd have to wait.

He had another girl to see.

The sound of the pounding he'd heard earlier had resumed. "What's that noise?"

"Peter's fountain is being repaired," she murmured. "While he's busy supervising, I think I'll run a couple of errands."

"Can I catch a ride to midtown?"

She frowned. "Shouldn't you rest?"

"It's important. Besides, I feel better than I have in a long time."

"Okay. I laundered your clothes—they're in the closet in your room. Can you be ready in twenty minutes?"

"Fifteen," he said, then raced downstairs for a quick shower. He checked his accumulated cell phone messages. One Meg had left Wednesday night saying she was at the movies and had he changed his mind? The rest were from Carlotta, Chance, Hannah, and Liz, all wondering where he was and would he please call. Kendall Abrams had called several times asking for his help with body pickups. The guy sounded desperate.

As Wesley tucked in his shirt, he conceded Meg was probably furious that he hadn't showed up for their date, but maybe she was a little worried about him since he'd missed work Thursday and Friday.

On the drive, he was especially aware of sensory details—the new-car smell of the rental, the sound of Carlotta's buoyant laughter, the indigo hue of the sky, and the cloying moisture in the hot summer air. He had thought the Oxy made everything better, but it was so damned good to have a clear head again.

"Where shall I drop you?" Carlotta asked.

"Um…somewhere close to Georgia Tech would be fine."

She gave him an amused smile. "Which dorm is Meg's?"

Sheepishly he gave her directions and when she slowed the car, he jumped out. "I'll get a ride back," he said.

"Okay. Wes?"

"Yeah?"

"I keep forgetting to thank you for getting rid of the fire ants in our yard. Mrs. Winningham was impressed."

Wes frowned. "Sorry, Sis. I meant to take care of it, but I forgot. The ants must've found a better yard. See ya."

He turned and jogged up the sidewalk to Meg's dorm. Passing coeds stared at him, and he wondered if he still looked a mess from the detox. He'd lost at least five pounds, and he didn't have many to spare. He walked into the lobby and punched in Meg's number on his cell. His hands were shaking, but at least it wasn't from drugs.

"Hello," she answered.

"Hey, it's Wes."

She scoffed. "Not the Wes who stood me up Wednesday night. Because he would know better than to call me *four* days later with some lame excuse."

"I'm sorry about that. Something came up."

"I gathered as much when you ditched work Thursday and Friday."

"Can I see you? I'm in the lobby of your dorm."

She sighed. "I'm actually on my way down."

He smiled into the mouthpiece. "I'll be waiting." He ended the call and paced the length of the room, eager to tell Meg that he was clean and they could start over.

When the elevator doors opened and she stepped off wearing a yellow sundress and pink sandals, he couldn't hold back a sappy smile. "Hi."

She looked somewhat less happy to see him. "What, are you stalking me now?"

"You look nice."

"Thanks," she said. "I'm going out."

He balked. "On a date?"

When she smiled at someone behind him, he turned to see Preppy Mark standing there, dressed like a Ralph Lauren magazine ad…in a gay magazine. He smiled at Wes. "Hey, Schwinn."

Wes glared at him.

"Wes," Meg said, "did you want something?"

He looked back to her, suddenly tongue-tied. "I, uh, wanted to apologize for…Wednesday night."

"No biggie," she said with a shrug. "Is that all?"

"No. I…I got clean, like you said."

"Good for you. See you later." She turned away and walked up to Mark, giving him a blinding smile. "Ready?"

Wes watched them walk out the door and rubbed his breastbone. The detox had done a number on his body. He was feeling strange things in strange places that he'd never felt before.

Carlotta handed money to the clerk at the dry cleaners drive-through and her charm bracelet clinked. She stared at the charms and mentally ticked back through the ones they'd found on all the victims of The Charmed Killer. Wesley was right—except for the lipstick charm found in Maria's mouth, they all pointed to Coop. The GBI would say that he was taunting them, daring them to figure out his clues.

But what if the charms were a clever way to frame Coop?

And why did the charms before Maria's murder skew neutral or masculine, and then suddenly skew feminine? It didn't track…just like the fact that the victims had seemed random, or at least innocent, up to that point.

Then a thought curled into her brain. What if Maria's murder had been a copycat crime, meant to *look* as if The Charmed Killer had done it?

Her pulse raced. If so, the obvious culprit would be Rueben Garza. What if Garza was the kind of man who wouldn't accept Maria's decision to leave? He was a police officer, who would naturally be following The Charmed Killer case. He'd have the strength and the know-how to kill…and a unique signature under which to disguise his deed.

Comments that Maria had made came back to her. *I was married, but that's over… You're putting your faith in the wrong guy, and I know what that's like.* It would explain why Maria had always seemed withdrawn, and why she would shy away from a relationship with Jack.

Jack…

She thought back to the night at the restaurant. Jack had said Maria had invited him, but Maria had gone out of her way to assure Carlotta they weren't on a date. And when they'd heard a noise from the tree line, Maria had instantly drawn her weapon, telling Carlotta to go inside, and not to get Jack—that she could handle it.

What if the noise hadn't been made by a dog, as Maria had claimed? What if she thought she was being stalked…by her ex-husband? Maybe she'd invited Jack to dinner thinking that if Garza confronted them, Jack could take care of himself.

Or shoot the man, if necessary.

If Garza was getting his information from the newspaper, or from inside sources, he might not have realized that all the charms had been of a neutral or male bent.

And then she remembered a small detail—the charm removed from the mouth of victim number five, Marna Collins, was a pair of handcuffs. But it had been reported erroneously in the paper as being a woman's shoe.

With that piece of flawed information, planting a lipstick charm would seem believable.

Carlotta itched to tell Jack her theory, but without proof, she knew he would blow her off.

"Ma'am?"

She jerked her head around to see the irritated clerk waving her change. "There's a line behind you."

"Oh. Thanks." She took the money, then pulled over in the parking lot and called the midtown police precinct.

"Atlanta PD," a woman's voice said.

"Brooklyn?"

"Yeah, who's this?"

"Brook, it's Carlotta Wren. I need a favor."

"What?" the woman asked in a voice that was more interested than cautious.

"Do you know if the police department covered the arrangements for Maria Marquez's ex-husband Rueben Garza to come to the funeral?"

"Yeah, we paid for it, him being a cop and all. Professional courtesy."

"Can you find out if he's still in town and where he's staying?"

"Hm. Might take me a few."

"Call me back on this number." She ended the call and tapped on the steering wheel nervously until Brook called her back.

"He's at the Four Seasons, girl, room 535, paid for through tonight."

"Thank you so much. And, Brook...don't mention this to Jack."

"I kinda thought you might say that. Don't worry. I don't wanna know what you're up to and if I get called to the stand, I have no problem committing perjury. Goodbye."

Carlotta smiled, then disconnected the call and headed to the Four Seasons. The last time she'd been at the hotel, she'd crashed an upscale party and had been reunited with Peter. That seemed like ages ago, but in reality, it had been only a few months.

So she remembered the layout of the hotel perfectly.

After parking along the street, she jammed on dark sunglasses and walked to the entrance. It was a lovely place—the doormen were gracious, the lobby was luxurious, the air was perfumed. With her chin held high, she walked through the lobby to a house phone and dialed room 535, prepared to hang up if Garza answered. But if the man had done what she suspected him of, he would not be holed up in his room on a pretty Saturday, mourning his dead ex-wife.

She let the phone ring until it rolled over to voice mail. The she hung up and called again, just in case he was sleeping. Again, no answer.

Carlotta returned the receiver and headed toward the elevator bay. Then she walked around the corner to a service elevator and rode down to the basement. There she followed the hum and the heat to the laundry room and knocked on the half door that led into the humid, noisy place. A sweaty man hurried over, his expression concerned.

"Yes, ma'am?"

She sighed dramatically. "I've called housekeeping three times for a robe with no response, so I decided to come down and get one myself."

He winced. "Your room, ma'am?"

"535."

"Last name?"

"Garza."

He hurried to a phone and made a quick call, presumably to the front desk. Then he came back, looking contrite. "Sorry, ma'am, how many robes do you need?"

"Just one will do," she chirped.

He left and came back with a white waffle-weave robe, freshly laundered and folded to crisp perfection. "Here you are, ma'am. So sorry."

"Thank you." She handed him a five dollar tip, then turned on her heel and made her way back to the service elevator.

She rode to the fifth floor and found the ice machine room. There she quickly removed her clothes down to her underwear and shrugged into the robe. Her cell phone and wallet went into the pockets of the robe, then she stuffed her clothes into her purse and stowed it behind the ice machine. Someone had left a glass sitting on top of the machine, so she grabbed it and filled it with ice before making her way back down the hallway until she spotted a housekeeping cart.

"Excuse me," she said to the maid, who was writing on a form on a clipboard. "I'm so sorry, but I went to get ice and I locked myself out of my room." She held up the glass of ice as proof, then pulled the robe tighter around her. "I can't go down to the lobby looking like this. Can you help me?"

The housekeeper looked dubious.

"It's room 535, Garza," Carlotta said, pointing to the clipboard. "Please?"

The woman checked, then looked back and nodded.

"Oh, thank you. I'm so embarrassed," Carlotta gushed. She stealthily snagged a pair of latex gloves from the cart and stuffed them into the pocket of the robe before following the maid to the room.

The woman unlocked the door and pushed it open.

Carlotta held her breath, hoping that Garza wasn't there, but the bed was made and the room was silent. She thanked the woman profusely, then elbowed her way inside, taking care not to touch the doorknob. She didn't want to leave fingerprints.

Once inside, she set the glass of ice on a table and pulled on the latex gloves. Then she set about snooping, not sure what she'd find, or if she'd find anything at all, but systematically opening drawers and cabinets.

Mr. Garza had gone shopping, she noted, fishing through bags from Hugo Boss, Versace, and Gucci. Not exactly the behavior of a grieving man, although she begrudgingly admitted he had good taste.

In the bathroom, the vanity was crowded with moisturizers and creams. The man was a bit of a metrosexual who was obviously in preservation mode. She picked up a bottle and made a face. She wondered if Garza's fellow police officers knew he used a pore minimizer.

Carlotta opened his toiletry bag and sorted through razor, tweezers, nose-hair clippers, and a manicure set. She was about to move on when she spotted the glimmer of a silver chain in the corner of the bag. She grasped it between two gloved fingers and pulled it out.

Then almost dropped it.

It was a charm bracelet featuring "girly" charms—a purse, a high-heeled shoe, a hat, a hairbrush...and a noticeable gap where a charm was missing.

A lipstick?

Her hand began to shake.

The bastard had done it. He'd killed Maria and blamed it on The Charmed Killer.

From the other room, she heard the sound of a card key being inserted in the door. Alarm seized her. She dropped the bracelet back into the toiletry kit and weighed her options: Hide or get caught.

She hid.

In the shower. She barely had time to pull the curtain closed before the bedroom door opened, and the sound of upbeat whistling reached her ears.

She gritted her teeth. He'd just killed a woman and he was *whistling?*

Because he thought he'd gotten away with it.

As he moved around the room, she closed her eyes and prayed she'd get out of there alive. She was starting to think that hiding in a bathtub from a man who'd just drowned a woman in her bathtub might not have been the smartest move. She thought wistfully of the stun baton in her purse—why hadn't she brought it with her?

Then she remembered she had her phone. She couldn't make a phone call without being heard, but she could text.

She pulled out the phone and frantically typed a cryptic message to Hannah: *urgnt cll 4 seasns get man out rm 535.* She hit Send and prayed Hannah was available and that she understood.

The whistling grew louder and to her horror, Rueben Garza came into the bathroom and proceeded to take a leak. She held her breath, but was sure he could hear her sweating. Through a sliver in the shower curtain, she could see his reflection in the mirror. He was tall and dark-skinned. He wore swim trunks and fussed with his blue-black hair with the hand that wasn't holding his dick.

Nestled in his chest hair was a gold medallion—maybe a St. Christopher medal.

The same size and shape of the metallic flash she'd seen from the tree line outside the restaurant. Blood rushed in her ears.

Garza finished and shook himself off, then flushed the toilet and walked back into the bedroom.

She exhaled and wondered how long she could stay in here. What if he decided to take a shower? How would she explain her presence in his room, in a robe?

From the next room she heard him scoff. "What the—?" Then she heard the sound of ice clinking in a glass. She winced—he'd found her glass.

He walked back into the bathroom. "Damn maid," he muttered, then he reached inside the shower curtain and dumped the ice.

On her bare feet.

She swallowed a gasp, but when he twisted the knob to turn on the shower, she nearly swallowed her tongue.

The icy spray blasted her in the face. She stood stock still, but her mind raced. Her only hope was to wait until he was naked, and then he might not run after her—if she could make it to the hallway. Her heart stampeded her lungs.

She could hear the sounds of him pushing down his swim trunks. And then from the other room, the sound of the ringing phone.

The cavalry.

Garza cursed.

Answer it, she silently begged. *Answer it.*

He stomped into the bedroom and answered the phone. She could hear him arguing with whoever was on the other end. She thought about making a run for it now, but then remembered she needed that glass—her fingerprints were all over it.

He slammed down the phone and came back to get his trunks, grumbling, then reached in and turn off the shower. The sudden absence of the water was more shocking than the initial spray. Her robe, cold and sopping wet, clung to her and weighed a ton.

She heard more shuffling, then the blessed sound of the room door opening and closing.

Carlotta shoved aside the shower curtain and jumped out of the tub as fast as the sodden robe would allow. She ran into the bedroom, leaving a trail of water, scanning for the glass. When she found it, she shoved it in her pocket and dashed to the door. She opened it and slipped out into the hall, smiling at the couple coming down the hall toward her. They squinted at her drenched appearance and hurried into their room. Carlotta sprinted back to the ice machine room and yanked out her purse. She made a split-second decision that putting her clothes on over wet underwear would draw more attention than if she wore no underwear at all, so she stripped naked and redressed. Then she pulled out her phone and wallet—now waterlogged—and stuffed the wet robe in a trash can.

She took the stairs down to give herself a few minutes to repair her appearance. She skimmed her wet hair back into a ponytail and removed mascara streaks with a tissue. By the time she walked out into the lobby, her sunglasses and attitude were back in place. Rueben Garza stood there dressed in swim trunks, T-shirt and sandals. When she passed him, he ogled her in between shooting exasperated glances at his watch as he looked for someone who hadn't yet shown up.

Carlotta walked quickly to her car, unlocking it from a safe distance. Just as she opened the car door, Hannah's van pulled up and the window zoomed down. "I had to come see."

Carlotta's shoulders fell. "How did you get him out of the room?"

"I told him he had to come to the lobby to sign for an ostrich egg."

"What?"

"I panicked…it was the only thing I could think of. You didn't give me a lot to go on."

"It worked. You saved my life."

"What happened?"

"I'll tell you in a minute. Can I use your phone? Mine took a shower."

Hannah handed over her cell. Carlotta punched in Jack's number.

"Terry," he barked after the second ring.

"Jack, it's Carlotta."

"Carlotta, my plate is pretty full right now."

She frowned. "This is important. Before you dismiss me or hang up, promise me you'll hear me out."

He sighed. "I'm listening."

"Maria's ex-husband murdered her."

"What? Are you out of your mind?"

"Maybe, but that's beside the point. Rueben Garza killed her and he made it look like The Charmed Killer did it."

He made a disbelieving noise. "Have you been drinking?"

"Jack, shut up for a minute and think about it. Maria knew he was stalking her. That's why she asked you out to dinner, because she expected a confrontation and knew you'd protect her. It was Garza watching us from the trees that night, I know it. He knew Maria smoked and that she would come outside eventually. The charm is all wrong, Jack—it's feminine, not like the others. Besides...I know for certain he killed her."

"How's that?" he asked. But the absence of sarcasm meant he was, at least, listening.

"I found proof in his hotel room."

A strangled noise sounded over the phone. "You *what?*"

"A charm bracelet, missing a charm. He did it, Jack. So you should be able to find evidence other than the charm bracelet, proof that he was in town the night the murder occurred, that there's a history of violence, something. But he's checking out tonight, so you'll need to move fast."

"I can't believe you!" he bellowed. "Have you not heard a single word I've said about staying out of police work?"

"Okay, before you have an aneurysm, I have something else to run by you."

"I don't suppose there's any way I can stop you from telling me?"

"No. I've been wracking my brain thinking about how someone could've framed Coop for these murders."

"Carlotta, don't."

"Just listen, Jack, please. If someone wanted to incriminate Coop, they would've had to know where he goes— the bookstore where Shawna Whitt worked, the block where Pepper hung out, the gym Cheryl Meriwether belonged to, the grocery store where Marna Collins shopped, the cigar shop. And when I started thinking about how you tracked down Wes, it occurred to me—maybe there's a GPS chip on Coop's van somewhere."

"You can't honestly believe—"

"The van has probably been impounded, right?"

"Yes," he said through gritted teeth.

"Then can't you wave a wand over it or something to find a chip if there is one?"

"Yes, I'll get out my magic wand," Jack said dryly. "Are you hearing yourself? This is crazy talk, even for you."

Carlotta bit her lip to stem tears of frustration. "Okay, Jack, don't do it for me. Do it for Maria and for Coop. If I'm wrong, I'm wrong. But what if I'm right?"

He expelled a burdened sigh. "Oh, well…I wasn't planning to sleep tonight anyway."

28

Wes was awakened early Sunday morning by his ringing cell phone. He cracked an eye at the clock—6:15 a.m.—and brought the phone to his mouth. "This had better be Jesus."

"Wes, man, it's Kendall. Where have you been?"

Wes winced. "I've been sick. Dude, it's not even dawn. Go back to sleep."

"That's the problem," Kendall said, his voice small and squeaky. "I can't sleep. I have nightmares. I don't think I can do this job anymore, Wes. I'd rather work with roadkill."

Wes rubbed his eyes. "Moving bodies isn't for everyone."

"So why do you do it?"

Wes sat up and swung his feet over the edge of the mattress simply because the idea of lying in bed talking on the phone to another guy weirded him out. He sighed. "I used to do it because of Coop. He made it interesting, he made it seem…I don't know—like we were doing something that mattered."

"You miss him, don't you?"

"Uh, yeah, I guess." More than he would ever admit

to Gomer. "Dude, did you call for a reason or are you just PMSing?"

"Will you help me tell my uncle?"

"Tell him what?"

"That I'm just not cut out for this job. I've tried so hard to make him proud of me, but…I miss my squirrels."

"Squirrels?"

"It's hard to explain, but there's just something really beautiful about them when they're all flat. Did you know that most of them die in a perfect silhouette?"

Wes squinted. "Uh…no."

"Their tails bush out—"

"Dude, no offense, but I couldn't be less interested."

"Aw, okay. Can you help me make some pickups today?"

"You mean after the sun comes up?"

Kendall laughed. "Good one. I can pick you up at noon."

Wes gave him the address. "Wear a coat and tie, how about it?"

"Why?"

"Just do it," Wes said, remembering the lecture Coop had once given him about professionalism. "And Kendall?"

"Yeah?"

"I'll go with you to talk to Dr. Abrams if you want, just let me know."

"Okay. Thanks, man."

Wes ended the call and shook his head. There was something wrong with that boy.

He lay down and tried to go back to sleep, but his mind was wide awake—the one downside of being clean of the Oxy was the burden that came with thinking clearly.

Where was Coop? How could the man who had raked him over the coals for conspiring to have a body stolen do all the things he'd been accused of? It just didn't add up. But if Coop was innocent, why run?

Just like his own father…

Then he was tormented by images of Meg with that other guy. He'd totally blown it with her.

He needed to call Liz.

And repair the townhouse.

And thank Mouse.

At this point, he was glad that the identification of the headless corpse in the morgue had gone cold. Because if one of the three names on the list he'd sent anonymously to the APD actually panned out, they might link the dead guy back to Mouse. And he owed Mouse one. A big one.

He finally managed to doze for a couple of hours, then showered and took the vitamins and minerals that were supplementing his energy and his full recovery. When he went upstairs, Carlotta and Peter were having brunch out by the pool. Through the glass door he watched them interact for a few minutes, nursing guilty pangs about pushing Peter on Carlotta when it was so clear to him her heart was elsewhere. He'd explored the rest of the house and suspected their separate sleeping arrangements had little to do with appearances.

But Peter had really helped him out of a jam, and he did seem to care for Carlotta. He would give her the life she deserved, the one their parents had yanked out from under her.

Wes walked outside and joined them. He snagged a strip of bacon and a banana, then noticed the brochures they were studying.

"Who's going to Vegas?" Excitement stirred in his stomach as he picked up one of the flyers.

"Peter bought a trip to Vegas for charity. We're leaving Tuesday for five days."

"You're welcome to stay here while we're gone," Peter added.

Envy stabbed Wes. He'd always dreamed of going to Vegas. Any poker player worth their salt played the strip. "Thanks for the offer, Peter, but I'm heading back to Chance's place tonight." He glanced at Carlotta. "I'm going with Kendall Abrams on a few body pickups this afternoon. I'll have him drop me off there when we're done."

She looked sad, but she nodded. He wondered briefly if she was lonely living with Peter. There was a feeling of detachment here in the suburbs that didn't seem to fit his sister's personality.

"Have you called Liz?" she asked.

"Not yet."

"So…" Carlotta grinned. "How did it go with Meg yesterday?"

Wes frowned. "It didn't. She's going out with someone else, someone in her own league."

"Well, if you're giving up, that will definitely make her decision easier," Carlotta said lightly.

A honk sounded from the front of the house.

"That's my ride," Wes said. "Later." On impulse, he dropped a kiss on his sister's cheek, then bolted.

The body pickups were rote—four nursing homes and the veteran's hospital, six trips to the morgue.

Kendall Abrams was as morose as the country songs he insisted they listen to. Dr. Abrams wasn't at the morgue, so the dreaded, "I gotta be me," meeting with Kendall and his uncle was postponed. As Wes maneuvered around Kendall's shortcomings on the job, he realized how much he'd learned from Coop. But it wasn't the same making calls without him.

The afternoon turned into evening and they were still stacking bodies in the back of the van. An influenza outbreak in one of the nursing homes had taken its toll. They were completing their final run to the morgue when his cell phone rang. At the sight of Meg's name on the screen, his pulse kicked up. Uncaring of how uncool it was, he answered on the first ring.

"Hi, Meg."

"Hi. Are you busy?"

"Just moving bodies."

She grunted. "Are you going to be busy all night?"

Hope stirred in his chest. "No. We just finished."

"Why don't you come over?"

"To your dorm?"

"Yeah. My roommate's gone. We can hang out and watch TV."

"I thought you girls weren't allowed to have guys in your room this late."

"We're not. If you want in, you'll have to think of something creative. Room 2011."

He swallowed hard. "What time?"

"That's up to you," she said, then clicked off.

He snapped the phone closed and looked at Kendall. "We're done. I'll buy pizza."

Twenty minutes later, Kendall dropped him off in front

of Meg's dorm. Wes pulled out the hat he'd bought from the guy at the counter of the pizza joint and walked in with a pie propped on his shoulder. "Pizza for room 1911," he told the dour-faced woman manning the lobby desk.

"The girls have to come down and pay for it here," she said primly, as if she were personally responsible for guarding their hymens.

"I've been calling and calling from the parking lot, and it's busy." He tried to look pitiful. "Please, ma'am. I got fifteen more of these things to deliver in the next forty minutes, or it all comes out of my paycheck."

She frowned. "All right. But if you don't come back, I know which room you're in."

"That's what you think," Wes muttered under his breath as he stepped onto the elevator.

When Meg answered the door, she burst out laughing. "I knew you'd think of something."

He was kissing her before the door closed.

She kissed him back, then lifted her head. "No sex, do you hear me? This is still our first date."

He nodded. He just wanted to be in the same room with her.

They sat on the couch watching TV and sharing the pizza with her leg crossed over his, and his hand on her knee. In between talking, they kissed and petted, but despite a persistent hard-on, Wes didn't let things go too far. He didn't want to mess up again.

Around two in the morning, they stretched out on the couch, their warm bodies pressed together. She had her hand under his shirt, caressing his stomach. As Wes stroked her hair, a fierce possessiveness welled in his chest.

"So, what's up with you and this Mark guy?" he asked.

Meg's hand stilled, and for a few seconds, he thought he'd angered her. Then she sighed. "Mark was my brother's best friend."

"Was? Meaning they're no longer best friends?"

"Meaning, I no longer have a brother."

Wes twisted to see her face. "What happened?"

Her eyes shimmered with tears. "He died of a drug overdose about three years ago."

So that explained why she'd given him such a hard time about the Oxy. It also explained the air of fragility he'd detected around Meg's mother when he'd met her.

"I'm sorry," he murmured. "That must have been awful."

"It still is. I'm glad you decided to get clean."

"Me, too," he said, and meant it. He felt like he had a new lease on life.

She snuggled closer and that odd pain stirred in his chest again. An alien thought invaded his mind, but he pushed it away. No, he was *not* in love with Meg Vincent. He just wanted in her tight pants.

"I'm going on vacation with my folks for a few days," she said. "I'll miss you while I'm gone."

Christ, he missed her already. With a sinking sensation, he conceded that this miserable anguish wracking his body must be love. Like a drowning man, Wes closed his eyes and gave in.

29

"Last day before vacation?" Patricia Alexander asked Carlotta.

"That's right," Carlotta sang, walking through Shoes on her way up to her department. "Have fun doing inventory."

Patricia stuck out her tongue good-naturedly.

Carlotta frowned at Patricia's bare wrist. "Hey, where's your charm bracelet?"

"Oh…I just realized how silly it was to believe that a bunch of random charms can predict the future."

"Did you break it off with Leo?"

Patricia nodded. "I don't know, Carlotta. There's just something about him that I can't put my finger on. It's like he's keeping something from me."

"You did the right thing," Carlotta assured her. Then she held up her own bracelet with a smile. "But who cares whether the charms can predict the future? It's a pretty bracelet."

Patricia laughed. "You're right. I'll start wearing mine again." She gestured to the array of fall shoes that had just arrived. "Have you seen the Valentino leopard-print platforms?"

"Yes," Carlotta said wistfully. With a pang she remembered how much Maria Marquez had admired her silver Valentino sandals.

She glanced at all the beautiful, shiny shoes that bloomed like flowers in a garden. She'd love a new pair of sandals for the trip to Vegas, but resisted, knowing she and Wes would need money to repair and repaint the townhouse. Besides, she had plenty of shoes. She planned to stop by the townhouse tomorrow on the way to the airport to pack some of her more dressy clothes.

"Maybe later," she said to Patricia with a goodbye wave.

"Have fun in Vegas," the blonde said slyly.

Carlotta returned with a smile, then turned toward the escalator. She was looking forward to getting away, she just wished it were under different circumstances. She couldn't shake the feeling that she was abandoning the situation here in Atlanta when too many ends were still loose.

Which was ridiculous, since Jack and everyone else had so often reminded her that it wasn't her place to try to fix things.

"Carlotta Wren, line two," said a voice over the P.A. system. "Carlotta Wren, line two."

Carlotta hurried to her station and picked up the phone. "This is Carlotta."

"Hello," said a quiet, warm voice she recognized with a thrill.

"Coop?" she asked, stunned. She turned her back to Herb, her bodyguard. "Are you okay?"

"I'm fine. How are you?"

"Worried sick about you," she whispered. "Where are you?"

A rueful noise sounded over the line. "I can't tell you where I am, but I'm okay. A friend of mine died."

"Sarah Edlow?"

"I see you've been keeping up with the media coverage. Yes, Sarah—the woman I almost killed because I was so drunk on my ass."

"She recovered, Coop."

"Only to get a brain tumor. That doesn't seem fair, does it?"

"No," she agreed, marveling over how calm, how normal, he sounded in the wake of the accusations against him.

"I even wondered if something about her injuries, or the medicine she had to take because of them could've caused the tumor."

"No one could know that," she murmured.

"Still, after I was arrested, I started thinking all these horrible things were happening to me because of what I did to Sarah, like karma. Some part of me thought I deserved it."

"But you didn't kill those women, Coop."

"No, I didn't."

She closed her eyes in abject relief just to hear him say the words. "Then why did you leave?"

"Because I promised Sarah I would do something for her, something she wasn't able to do herself. I'll be back tomorrow to face the music. And I'll call Liz later, but I wanted to talk to you first. I miss your voice."

Carlotta smiled into the phone, then looked up and saw Jack striding toward her.

"Jack's here," she whispered. "I have to go. Take care of yourself." She replaced the receiver just as Jack walked up.

"Who was that to put such color in your cheeks?" Jack asked.

"Uh…it was Wes." She clasped her shaking hands behind her back.

"How's he doing?"

"Great, just great." Then she angled her head. Jack had a sparkle in his eye. "Speaking of color in your cheeks… What's up?"

"Well, it'll be all over the news soon, but I thought you should be the first to know. This morning Rueben Garza confessed to Maria's murder."

She gasped. "You're kidding."

"No. We questioned him and it wasn't long before his story fell apart. You were right—Maria must've known she was being stalked. I'm just sorry I wasn't as astute as you were in picking up on it."

"Jack, you can't blame yourself."

He pressed his lips together. "No. But I shouldn't have blamed you, either. I'm sorry I lashed out."

"I know you didn't mean it. We were all grieving."

He nodded, then he gave a little laugh and shook his head. "I feel like a cheesy TV pitch guy, but…*wait, there's more!*"

She smiled. "What?"

From his pocket he removed a small plastic bag. In the corner was a square black chip, less than half the size of a postage stamp.

Carlotta squinted. "What is it?"

"A GPS chip found attached to the inside fender wall of Coop's van."

She covered her mouth with both hands.

"The van had already been processed," he said. "The chip would've never been found if we hadn't been looking for it."

"So someone was keeping track of Coop's movements?"

"Absolutely. We don't know who, but at least now we have a place to start. In light of Garza's confession and this new evidence, the D.A. is reviewing the charges against Coop."

She squealed with delight.

"That doesn't mean you should let your guard down," he warned. "Lane is still out there. I have some leads, but nothing definite. And now we have to find Coop, too, and convince him to turn himself in so we can get this all straightened out." He smiled. "But since the state boys created this mess, I'm going to let them handle it."

She considered telling Jack about Coop's call, but decided that once Coop called Liz, it would all get sorted out.

Jack returned the chip to his pocket and grinned. "Aren't you going to say I told you so?"

She shook her head. "No. Thank you for believing me, Jack."

He reached forward and picked up a lock of her hair, his pet gesture when he wanted to say something. He fingered the strand, rubbing it between forefinger and thumb. "You are something, you know that?"

She didn't respond, just soaked up his words and

basked in the happiness of knowing that she'd helped Coop…and Maria.

He dropped his hand and cleared his throat. "So…are you all packed for Vegas?"

"Almost," she said. "But I'm running low on underwear."

"Wow, it's a good thing you work in a department store," he said with a little smile. "If I don't see you again…have a safe trip."

She smiled. "Thanks, Jack."

He turned and walked away.

He was always walking away, she realized.

But she refused to be the least bit sad about anything. She finished her shift, said goodbye to Herb, and stopped to pick up the rest of the dry cleaning for her trip. Then she drove home listening to the radio as news broke that split The Charmed Killer case wide open and sent reporters scrambling.

When she got home, she pulled the dry cleaning from her car. One of the bags contained the bathing suit that Hannah had worn in the hot tub. Carlotta decided to write Hannah's name on the garment bag so she'd always have a suit when she came over.

And just like that, Carlotta realized that she was planning on staying at Peter's home for a while.

When she walked into the house, she grabbed the key to the pool house and kept going, out onto the patio, past the pool, sorting through her mail that had been forwarded to Peter's address. Bills, bills, bills.

She sighed, juggled envelopes and the garment bag as she unlocked the door to the pool house. She walked in and went directly to the changing room, where she hung the suit in the armoire. When she turned around, she stopped and frowned. Something was out of place.

Her gaze landed on a picture propped up on the vanity. A picture of her, taken by Michael at an employee party. It was the same photo that he'd swiped from the bulletin board in her bedroom when he'd hidden in the townhouse under their noses.

And he'd been hiding right under her nose again, here in the pool house. Terror seized her. She should've given in to the urge to check the closet the other day for Angela's lingerie and props. Although, if she had, Hannah might have gotten hurt.

She turned to run, but Michael Lane stood in the doorway, newly blond, dressed in chinos and a dress shirt, as if he were going to work. Strangely, though, his pants pockets bulged—perhaps with coins? In his hand he held what looked like a surgical knife, probably the same one he'd escaped with from the mental ward of the hospital.

She screamed and backed up to the wall.

Michael looked confused. "Why would you scream? No one can hear you."

Carlotta found her voice. "You startled me, Michael, that's all."

He laughed. "You should see the look on your face. You look like all those other women."

He was completely mad. His eyes were vacant, darting. "Wh-what other women?"

"All those women whose pictures are on TV," he said. "I'm really sorry about that," he said, then grimaced. "I'm really sorry about a lot of things. I wasn't a very good friend to you, Carlotta."

"It's okay," she soothed. "We can work this out.

Why don't you let me call someone?" She reached into her purse.

"No!" he shouted, holding the knife blade toward her. "It's too late for that. They're looking for me, did you know?"

"They want you to get help, Michael."

"No, they want to kill me in a dozen different ways."

Carlotta wet her lips. "Is that what you were doing, Michael? Killing women in a dozen different ways?"

He looked up and squinted. "I was always smarter than people gave me credit for, Carlotta. And charming. I was so charming, wasn't I?"

Her throat convulsed. "Yes, Michael…you've always been charming. And helpful." She shifted to shove her hand deeper into her purse. "I didn't get to thank you for all the things you did around the townhouse to help out."

He looked confused, then he nodded. "What did I do?"

"You know—laundry, running the dishwasher, that kind of thing."

"Oh…right. I thought it was the least I could do since you allowed me to live there."

"And you got rid of the fire ants in our yard," she said, curling her fingers around the baton.

He frowned. "No. I don't like ants." Then he pointed the knife at her. "Hey, stop talking. You're trying to mess with me. You're trying to get me sent to prison for the rest of my life."

"No, I'm not, Michael."

"Yes, you are!" he shouted. "You were going to testify against me, say that I tried to hurt you."

"You did hurt me, Michael. Remember, you threw me over the balcony of the Fox Theater?"

"That was self-defense. What else was I supposed to do?" He stepped closer, holding the blade. "You can fix things. You can tell the police I didn't mean to kill those women, but I had to."

She nodded. "Okay, I'll tell them whatever you want, Michael. Just put down the knife."

He looked at the weapon, then up at her again. "You're trying to trick me." He lunged toward her and she pulled out the baton. She groped for the button, and was able to make contact with a *zzzzt* just as he stabbed at her. His body stiffened and the knife fell. Then he dropped to the floor.

As he lay there twitching, Carlotta dissolved in sobs. She reached for the phone and fumbled with the buttons until Jack's number popped up. She pushed Send, and he answered on the second ring.

"Did you decide to gloat after all?" he asked.

Her teeth chattered. "J-Jack…J-Jack…"

"What's wrong?" he asked, instantly serious. "Where are you?"

"P-Peter's p-pool house. It's Michael…it was Michael…"

"Stay on the phone. I'm coming."

30

If they had any questions about Michael's guilt, it was put to rest by the contents of his pockets—handfuls of charms of all kinds.

Carlotta stood inside the house, looking out the sliding glass door, watching Michael being hauled away on a gurney. He was handcuffed and shackled—the authorities weren't taking any chances this time. Rainie Stephens stood nearby, directing a photographer to get the photos needed for the exclusive Carlotta had promised her.

"Are you sure you're up to giving a statement?" Jack asked.

Carlotta turned and nodded. "I want to get this over with." She retraced her story and her steps for Jack as he took notes. When she was finished, he put away the notebook. "When you get back from your trip, we might have a few more questions for you."

"Of course. But you've got enough to hold him, don't you?"

"Yes. And I finally picked up a lead on one of the parts for the explosive that was planted under your car. If it tracks back to Lane, we'll have more federal charges to file. If the man is sane, I'd say he's looking at the needle for sure."

"He didn't seem sane to me. He was confused, as if he couldn't tell the difference between what was real, and what was happening on television."

Jack grunted. "Then he'll probably be institutionalized for the rest of his life."

"But why would Michael want to frame Coop? It doesn't make sense."

"I don't know. If Maria were here, I'm sure she could help us understand."

Carlotta stepped back to the sliding glass door and looked out on the pool house. A CSI team was processing the building. She couldn't help feeling that something wasn't right, but she reasoned that everything would be explained as Michael relayed details of the crimes. It would still be a long time before the city felt normal again.

Jack came to stand behind her. "What a day, huh?"

She hugged herself. "Yeah, what a day."

He reached up and pulled her hair over one shoulder. "Carlotta, about your trip…"

She looked back at him. "What, Jack?"

He moved up behind her and wrapped one arm around her. "Don't go," he whispered hoarsely.

She closed her eyes as emotions coursed through her. She swallowed hard. "Don't go…or stay here with you, Jack? It's two different things."

He pulled back and she could sense his emotional retreat. It would always be that way with Jack, hot and cold. Down the hall, the sound of the front door bursting open broke the silence.

"Carly?" came Peter's frantic voice.

She and Jack moved in opposite directions as Peter strode into the room and pulled her into his arms.

"Are you okay?" He leaned back and cupped her face. "I can't believe I almost lost you. I love you so much." He held her tight and rocked her back and forth, murmuring little contented sounds.

This was the man she could count on, she realized, the man who wanted her so much, he wasn't afraid to let the world know. "I love you, too," she said.

When she opened her eyes, she caught a flash of resignation of Jack's face just before he turned to go.

31

Wes sighed and stared at the clock on the wall. Was the damn thing even working? It had been five minutes til noon for what seemed like over an hour now. Christ, with Meg gone on vacation, his time at ASS *did* seem like a sentence.

"When does Meg get back?" Jeff Spooner asked.

Ravi Chopra paused in his keyboarding. "Yeah. Do you know, Wes?"

Wes looked at the guys who shared the workstation, equal parts sorry for them and irritated with them. He wanted to say, "She's mine, losers, back off." But he understood where they were coming from. Meg had them all tied up in knots.

"It's only been two days, guys. She'll be back next Monday." He was reassuring himself as much as them. Wes pushed to his feet and grabbed his backpack. "I'm outta here."

As he exited the building, his cell phone rang. He reached for it, hoping it was Meg. Instead, Liz Fischer's name came up on the screen. He winced, but he had to answer it. They'd been playing phone tag because she'd been so busy taking care of Coop's case since it had blown up in the D.A.'s toady face.

"Hey, Liz."

"Hi, Wes. Is this a good time to talk?"

"Sure," he said, walking toward the bike rack. Mouse would be there soon to pick him up. "How's Coop?"

"Good," she said. "The initial charges have been dropped, and I'm pretty sure I can get the fugitive charges dropped, too. It's going to take a while to get everything sorted out, but Coop seems to have a champion on the staff of the *AJC*. We have interview requests from all the networks. Everyone's backpedaling, trying to repair the damage to Coop's reputation. I think he's going to come out of this on top."

Wes grinned. "That's great news." Carlotta had been right about Coop all along…and right about Wes getting clean. "Uh, Liz…I need a favor."

"Shoot."

He told her about the blood test taken the previous week at his probation meeting. "I'm not going to lie to you—I know it tested positive for Oxy. But I went through detox over the weekend, and I'm clean. I was hoping you could talk to my probation officer and arrange for me to take another blood test when I go in tomorrow."

"Ah, so that's why I have three messages from your probation officer. Don't worry. I'll take care of it."

His shoulders fell. "Thanks, Liz, you're the best."

"Wes, there are a couple of other things I need to talk to you about."

"Okay." The black Town Car pulled up and Mouse threw up his hand in a wave. Wes waved back and held up a finger to indicate he'd be a minute. He was still amazed at what the big man had done for him.

"I got a call from Jack Terry this morning," Liz said.

"He wants to know why your fingerprints are on an anonymous note the APD received listing possible names identifying a headless corpse in the county morgue."

Wes's stomach dropped to his knees. "Uh...I don't know what you're talking about."

"Okay, well, Jack wants to meet with us as soon as possible to get this all straightened out."

Holy crap. Anything he said now would incriminate Mouse...and how could he do that after what the man had done for him? He glanced up and Mouse nodded. Wes stiffly nodded back, offering a weak smile.

"And...there is one more thing," Liz said. "I was hoping I wouldn't have to tell you this over the phone, but here goes. I'm pregnant."

Wes's stomach, still dangling at his knees, fell to his ankles. Bright spots obscured his vision. Too bad the starbursts couldn't erase the memory of standing in Liz's bathroom after they'd had sex a few weeks ago, staring down at a busted condom.

Wes opened his mouth to say something...anything. Instead, he fainted.

32

Carlotta walked up the stairs, holding her cell phone to one ear. "Peter, I'll just put your suitcase in my rental car. That way you won't have to come by the house before going to the airport."

"If you don't mind getting it from my bedroom, that would save me a trip," Peter admitted. "I didn't expect this meeting to run so long."

"We still have plenty of time," she said. "I'll check our bags curbside under my ticket, then I'll turn in the rental car, and meet you at the gate."

"Sounds good. Are you leaving now?"

"In a few minutes. I want to stop by the townhouse and get a few things I didn't bring with me."

"Sounds intriguing," he murmured. "I can't wait to get you alone in Vegas."

She smiled into the phone. "We're going to have fun. See you in a bit."

Carlotta ended the call and at the top of the stairs, she turned toward the double doors leading to Peter's bedroom. She walked in, always impressed by the opulence of this room, a master suite in every sense of the word, with custom furniture, inlaid wood floors, and every amenity imaginable, from the flat-screen TV on one wall to the heated massage chaise in the spa-quality bathroom.

Peter's suitcase was lying open on the bench at the foot of the massive bed. His luggage, like everything else in his life—with the exception of her—was top quality. Inside, his clothes were packed in little winged mesh containers designed to keep everything compact and wrinkle-free. It was all very organized and orderly, just like Peter.

She lifted one side of the suitcase to fold it over, but the containers dumped out. With a sigh, she started to restack them, then froze.

In the corner of the suitcase was a familiar red Cartier ring box…the ring Peter had first given her when she was eighteen years old. She picked up the box and opened it to reveal the spectacular redesigned ring. Peter had located the original solitaire she'd pawned, magnificent in its own right, and added large diamonds on either side of the center stone. He told her it represented their past, their present and their future, and that he would hold it for her until she was ready.

Obviously, Peter meant to use their Vegas getaway as an opportunity to propose.

What would she say?

She remembered what the white-haired jeweler had told her. *An engagement ring is just something nice to wear while you make up your mind.*

Carlotta removed the ring from the box and slid it onto her left ring finger. After more than ten years, the original band was snug, but the dazzling trio of diamonds took her breath away.

The doorbell sounded, reverberating through the big, empty house. She tugged on the ring, but it was stubborn and would have to be loosened with soap. She jogged down the stairs, thinking there must be a delivery, or maybe the housekeeper had misplaced her keys.

When she checked the window next to the front door, her heart vaulted.

Coop.

She flung open the door and soaked in the sight of him—he wore dress jeans, a black T-shirt and low-heeled boots. His longish hair and sideburns were trimmed, and the color had returned to his cheeks. More than that—behind the funky heavy-rimmed glasses he wore, the life was back in his bright brown eyes. He grinned. "Hi."

She launched herself at him and he caught her in a hug.

"I can't believe it's you," she said, laughing and crying and hanging on for dear life. "It's so good to see you, Coop. Really."

He set her gently on her feet, but his hands lingered on her waist. "It's good to see you, too."

"Please, come in," she said, pulling him toward the door.

"I can't," he said with regret. "I heard through the grapevine that you're taking off for a few days, and I just wanted to come by to thank you before you leave."

She smiled. "You're welcome, Coop, to anything I've done."

He pressed his lips together. "Jack told me you believed in me…when no one else did."

Carlotta winked. "Maybe I know you better than everyone else."

"I think you do," he agreed quietly.

"Coop, what was it you had to do for Sarah Edlow that was so important?"

He wiped his hand over the back of his neck. "I wouldn't want this to go any farther."

"It won't."

He sighed and nodded. "After the…accident, I kept up with Sarah. We got to be friends. When her tumor was diagnosed, she asked me to help her select a surgeon. I even went with her to appointments sometimes, to talk to the doctors. When it became clear she was terminal, Sarah revealed that she had put a son up for adoption when she was a teenager. Her family didn't know. She had managed to locate him, but she didn't want to meet him when she was on death's door. So Sarah put together a box of things she wanted her son to have. She asked me to take it to him and explain to him and his adoptive family why she couldn't be there herself."

Coop stopped and his expression became haunted. "I gave her my word. When it looked like I was going to be in jail indefinitely, I panicked. After I was granted bail, I knew it would probably be my only chance to keep my promise to Sarah." He shrugged. "After what I'd taken from her, it seemed like a very small request."

Carlotta blinked back tears. "That sounds just like you."

He looked down and picked up her left hand. "Wow, that's a much nicer engagement ring than the one I gave you," he teased in reference to the butterfly band she'd used to convince the officer at the City Detention Center to let her see her "fiancée."

Carlotta blushed and she shook her head. "It's not an

engagement ring. I mean—it's an engagement ring, but I haven't accepted it."

"You're just wearing it?" he asked in an amused voice.

"Actually, I was just trying it on," she said, feeling like a complete idiot. "Um…it's complicated."

He grinned. "With you, I wouldn't expect anything else." Then he nodded toward his white Corvette convertible sitting in the driveway. "I should go and let you get ready for your trip."

"I'll call you when I get back," she said. "Maybe we can have coffee and catch up."

"I'd like that," he said. Then he leaned forward and gave her a brief kiss on the mouth.

Her lips remembered his, sending a little shudder of happiness through her chest. She was ecstatic to see him free…sober…back to his old self. It was especially sweet because a few days ago she couldn't have imagined things ending so well.

She waved until he was gone, then walked back into the house feeling strangely…let down. It was the lull, she decided, after what seemed like a constant rush of adrenaline over the past few weeks. Her step was lighter, though, going back upstairs to retrieve their suitcases because now she could go on her trip knowing that everything was okay.

Michael was in a maximum-security mental institution.

Wes was drug-free and seemed to be head over heels for his Meg.

Coop had been vindicated.

Peter was making plans for their future.

Jack was…Jack.

And she…

Carlotta frowned. What was *her* next step? Marriage? Maybe a new career? College? She toyed with the charms on her bracelet—a puzzle piece, an aloha charm, three hearts, two champagne glasses, and a woman whose arms were crossed over her chest.

Maybe the charms didn't have prophetic power…but it was fun to think of all the possibilities.

She loosened the Cartier ring with soap and returned it to the box, then repacked Peter's bag and zipped it. His suitcase was light because he hadn't packed much. Hers was light because she still wanted to add things to it, so she had no trouble getting them into her rental car.

On the drive to the townhouse, she called Hannah.

Her friend answered on the second ring. "Hey, what's up?"

"I'm on my way to the airport. I just called to say goodbye."

"Try to enjoy yourself," Hannah said dryly.

"Now, now," Carlotta chided. "I intend to forget about everything else for a while and just let go." She frowned at what sounded like intimate noises in the background. "Did I call at a bad time?"

"Nah, this is fine," said Hannah. "I told you, Fat Boy can give head for hours. I just paid all my bills and gave myself a manicure."

"Eww. I'm hanging up."

"Are you sure? This might be as close to an orgasm as you're going to get for a while."

"Goodbye, Hannah. I'll call you when I get back." Carlotta ended the call, shaking her head, unable to suppress a laugh at her bawdy friend.

When Carlotta got to the townhouse, she grabbed her suitcase and practically ran across the yard and up the steps to avoid Mrs. Winningham. Luckily, she managed to unlock the door and get inside with no interruptions.

She dashed in, wincing at the warm, stale air of the closed-up house, and opened the suitcase on her bed. She went through her closet and quickly picked the dresses, shoes, and evening bags she wanted, plus a few pieces of lingerie she hoped would help to get her and Peter over their hump.

And *hump,* already.

When she zipped her suitcase a few minutes later, she was getting a headache from not eating and too much excitement. She carried the suitcase into the living room and set it down, then went to the kitchen in search of aspirin and a bottle of water.

Carlotta was tossing back the aspirin when she was struck from behind. She went reeling sideways and careened into the breakfast bar, bashing her head on the counter. She gasped for air and choked on the bitter pills. When her vision cleared, she saw the flash of a knife.

The only thing worse than getting aspirin stuck in one's throat, Carlotta decided, was getting aspirin stuck in one's throat, and then having one's throat slit.

33

Carlotta lifted her gaze from the knife, to the hand holding the knife, to the arm holding up the hand holding the knife, to the shoulder supporting the arm that held the hand holding the knife, to the neck connected to the shoulder supporting the arm that held the hand holding the knife, to the head supported by the neck connected to the shoulder supporting the arm that held the hand holding the knife.

Dr. Bruce Abrams.

She screamed as if her hair was on fire.

He winced. "Stop it. No one can hear you. Your nosy neighbor is sleeping off a little chloroform coma…she won't be calling the police anytime soon."

"It was you," Carlotta murmured, marveling how a knock on the noggin could make one see things in a different way. "You set up Coop. You sent him to retrieve the bodies of the women you killed. You wanted him out of the way."

The doctor glared at her with beady eyes. "Out of my morgue, yes. He's a drunken body hauler, but he still acts like he owns the place. My people go to him behind my back. It's a disgrace."

A train was moving through her head. "Why? Why kill those women? They were innocent."

He shrugged. "Why not them? Everyone dies. They were the lucky ones—they were allowed to die famously. Victims of The Charmed Killer." He smiled, seemingly proud of his handiwork.

"Why the charms?" she asked, stalling. She was on the verge of passing out, but she had to keep talking. Keep *him* talking.

Abrams laughed. "Shawna Whitt gave me the idea. I saw her in the bookstore, flirting with other men, especially Coop. He never noticed her, but I did. I noticed she wore a charm bracelet and when I saw that chicken charm, it was like she'd handed me my answer. She chose me to kill her to set up Coop, don't you see?"

Carlotta saw that he was completely insane.

He sneered. "And everything was fine until you got involved. I knew you were going to be trouble. I tried to get rid of you early on, but you're like a damn cat with nine lives."

She tried to calculate which life she was on, then gave up in lieu of screaming again. "Help me! Help me, he has a knife! He's going to kill me!"

"You're right," he said, then glanced at his watch. "I have to be back to the morgue soon. I'm thinking about calling Coop to pick up your body, what do you think? Or maybe your brother."

She lunged for the doorway, but he body-slammed her against the wall and held the knife to her throat.

"I'll even do your autopsy myself," he whispered. "I'll get to touch every inch of your body, and cut you up, inside and out, any way I want to."

Tears slid down her cheeks. "Don't…please…let me go."

"Nope. You're going to be the random victim of a random crime in a questionable neighborhood. Your death probably won't even make the newspaper. Goodbye, Carlotta."

Suddenly the front door burst open and a man barreled inside, startling Abrams enough that he loosened his grip on her. Carlotta tore away, but felt a stinging slice to her shoulder. A shot rang out, and she heard the thud of a body fall. When she swung around, Abrams lay on the floor, clutching his bloody groin.

"Ja—" Carlotta looked up, but stopped short when she saw the shooter wasn't Jack.

She blinked, not trusting her eyes, still disoriented from the blow. But when the man didn't disappear or morph into anyone else, she tested the word on her tongue. *"Daddy?"*

34

Still tall and still handsome, Randolph Wren gave her a shaky smile. "Hi, Sweetheart."

"Where…how…?" She couldn't find the words.

"I told you I was keeping tabs on you and Wesley. I tried to do little things to help…like taking care of those fire ants."

"The listening device?"

He gestured to her shoulder and walked closer. "You're bleeding." He shoved his gun down in the waistband of his jeans and walked to the kitchen. He came back with a towel and pressed it gently against the wound. "Can you hold it?"

She nodded, drinking in the sight of him. She scanned his face, every feature, again and again, half thrilled, half terrified. It was surreal, having him close enough to touch.

"You should sit down," he said, leading her to a chair.

"Freeze."

Carlotta looked up to see Jack's broad shoulders silhouetted in the open door. He had a gun trained on Randolph. "Place your hands on your head and get on your knees."

"Jack—" she protested.

"Do it!" he shouted.

Randolph obeyed.

"Slowly, place the weapon on the floor," Jack said.

Randolph did, wordlessly.

Jack pulled out his radio and gave the address. "I need a bus, and I need backup." He replaced the radio. "Carlotta, are you okay?"

"She's bleeding," Randolph said. "That man stabbed her."

"Shut up," Jack said. "Carlotta?"

"I'm bleeding, but I don't think it's serious." She looked down at Abrams, who was either dead or had passed out. "He framed Coop, Jack. He admitted everything to me."

Jack nodded as the sound of sirens rent the air. "I know. I traced the bomb parts to Abrams, too."

So that's what Abrams had meant when he said he'd tried to get rid of her. "How did you know I was here?"

"Peter told me you were stopping by on the way to the airport. I took a chance."

He took a chance... "Dr. Abrams killed all those women," she said, tears sliding down her cheeks.

"We'll sort it out later, darlin'," Jack soothed. He pulled handcuffs from his belt. "Get on your feet," he said to Randolph. "And turn around."

Randolph did as he was ordered, but with a little smile. "Do you know who I am?"

Jack holstered his weapon. "I should, you son of a bitch. I've looked at your photo enough in the criminal file that I've memorized." Jack snapped on the handcuffs. "Randolph Wren, you're under arrest. You have the right to remain silent. Anything you say can and will be used against you in a court of law in which I will be in the front row. You have the right to an attorney. If you can't afford an attorney, one will be appointed for you. Do you understand these rights?"

"Yes," Randolph said, darting a look to Carlotta as Jack led him toward the door.

She lunged to her feet, but she was light-headed and had to lean into the wall for support. "Jack, he saved my life."

"He's still a criminal."

"Don't take him yet," she pleaded.

"I have to," Jack said, leveling his gaze on her. "Don't make this harder than it already is."

Carlotta stumbled to the door and caught herself to keep from fainting. She watched Jack lead Randolph to the police car and realized that her life had been leading up to this moment all along. She'd always known that Jack would be the one taking her father into custody.

"Daddy!" she yelled, feeling as if her heart was being wrenched out of her body.

Randolph turned and gave her a bittersweet smile. "Come and see me, Sweetheart. We have a lot to talk about."

* * * * *

Don't miss a move!
Keep up with all the BODY MOVERS news at
www.MIRABooks.com *and* www.stephaniebond.com!

HARLEQUIN® *Blaze*™

Seduction by the Book

by STEPHANIE BOND

When four Southern wallflowers decide to get together
and form a book club, they never dream where their
literary wanderings are going to lead them. Because in
this club, the members are reading classic erotic volumes,
learning how to seduce the man of their dreams....
Atlanta's male population won't stand a chance!

Encounters—
1 blazing book, 4 sizzling stories

*Available only from Harlequin Blaze
in October 2009, wherever Harlequin books are sold.*

red-hot reads

www.eHarlequin.com   HB79504

REQUEST YOUR FREE BOOKS!

2 FREE NOVELS
FROM THE ROMANCE/SUSPENSE
COLLECTION PLUS 2 FREE GIFTS!

YES! Please send me 2 FREE novels from the Romance/Suspense Collection and my 2 FREE gifts (gifts are worth about $10). After receiving them, if I don't wish to receive any more books, I can return the shipping statement marked "cancel." If I don't cancel, I will receive 4 brand-new novels every month and be billed just $5.74 per book in the U.S. or $6.24 per book in Canada. That's a savings of at least 28% off the cover price. It's quite a bargain! Shipping and handling is just 50¢ per book.* I understand that accepting the 2 free books and gifts places me under no obligation to buy anything. I can always return a shipment and cancel at any time. Even if I never buy another book from the Reader Service, the two free books and gifts are mine to keep forever.

185 MDN EYNQ 385 MDN EYN2

Name _____ (PLEASE PRINT) _____

Address _____ Apt. # _____

City _____ State/Prov. _____ Zip/Postal Code _____

Signature (if under 18, a parent or guardian must sign)

Mail to **The Reader Service:**
IN U.S.A.: P.O. Box 1867, Buffalo, NY 14240-1867
IN CANADA: P.O. Box 609, Fort Erie, Ontario L2A 5X3

Not valid to current subscribers of the Romance Collection,
the Suspense Collection or the Romance/Suspense Collection.

Want to try two free books from another line?
Call 1-800-873-8635 or visit www.morefreebooks.com.

* Terms and prices subject to change without notice. Prices do not include applicable taxes. Sales tax applicable in N.Y. Canadian residents will be charged applicable provincial taxes and GST. Offer not valid in Quebec. This offer is limited to one order per household. All orders subject to approval. Credit or debit balances in a customer's account(s) may be offset by any other outstanding balance owed by or to the customer. Please allow 4 to 6 weeks for delivery. Offer available while quantities last.

Your Privacy: Harlequin is committed to protecting your privacy. Our Privacy Policy is available online at www.eHarlequin.com or upon request from the Reader Service. From time to time we make our lists of customers available to reputable third parties who may have a product or service of interest to you. If you would prefer we not share your name and address, please check here. ☐

BOB09

STEPHANIE
BOND

32659 BODY MOVERS:
      3 MEN AND A BODY   ___ \$6.99 U.S. ___ \$6.99 CAN.
32606 BODY MOVERS: 2 BODIES
      FOR THE PRICE OF 1   ___ \$6.99 U.S. ___ \$6.99 CAN.
32482 BODY MOVERS   ___ \$6.99 U.S. ___ \$8.50 CAN.

(limited quantities available)

TOTAL AMOUNT   \$_____
POSTAGE & HANDLING   \$_____
(\$1.00 FOR 1 BOOK, 50¢ for each additional)
APPLICABLE TAXES*   \$_____
TOTAL PAYABLE   \$_____

(check or money order—please do not send cash)

To order, complete this form and send it, along with a check or money order for the total above, payable to MIRA Books, to: **In the U.S.:** 3010 Walden Avenue, P.O. Box 9077, Buffalo, NY 14269-9077; **In Canada:** P.O. Box 636, Fort Erie, Ontario, L2A 5X3.

Name: _____
Address: _____ City: _____
State/Prov.: _____ Zip/Postal Code: _____
Account Number (if applicable): _____

075 CSAS

*New York residents remit applicable sales taxes.
*Canadian residents remit applicable GST and provincial taxes.

MIRA®

www.MIRABooks.com   MSB0409BL